I0762849

SHE DRINKS THE LIGHT

SHE DRINKS THE LIGHT

YASMIN ANGOE

FEIWEL AND FRIENDS
NEW YORK

A Feiwel and Friends Book
An imprint of Macmillan Publishing Group, LLC
120 Broadway, New York, NY 10271 • fiercereads.com

EU representative: Macmillan Publishers Ireland Ltd, 1st Floor, The Liffey Trust Centre, 117–126 Sheriff Street Upper, Dublin 1, D01 YC43

Our books may be purchased in bulk for specialty retail/wholesale, literacy, corporate/premium, educational, and subscription box use. Please contact MacmillanSpecialMarkets@macmillan.com.

Library of Congress Cataloging-in-Publication Data is available.

First edition, 2026
Book design by Maria W. Jenson
Feiwel and Friends logo designed by Filomena Tuosto
Printed in the United States of America

ISBN 978-1-250-87268-5
10 9 8 7 6 5 4 3 2 1

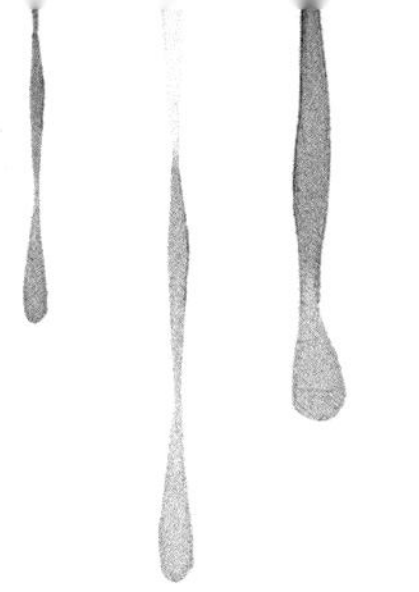

To the readers who are unafraid to read widely and diversely, who can let their imaginations run free and get deeply lost in stories about others

PRONUNCIATION GUIDE

Addae Ewiem	Ah-Dye-Yee Ehh-We-Em
Nana Ama	Na-Na-Ma
Sekou	Say-Coo
Naira	Ni-Rah
Adze	Ah-Jay
Nyame	Neya-May
Awuraa	Eh-Rah
Abalsom	Ah-Bahl-Som

CHAPTER ONE

IT WAS THE SHAKING THAT WOKE ME.

Again.

Didn't come from a single place, but everywhere all at once. The floor, the ceiling, my bed. The fan overhead, the chain switches on it swinging like pendulums, and the lights I'd strung all over my walls, swaying like twinkling stars, confirmation that this was not a dream.

Then it was quiet. Heavy. Total. The kind of silence that is louder than noise, as though the island was holding its breath along with me, like we were waiting for the other shoe to drop.

It took a minute for my mind to catch up to what was happening. Earthquake. Another one, as strong as the one six months ago. That one made my grandmother cry out into the night and mumble things I didn't understand and that she wouldn't talk about. I left it alone, but I never forgot.

Lately we had been having more earthquakes. The geologists called them "normal" because South Carolina includes a number of fault zones, and even though we were on a tiny sea island off the coast, we still felt them. But Nana Ama, my grandmother, said it was the spirits and the gods angry about something. About what? She wouldn't tell me. She'd stop talking and retreat into herself or lock herself away in her tiny cabin behind our house. It was set deeper into the woods, a place where she made her elixir and tinctures and sachets filled with herbs for islanders who needed healing or blessings. She never told me anything that mattered.

Storms, floods, hurricanes were what our sea island knew best. Not earthquakes like they had in California. The first was the big quake six months ago—the only one I'd ever experienced at the time. It was big enough to tear open the land in some places. Big enough to make our power go out and on again. Big enough to crack open something deep within my grandmother.

She had wailed into the dark. When I'd found her in her room, her sheets were damp with sweat and twisted around her legs. She climbed out of bed, barely registering I was there, and shot out of her room. All I could do was grab her robe and follow, desperately calling her name. She spoke to herself in dialects I didn't recognize and had never heard her speak. She walked the perimeter of our home, murmuring to the trees, to the ground, to the land, like she was trying to soothe something ancient and angry. Our land, this island we'd owned for centuries—she believed it was offended. That we'd somehow broken a promise our blood had once made and the earthquakes were a result of our offense.

Her eyes darted left and right, like something was about to jump out at her from behind a tree. I'd never seen her show fear. I'd never seen her in pain. I didn't know how to help her. She'd always been the one who healed others.

I had followed her through the winding path from our home, through the peach groves she cherished and got rich from, through the thatch of woods that separated us from the Atlantic Ocean.

She stopped on the cliff, that high ledge where she usually went to be for hours. I could hear the waves crashing against the rocks below. As she always did, she was looking up at the sky. But this time more intently, urgently, as if waiting for an alien mother ship to come down and swoop her up. I called her name. She didn't reply. Just looked so intensely at the sky, at the clouds that were gathering, as if she was trying to peer through them into something beyond. She had started mumbling again, and this time I heard what she said, the words I hadn't been able to decipher earlier when I'd found her in bed. My blood felt like ice in my veins because, when she said them, she spoke as if her heart had been torn from her body and smashed into nothing.

"Born to be the cure but instead became the disease."

Something had lurched in me, and I shivered as her words slid around me like a constricting snake. I had no idea what she meant. It made no sense why she'd say that, because Nana Ama was a healer, had always been. She had spent her life, her energy, had gone hungry and without rest taking care of everyone else, including me. Magic happened in that tiny cabin of hers where she concocted her special elixir, tinctures, poultices, and herb-filled sachets.

There was no ailment Nana Ama couldn't catch before it was too late. There was nothing she couldn't diagnose from a mere perceptive look, a touch, or a feeling—a vibe she gleaned from the afflicted. Healing was Nana Ama's gift. She just . . . knew when something was wrong. And if the illness was too complicated for her to take on without too many questions asked of her, then she'd send the patient across the sea to the mainland to seek help from doctors.

So to talk about a cure becoming a disease rattled me. But she never spoke those words again. Didn't acknowledge them the next day, when I'd asked what she'd meant. Instead she totally shut me out. Like she always did when she thought something was over my head. Well, it wasn't.

Now here we were again—six months later and another Nana-shaking quake. The jostling stopped, but the tension, the dread, lingered, wrapping around me like a mummy.

She wasn't in her bedroom like the last time. Or in the kitchen. Or in her favorite chair on the lanai, *getting her thoughts together* as she sipped warmed, honeyed coconut water or palm oil to replenish the energy she'd used managing this island and its people. She wasn't in the front yard, or in her cabin. She wasn't on the cliff. She was nowhere.

The threads of fear tightened around me, making it harder to breathe.

I finally found her when I doubled back and went through the peach grove. I don't know how I'd missed her before. Maybe it was my panic. Now all I knew was relief. I weaved through the trees that stood like small guards at the edge of our land, their short trunks and stubby branches reaching to the sky as if in celebration. Usually, seeing them, the fruit that built Nana Ama's peach empire on the mainland, comforted me. Their thick, shiny leaves would be like a thousand hellos in the breeze. But tonight the grove looked anything but comforting.

Nana stood among the trees as stiff as stone with her head canted to the side. One arm was wrapped across her chest, fingers gripping her shoulder, while the other hand hung limply at her side. If she heard me coming, she didn't show it.

She stared deep into the trees, beyond the grove, past where I'd come from. Again, she looked like she was searching for something that wouldn't show. I did a quick check just to make sure.

She once told me that if you stood in the right spot in the grove, you could see through it and the woods, straight to the cliff, and catch a glimpse of the sky. She said that blue reminded her of home. *Home*, home, the place across the sea where millions of our ancestors had been stolen, never to return. Being on our Golden Isle was like being in two worlds, Nana said. The worlds of then and now. It was the closest thing she felt to the culture she'd grown up on.

The air around her was charged with a strange energy, and I hesitated before interrupting her in this state.

"Hey, Nana," I said softly, carefully, so as not to startle her. You weren't supposed to surprise your elders, and my grandmother was the eldest of elders—though you wouldn't hear that from me—but to everyone else she looked ageless.

Her quilt had slipped from one shoulder, its tips dragging in the dirt. I stepped closer to gently put it back in place, finding her body wound up beneath my fingertips. Her muscles were coiled tight, like she was ready to spring. The weird energy continued to radiate. Red and pulsing in waves. Keeping me at bay.

I didn't think I'd done something lately to piss her off. And she didn't seem sick. Nana never got sick, even though she was old. Healers were strong, and the powers she'd been blessed with made her invincible.

When her face came into my view, my heart thumped in my chest and my breath caught. Her brows tented up in the middle of her forehead. Her lips were pressed so close together they nearly disappeared, replacing the warm, easy smile that was her trademark.

Nana wasn't staring into the grove. Wasn't really staring at anything at all. It was like she was here, but . . . not.

I was about to say something to break the eerie silence when she spoke first.

"The Oosoro. The Asase. The Asamando."

My mouth ran dry. The *Skies*. The *Earth*. The *World of Spirits*. Her voice was flat, not like the vibrant, melodious one I'd known all my life.

"They are gathering," she said, her voice low, almost baritone. "*She* is gathering."

I clutched Nana tighter to shake her out of this terrifying trance, but then the world changed. Gone was the sky that had been clear, pinkening and brightening as dawn began to break. Gone was the tiny peach grove Nana carefully maintained. Gone was our house with its wraparound, enclosed lanai; gone was her tiny shed. Gone were the smells of the morning dew on plush green leaves and the distant sounds of our families of Kinfolk or the rest of the islander locals who lived beyond the front gates of Kin's Landing.

All of it fell away into some ethereal place of mist, too thick to make out anything except the outline of an enormous mountain, bigger than I'd ever seen. And circling the majestic mountain with a golden band were all the Adinkra symbols, glowing like individual beacons of light.

I grew up with the Adinkra. These centuries-old Akan symbols that Nana said were gifted by the gods to serve as both guides to live by and an indication of one's purpose in life were infused into our cultural heritage and everyday life on the Golden Isle. Etchings of them were carved into every structure for protection, blessings, and reminders of where the Kinfolk had originally come from.

I stared at my grandmother as the image of the mountain with the gleaming symbols eclipsed her, and saw that it wasn't just Nana standing there, but a large shadow with shapes resembling limbs protruding from its sides, making Nana look like she was a spider.

I stared hard at the image in front of me . . . the mountain, the shadow, the symbols . . . Was this all a dream and I was still in my bed? But it was too real. I could feel the heat from Nana's skin beneath my fingers.

The shadow loomed over her, or emanated from her—I couldn't tell which. It was hard to figure out where the shadow ended and my grandmother began. The symbols glowed so brilliantly, as if I were looking into the sun, that I had to shield my eyes with a hand. That is, until Nana Ama began to speak.

But her voice was not hers. It was a mix of her melodic tone and the deep baritone of a male. I tried holding on to her, but her skin became so hot I snatched my hand away, as if I'd touched a flaming-red stovetop.

Nana's voice filled up all the space inside my head. I slammed my hands over my ears, but nothing could dull the intensity and the volume of her voice.

"*She* is . . . gathering," Nana said.

"Who?" Panic climbed my throat. I had no idea what or who Nana was talking about or what was wrong with my grandmother. She had never been like this before.

I asked again, "Nana, who is gathering?"

"What has been done is now undone" was her reply. "Stand and be ready. Stand."

As quick as it came, the image of cloud and mist faded. The gigantic mountain behind Nana became lighter and lighter until it was gone, leaving Nana Ama still in her trance.

"Nana?" I backed up a step. I'd left my phone in my room so I couldn't call for help. I looked around, but we were alone. No one dared come to our part of the Isle, which took up the back half of Kin's Landing, unless they were invited.

I psyched myself up enough to shake my grandmother back to her senses when she blinked. Her body relaxed, and instantly, the danger-red vibe that had emanated from her downgraded to a safe green. She focused on me, eyes sparkling and clear.

"Do you feel okay?" I asked, searching for any remnants of seconds ago.

Nana smiled sweetly, as if those last moments hadn't happened. I considered telling her what she'd said and what I'd seen. She would believe me, I thought. Nana was a firm believer of the gods and spirituality and earth magic. We lived on and protected an island that was more than just sand and rock.

Nana Ama took in her surroundings as if she were seeing them for the first time. I joined in, searching the skies for the mountain or the shadow, straining my ears for that voice so deep it seemed bottomless. Could we have suffered from something like carbon monoxide poisoning and Nana and I were having one of those—what did they call them—shared hysteria? Except I was aware and Nana was . . . not? I waited for her to say something, but she acted as if nothing happened. Like everything had all been just a dream and maybe I was the one who'd been sleepwalking.

She eyed me critically, her once delighted-to-see me smile slipping into a Addae's-about-to-get-it scowl.

"Addae, what'd I tell you about not wearing shoes outside?"

As if on a shared string, we both looked down, staring at my bare feet coated with dust and wet grass. I wiggled my toes at the sudden attention called to them. Maybe I would have remembered to put on shoes if I wasn't running around looking for her.

"And don't you track any dirt and sand up in my house either. I swear you're so hardheaded."

Nana rubbed my arm, giving it a tiny squeeze, and turned on her heels. Wordlessly, she started back toward the house. I was about to follow her when something on the ground caught my attention. I bent, my breath catching as I got closer and recognition took hold. First "born to be the cure but instead became the disease," and now . . .

The Adinkra symbol of Nsoromma, *Child of the Heavens,* was etched in the dirt where my grandmother had been standing.

So much for what was supposed to be an ordinary graduation day.

CHAPTER TWO

"Fake it till you make it."

I'd been repeating this mantra all morning, pretending I'd also been breathing the same air of anticipation like everyone else on the Isle, Nana included. I'd been giving her side-eye all morning, checking if she'd show any signs of being weirded out about what had happened at the ass crack of dawn this morning. Maybe she had a reasonable explanation for what I thought I'd seen. But she acted like everything was normal. And if she was going to be like that, then I would be too. I was going to pretend the hell out of this day, if not for Nana, then for Naira and Sekou.

Today, Naira, Sekou, and I were graduating. Finally. Along with the other Isle seniors, we'd spent the last four years commuting by ferry twice a day, rain or shine, to attend Calibogue High on the mainland. I didn't love much about the mainland. To me it was overrated, overpopulated, and very overstimulating. Too much of all that was draining. But today was different, and even I, the self-proclaimed eternal pessimist, felt flutters of excitement. The thought of walking the stage in a cap and gown, tassel swinging as I stepped toward something new—claimed something new—sent jolts through my chest. Graduating meant more time on the Isle together and less time dealing with obnoxious mainlanders who either thought we were an anomaly or a spectacle they wanted to explore and understand how we, descendants of formerly enslaved people, could own the Isle all by ourselves.

But whatever we wanted to do, we'd figure it out together and do it together, the three of us. Ever since we were little, Sekou, Naira, and I believed the Golden Isle was our whole world. Back then promises of staying on this little bit of land forever felt unbreakable. Like a friendship bracelet, threads woven together, swearing never to come apart.

I maneuvered our golf cart, the Isle's preferred mode of transportation, through the small dirt roads leading to the public dock where we were supposed to meet up with the rest of the island's families—both Kinfolk and non—to ferry over and attend the ceremony. Beside me, Nana Ama sat regal in her usual flowy skirt and peasant top. Folded neatly in her lap was her woven wrap of a dark blue traditional African cloth with asymmetrical lines of black, circles of white. She rarely went without a wrap, as the Isle's climate shifted from hot to cold at the snap of a finger. Her wrists were adorned with bracelets of cowrie shells, not with the golden heirloom cuffs that had been in our family for generations. Those she normally saved for special ceremonies on the Isle.

She hummed an old tune that let me know her mood was a happy one. At least that made one of us. I studied Nana, wondering if there was anything at all she remembered from this morning, if there was anything she'd admit to. She was so good at pretending away problems. So good at putting things away in neat little boxes and focusing on the big picture.

That was not one of my gifts.

Matter of fact, aside from a little bit of intuition here and there, vibes about people or things, I didn't know if I'd be a healer like Nana or something else. I couldn't become Lighted. But that was a whole other story.

"Nana," I started, making a right at the sign for the public pier. "This morning."

Nana's humming slowed to a stop, and she lifted her head from where her temple had been lightly resting on the tips of her fingers. She looked worn, like she hadn't slept well. Well, neither had I, but at least I hadn't been possessed by a creepy shadow figure. That was some next-level shit. Instantly, I was hit with guilt at the long day ahead and trying to make her talk when clearly she wasn't at 100 percent. I considered turning the cart around, back toward home. Nana was pushing herself to be there for me. Going to the mainland and being around many people was draining for her.

"What about this morning?" There was slight edge to her tone. She looked at me expectantly, and any bravery I had mustered up melted away. If my grandmother was going to push herself to attend my graduation on the mainland and deal with people all day, the least I could do was hold my tongue.

"Never mind, Nana." I pivoted, lightening my voice. "I hope you're ready for a whole night of partying on the Isle. Maybe try some Peach Lightning if you . . ." I chose my words. "Decide to stay in tonight?"

She chuckled as I pulled the cart into our reserved parking spot by the docks. The ferry bobbing on the light waves was already full of a sea of blue. Grads on one ferry, family on the other.

"Nothing a cup of warmed coconut water or palm oil won't cure." She waited a beat, then snuck in, "I'm not messing with the brothers' shit."

Nana said it so smoothly her curse didn't hit me until a second later, the shock of it causing me to stomp on the brake before the cart bumped hard into the stone parking marker.

"Nana Ama, are you alright?" I asked, shifting the cart in park and turning to her.

"Oho!" she said. "Stop your fuss. Worry about your awful driving!"

She brushed imaginary dust from her pristine flowy yellow skirt and then held out her dainty hand as I came around to her side. Her hazel eyes with flecks of deep gold, the same as mine, were full of amusement.

"Nana, when'd you learn to talk like that?" I asked, feigning shock.

"You don't tell me what I do or don't do, child."

I did a quick check, wondering if anyone had heard. Ama was regarded as the mother of the Kinfolk. Though Golden Isle was all of the Kin's, our family actually owned the land. Ours, along with the other founding families, had run from enslavers and come across an abandoned island off the coast of what's now Hilton Head, South Carolina. It was named the Golden Isle for the fireflies on it who, the story says, had helped guide the way, and was a new life for them and generations after, for anyone who needed a safe space. The founding families had come from all parts of Africa, had maintained their various cultures and traditions, and could be traced back centuries, maybe longer.

When Nana stepped down, I would inherit the title of leader and the land, and according to homeland traditions that had been passed down for generations, I'd be enstooled in her place (if I ever got it together and managed to become Lighted), continuing the same traditions and cultures our ancestors sacrificed to keep alive. Aside from the deeds to land and traditional matriarchal systems that gave Nana Ama the title of leader, her healing gifts set her—and our island—apart.

Nana chuckled, low and earthy, unlocking the worry building in my chest. "Unclutch those pearls of yours, girl. There's more to this old lady than you can imagine."

I followed my grandmother, finally allowing the bug of excitement intermingling with the sweet and salty scent of the Isle to grab me too.

The Golden Isle's famous peaches were first cultivated from Nana Ama's tiny grove behind our home. The harvests had supported our family, and the Kinfolk, for decades. When the demand for Golden Isle fruit became too great for the small batches grown here, my grandmother purchased property on the mainland, where she established larger farms to support the demand, eventually building enough wealth to maintain the Isle, which my family had owned since way before my time. It was something unheard of back then, Nana often reminded me, a Black family owning land, much less a whole island. "Us owning the Isle, refusing to give it up, blew those white folks' minds." She'd laugh but her eyes never did. Then came the warning. "And it damn sure better stay that way."

AS GRADUATION DAY WENT ON, I THOUGHT ABOUT HOW HARD it had been for me to get to this point. School was a struggle; tests weren't my strength. Naira and Sekou helped get me through. Sekou was nearly a whiz at math, and Naira had an affinity for memorizing and loved reading and research. Even when I kept saying I wasn't going to need stuff like trig and the five-paragraph essay.

"Not everyone is meant for college," I'd once complained. "How is any of this even important?"

Sekou said, "You never know. You might change up and want to travel the world."

I pulled a face. "Trig, though? Where?"

He shook his head. "Don't worry about that one."

I shuddered at the thought of college. Being confined within Calibogue's walls with the fluorescent lights and the massive amounts of highly emotional teens was too chaotic and always wore me out. I needed sun and space and quiet to give me life. I needed the Isle. "We all know my place is at the Isle. That won't change no matter what. This is my home. Like Nana."

"Doesn't have to be," Naira mumbled under her breath.

I ignored the quick pass of pity between them. Before I had a chance to overthink, she continued.

"Just because you may not go to college doesn't mean you

shouldn't try your best, right here and now. You freaking own an island. You need to know things, so pick up the damn textbook."

I picked up the damn book. And thought about chucking it at her damn head. But now, looking back, all I felt was gratitude that they hadn't given up on me, or let me give up on myself. I wouldn't have finished without my friends, and now we could move on with our lives together.

Nana Ama followed the other family members onto the boat, one of two chartered by Elder James, who happened to be Sekou's uncle and owner of one of the largest boat companies on the Isle, while I boarded with the grads and sat down between Naira and Sekou.

"Whatever you do, don't lose these," Naira said, pointing to our caps. "I worked hard to get them just right, and even if you two don't care, I do."

Sekou flicked her on the forehead lightly. "One drum is bigger than the other," he pointed out. "Don't do my djembes like that. But I guess you did good."

I peered over at his. Sekou's cap had the djembe drums, dark sunglasses because he thought he was so damn cool, and a replica of his favorite girl—his boat. Naira's had a few pics of her K-pop idols, a plane, and a stack of books. Then I studied mine—a firefly, and a tiny island with a palm tree I figured was Golden Isle. And all of ours had the year scrawled in gold sparkles and a small photo-booth picture of the three of us from the state fair in Columbia last year. My heart swelled. Naira had worked hard when I'd been too lazy to give it a second thought.

"They're great," I agreed. "Thank you."

The way she beamed back at me was the best gift ever.

UNDER THE PROUD EYES OF OUR CLOSEST FAMILY AND FRIENDS, Naira, Sekou, and I walked the stage on the football field. The stadium was nearly packed, as if it were a Friday football game, and once off the stage, I popped in my earbuds to dull the growing noise—too many unwanted voices clanging together.

The Russells, Naira's family of seven, cheered the loudest when Naira was handed her diploma. Nana Ama sat with them, but remained stoic and regal. I didn't expect the whoops and hollers like from the other families. Nana kept her feelings tightly tucked away, something I struggled with daily. She was always very careful—careful to speak, careful to act.

But when Principal Khan handed me the piece of paper and shook my hand, I would have loved to hear her voice crying out above the dutiful claps and cheers. The one person who I knew was mine.

When Principal Khan finally announced our graduating class, the sky became a sea of royal blue as Naira, Sekou, and I threw our caps in the air and cheered with the rest of our islander and mainlander classmates alike. We threw our arms around one another, and the sadness of earlier mixed with pure joy.

Through all the commotion, I managed to do exactly as Naira had instructed and found my cap in the chaos. As I trailed my fingers along the raised ridges of Naira's decorations, my eyes watered a little. I may have complained about attending Cal High every day, but I still planned to tack the cap to my wall of all my favorite things.

Sekou was nowhere to be found, though usually his six-foot-three frame of arms, legs, and head of dark brown natural coils sprouting several inches at all points was pretty hard to miss. He was the a total opposite of Naira, who was a foot south of him and, he liked to tease, "vertically challenged." But her waist-length goddess faux locs with their electric-blue tips stood out like beacons, and I spotted her in the midst of all the commotion tucked away in a small alcove near the concession stand.

I started toward her and saw she wasn't alone. In fact, her face was practically being swallowed whole by a preppy-looking guy with super-blond hair and even fairer skin. It didn't look like Naira would welcome my intrusion.

I hesitated, deciding to fall back and ignore the hurt and tiny flecks of betrayal creeping up. Why hadn't Naira told me about this guy? Was she ashamed of me? Maybe I was too country? Too backward being an island girl and not obsessed with getting the latest makeup trends from Ulta Beauty or chronicling every second of my life on TikTok?

Sekou, Naira, and I supposedly had no secrets from one another. Yet here was this pasty Abercrombie & Fitch model I'd never seen and knew nothing about. Thanks to my ancestry, in our world of superstition, everything was a sign.

And just like that, the unease I'd been fighting hard to push back from the night escapade with Nana came rushing back full force. It took ahold of me, making me wonder what change was coming, and if I was ready for it.

CHAPTER THREE

Our large group assembled to head back to Golden Isle after the brief postgrad reception and final pictures. I was half listening to Nana Ama discuss the art of peach growing with some guy she knew from the farmers market, until I caught sight of Naira returning, but not alone. I glanced around for Sekou, hoping he was around to figure out this whole scene with me, but he was in the wind. Probably chasing after some girl who swore he was Nyame's gift to women, if I knew my friend.

I tracked the trio as Naira approached, arm linked tightly with the prep from earlier, strolling along as if the rest of us weren't baking under this hot-ass June sun. A girl who shared his same features, delicate, very fair like they'd be sensitive to burning, with dark brown hair, walked with them, looking chummy. I studied them, a bunch of questions running through my mind like I was some detective on *Law & Order*. I joined Naira's parents as she walked up and introduced the two of them.

"This is Luke Hall and his older sister, Hailey," Naira announced.

"Only by a year and a half," Luke chimed in to Hailey's eye roll.

"Luke and I were in the same online history class from my dual-enrollment program. He goes to Charleston City University." Naira grinned sheepishly in my direction, but I only narrowed my eyes in response. I had never even heard of this guy.

Beside me, Sekou materialized, bumping me lightly with his arm. "What's this?" he half whispered in my general direction.

"No idea," I mumbled, watching the show and wishing I had a remote to turn it off.

Luke and Hailey—who looked about as out of place as I felt—took turns shaking hands with Naira's parents and waving at her younger brother and sisters. Naira turned to Sekou and me, her hands held out presentation style. "These are my best friends. Sekou and Ada." She giggled. "This is Luke and his sister."

"Yeah, Hailey," I said. "I heard."

Luke's face brightened, recognition breaking his expression. "Ada, short for Addae." He looked up like he was trying to get it just right. "*Ah-dye-yee*. Means *morning sun*. Last name Ewiem." He slowly enunciated each syllable, "*Ehh-we-em* for sky." His smile widened even bigger than Naira's, he was that proud of himself. "So, like, morning sun of the sky. That's beautiful."

I think I grunted in response, my gaze sliding slowly to Naira in disbelief. I felt my top lip start to curl, baring teeth, but I caught myself in time, remembering where I was and who I was with, and fixed my face.

"Naira talks about you all the time," Luke said, too enthusiastically for my taste.

Too bad we couldn't say the same, I wanted to shoot back, but another bump from Sekou signaled me to behave in front of company. My mouth slammed shut to imprison what I really wanted to say.

Meanwhile Hailey sulked, a step behind her brother, wearing a long-sleeved white button-down in this disrespectful heat. Luke was pretty covered up too. The only other people dressed in long sleeves and suits were Principal Khan and the other admin and faculty. Everyone else was decked out in short sleeves, khaki shorts, and sleeveless summer dresses. I guess Luke and Hailey didn't get the weather memo, or didn't care.

"Easy, killer," Sekou said under his breath, sensing my growing tension. "Play nice with the in-laws." The tips of Luke's ears reddened, signaling Sekou needed a lesson in proper whispering.

I turned to my so-called friend to remind him that I didn't need to be told how to behave. Somehow, I'd moved back when Luke was stepping forward. We crashed into each other, and my grad cap flew out my hand and onto the ground, landing in an especially thick pile of reddish dust.

As I reached for it, an icy hand met mine. Hailey. I shivered without meaning to—the sense, or vibe, I was getting from her was . . . no sense at all. She was a black void, and around me, no one ever was. Everyone always had something to say, even when they didn't speak.

Hailey caught me before I had a chance to play off my initial reaction and snatched her hand back. "Sorry." She sounded offended.

"It's fine," I muttered quickly, feeling like complete shit for her reading me wrong. She just startled me, that's all.

No one else caught the awkwardness. Everyone was still chit-chatting like they were all old friends. There wasn't a stranger Sekou didn't know or wouldn't get to know. I guess he never took to the "stranger danger" lessons we learned back in elementary school, or he forgot how we ended up on Golden Isle. We stuck to our Kin, and outside of Kin walls, in the rest of the island where Nana managed who lived there like a huge private community, we maintained our privacy and our distance.

History had taught Black people to move in non-Black spaces with caution, and when you had something everyone wanted—Golden Isle—we learned to be even more careful. Developers often tried to buy our land from us though it had been in our family for over two hundred years. We had to learn to be wary of strangers. You never knew their true intent.

I snuck a peek at Hailey. The elders have always said eyes were a window to one's soul. Looking into Hailey's dark coal-like eyes, I saw mystery instead. I wanted to dislike her from *hello* because she was a mainlander, or because I couldn't catch her vibe like I could most others. I couldn't put my finger on it. Maybe it was the way Hailey matched my stare with her own curiosity and without fear, like she was trying to read me like I was trying to read her.

She was the first to break away, handing back my cap. Her fingers were like icicles.

She turned on her heel and started toward the parking lot and called over her shoulder, "We need to head back to Charleston, Luke."

I dusted my cap off gently, even though I'd never be able to get all the dirt off. Someone from our group announced the buses were ready to head back to the dock, and we all began to move collectively to the parking lot too. I ended up trailing behind, using my cap as a distraction from having to talk, especially with Nana surrounded as usual and Sekou flitting around like the social butterfly he was.

"Text me when you get back?" Luke bent down close to Naira, sharing something private between them in the middle of this very public place.

I watched Mr. and Mrs. Russell, wondering if they were seeing their beloved daughter getting all cozy with a mainlander boy of the preppiest persuasion. They didn't seem to notice, too busy corralling the other four Russell kids from running around all over the place as if they'd never been out in public before.

Naira nodded, ducking her head shyly at whatever Luke was whispering in her ear.

He pulled away, saying wistfully, "Wish I could celebrate with you all tonight."

I stared her down, willing her to feel my vibe.

She wouldn't dare invite him . . .

"Maybe another time. This is for family."

That's what I thought. My body and attitude relaxed, and I felt relieved that Naira still had some sense. Sekou lowered his giraffe self until he was close enough to keep his words private. "If you death stare them any harder, you will make him combust. Chill out. You know it don't take much for Naira to clam up."

This was true. While Sekou was an open book, Naira was closed tighter than the leather over one of Sekou's sacred djembe drums.

I shrugged him away, punching him in the arm for good measure for his earlier crack. I knew how to act. I wasn't one of the Russell kids running around like no one ever took them anywhere.

And then I heard Luke say to Naira, "I'll call you tomorrow? Tell you about the big reveal my uncle Simon wants to show us back at the research lab."

Naira nodded. "Thanks for coming down."

Luke looked like he wanted to eat her up. He couldn't take his eyeballs off of her, even when we reached the parking lot and his sister was waiting in a cherry-red Camaro with its top down. The Russells waved their goodbyes at Luke, while Sekou and I hung back waiting for Naira because we were, like, good friends and all despite the fact that clearly we were kept in the dark about this online love connection.

Hailey called, "Luke!" I could tell from the single word she meant business.

Luke held up a finger asking for another minute.

He touched Naira's chin. "I hope you decide to come. I can show you everything."

She managed to sneak a quick peek at me and Sekou, both of us staring open-mouthed at her public display of affection with her parents and my grandmother in plain view. Luke kissed her lightly on the lips and my jaw dropped. I think I actually saw Naira melt. Okay, meeting a new dude was one thing, but when had they gotten so serious?

Luke finally made it to the Camaro before his sister up and left his ass. Luke twisted in his seat, glancing back at Naira as they drove off. She stared after that car, not moving until the red death trap NASCAR'd away. It was only after the roar of the revving engine faded that Naira finally snapped out of it and remembered the rest of us. Her shoulders sagged, as if the last thing she wanted to be doing was getting back on the bus with us. *Ouch.*

I opened my mouth, about to unload the boatload of questions that I had bottled up, but she held up a hand.

"Can we talk later?" she said. The space between us cooled in the sweltering heat.

"I didn't even say anything," I said, following her up the steps of the bus while Sekou brought up the rear.

"But it's coming," she said stiffly, looking for an empty seat and plopping in next to Peter Brooks, whose family ran the Bait and Tackle shop on the Isle. "I just want to cherish this moment for a little while longer, please. Then we can talk."

"My bad," Sekou said, bumping into my back when I'd stopped short, shocked at Naira's from-nowhere attitude. If I didn't know better, I would have thought she was mad at me, as if I were the one who made Luke go home.

I huffed. *Excuse me for intruding* was what I really wanted to say.

I nodded nice and dainty, while confused as hell about what was going on and how I'd become the bad guy. I hadn't even done anything yet. I kept my mouth shut, trying extra hard to keep it classy and be the mature one for a change.

And you know what *that* was called?

Growth.

CHAPTER FOUR

On our way back to Golden Isle, we passed Mr. Gilbert in his fishing boat, delivering his latest catch to sell to one of the restaurants. I waved to the old man, who had so often brought me and Nana Ama a bushel of crab or shrimp or oysters from his hauls. Fishing, shrimping, and growing peaches had been the main sources of livelihood since the Kin had lived on the Isle.

Later that night, a chorus of whoops and hollers rang out as a newly sprung Cal High graduate jumped from the deck of his catamaran into the water with a *splish*. We had all tied our boats together in a network of ropes and moored them to the docks. Parties on the water were something of an Isle tradition, and our graduating class had spent countless nights hanging out beneath the stars. Sometimes the boats would drift out farther, away from the inlet and into the Atlantic, but tonight we decided to stay close to the shore. That way, if some of us got too drunk, we wouldn't be too many clicks in to get them on land.

From where I stretched out in Sekou's sailboat, I watched as another islander, Davis, dove into the dark water. I swayed with

Sekou's boat, feeling pretty nice on the Peach Lightning moonshine that was our island's specialty. It was so good that even the mainlanders loved to come and have a glass or three of it. Had to take it slow, though, because that 'shine could sneak up on a person real quick and lay them out completely for two days.

"How long before Ada tells me to dock so she can go home?" Sekou asked.

I wasn't about to pay him any dust. I was relaxed and enjoying the night and everyone else having fun. I stifled a yawn, not willing to admit that I was a little tired and wouldn't have minded going home to bed. It was that moonshine. But I wasn't going to let Sekou Thompson, the eternal partier and playboy, have the satisfaction.

I turned to Naira, showing my saddest, most pitiful eyes. Since the bus, she'd mellowed out some and I wanted to keep it that way. This "being mature" took some getting used to. "Tell your friend to shut up."

Naira offered a patient smile from her corner of the boat, where she'd been hunched over her phone all night. I was reassured we were good, even if she seemed distracted since we'd gotten back. I hadn't mentioned Luke since we boarded the bus, listening to Sekou for a change. Growth, right?

I waited her out, hoping she'd be first to break and let us in on her love life. My growth was diminishing by the hour, though. There was only so much a person could take.

Naira said, "You've been sneaking home early for years already. Live a little."

My eyes narrowed. Traitor.

The boat rocked when Sekou heaved himself off it and into the water with a tribal yell.

"Try to look like you don't totally hate being here, please?" Naira slid her phone into her back pocket, stretching and wiggling her fingers at me and ignoring my groans.

"My bad." I bowed and remembered to smile hard enough to make my dimples appear.

"Maris stopped by the store the other day," Naira said nonchalantly. "I think she's hoping you'll hang out on the Fourth."

I forced myself to remain calm so Naira wouldn't notice how much I didn't want to discuss Maris tonight.

"She shouldn't have done that." I gritted my teeth. "Considering she's the one who ended things. She should be more focused on getting ready for that research trip with her college."

Here, the Fourth of July held a different kind of meaning. We celebrated big on the island with fireworks, food, and partying, but not for independence from the British. On the Golden Isle and to the Kinfolk, the Fourth was the day of our ancestors' independence. It marked the night the founding families saw a light in the distance out in the Atlantic and decided to follow it like the North Star, rather than die like the countless other stolen lives on the boats that were carrying them to hell. The founding families vowed never to be taken back again to live in bondage and used that mysterious blinking light in the water to guide them like a lighthouse. They landed on Golden Isle, the isolated island of fireflies, and flourished.

Naira shot me side-eye. "Maybe Maris figured out she screwed up. Don't you want to hear her out?"

"Nope." I popped the *p*. Maris was the cherry on top of an already annoying day.

"People make mistakes, Ada. People change. You can't always be so black and white about stuff."

It *was* black and white. Maris had shown me who she was when she refused to understand my priorities. She showed me I wasn't enough when she called it quits.

"How are you all into light and warmth when you're—"

I sat up quickly, striking what I thought was a sexy pose. "—some kinda Nubian goddess who bathes in blood to keep her youthful beauty?"

Naira pursed her lips, unimpressed as she watched me do a few more. "No. No, I wasn't gonna say that."

I flopped back down.

I could never share all of me. It came with the territory and the responsibilities to the island. To my grandma, especially since it was only the two of us left. To my legacy and the promise my family made to protect this land and everyone who lived here, which didn't leave much room for a love life.

"Love is overrated."

Naira smacked me. "Did you say that when you were with Maris?"

"Okay, now where is Sheriff Lyle because that was definitely assault." I swiveled around, looking for the Beaufort County sheriff even though it wasn't his day to check the island. Wouldn't be surprised if he popped up from behind the cluster of boats, ready to bust us. But we were policing ourselves. No excessive drinking. No boating if you were drinking. Each boat had a designated driver and Sekou was ours, though I didn't remember Naira taking a sip of anything other than water. I decided I'd had enough 'shine. I wasn't about to be the drunkest one on this boat and make an ass of myself.

"I just want you to be happy," Naira said, sounding like the world was on her shoulders.

I couldn't explain to Naira why Maris and I didn't work when I didn't fully understand it myself. We just didn't, and I had to believe that was okay sometimes. Plus, I was going through stuff. I had bigger things on my mind: like if this year was finally the one when I'd be able to Light and fulfill my role as the next matriarch to the Kinfolk and caretaker of Golden Isle. Nana had been preparing me since I could remember, teaching me how to make tinctures, salves and balms, protection charms, and mojo bags. How to make her most special elixir that she shared with the Kin every year, the elixir that kept them well and strong, if they wanted it, because on the Isle, there was always a choice. And each year so far, I'd failed at it miserably. Nana said I had to want it, that I hadn't accepted it, that I still feared it—the Light. She said I had to cultivate more.

"I *am* happy," I stressed, hoping she'd get it. "I don't need Maris to make me happy so maybe leave that one alone."

Giving my everything to someone was out of the picture. There were too many opportunities for danger, for them and for me, if the closely guarded secrets and gifts of the Isle were revealed. I couldn't invite my closest friends to share that burden, let alone a lover. Holding that part of me back *was* me giving my everything.

Naira pouted. The fire pits dotting the shore not too far off snapped and crackled, sending up sparks.

"You know . . ."

Please don't say it. Not tonight. I sucked in air. Nearly three years had passed, and I wanted one night when I wasn't reminded in some way.

"You know . . . ," she said again, "I just want you to be happy after . . . ," Naira choked out, her eyes shiny. I slowly exhaled. "Like, you never really talk about it."

Wasn't going to either. What was there to say? Naira was really on one tonight. All up in her feels and trying to bring me down with her.

You'd have thought it was *her* mother who was dead. My mother had to be. Because I didn't sense her presence here on Earth. Or maybe she was too far away and I was too weak to feel her. No, my mother was gone.

"What? Girl, come on," I scoffed, waving her off. It came out much louder than I intended, as I tried to pretend away any emotion.

"Who needs love when you and Sekou will always be by my side? We're done with Cal. We have the whole summer to chill, and come fall, maybe I'll even take classes at the community college with you. It'll be great. What else is there?" I shot her a big cheesy grin, ignoring the flash of guilt sliding across her face.

Love sure as hell didn't stop my mom from going and leaving me behind because the thoughts in her mind became too many. Love didn't keep me from wanting to launch into the stratosphere and never come back whenever I was forced to think of the moment Nana broke the news.

"Ada," Nana began that morning over a warmed cup of her treasured honeyed coconut water, "your mother has left."

The heaviness in Nana's voice and her ageless face, which now looked a hundred years old, told me what she meant without her having to say so. Mom hadn't gone to the mainland for an excursion. Mom wasn't coming back.

"How?" I asked, feeling surprisingly calm.

Nana looked beyond me to her groves that led to the cliff. "Out to sea."

I nodded because the huge painful lump growing in my throat wouldn't let me speak.

Nana sighed out her prayer for the dead. "May Mami Wata guide her to our ancestors, and may she finally find her peace."

Love didn't stop the anger and resentment of knowing I wasn't enough for Mom to stay, even though it had taken her so many years to have me. Nana constantly telling me how much my mother loved and wanted me for so many years wasn't enough. Not for me. Not for my mom. I was supposed to live with that. And I couldn't.

The only things, the *only* things that kept me from exploding were my grandmother and my friends. I couldn't take another person leaving.

Eventually, the water crowd joined the shore crowd, and that's when things got really live as we dried off in front of the fires. The music transitioned to a line dance, and the crowd went wild. Sekou spotted us, twirling an invisible lasso in the air and then throwing it at Naira.

She froze, caught for a hot second, then gripped the invisible rope in both hands and started under-handing her way toward him as he pulled on his end, her feet two-stepping and cowboy boogying effortlessly in time to the lyrics as she continued pulling herself along the rope. Her execution was so flawless, it was easy to see how Naira was the undefeated best dancer of the three of us.

Naira reached Sekou and he wrapped his long, muscled arms around her, twirling her as she cackled happily.

The two of them started dancing, jumping around, getting lost in the crowd. Sekou, who towered over most of the moving bodies, motioned for me to come over. I waved him off, opting to hang back and watch from the sidelines like I did best. I popped in my earbuds to block out the noise that could crowd my mind if I wasn't careful, facing the expanse of water that stretched out of the Calibogue Sound and into the Atlantic.

I gazed out to the blackness of the glass-like water as it reflected the sky. I could see the mainland's twinkling line of lights from where I stood on the beach as my friends danced the night away. I shivered, imagining someone across the three-mile stretch of Atlantic on the other side, doing just as I was doing. On the shore, staring over here and wondering about us too.

And for the briefest moment I thought my imagination was reality, and across the sea was someone staring back at me with two tiny red orbs where eyes should have been. I looked away to refocus, but when I returned there was no one. Another intense shiver ripped through me, clenching my bones, and I felt the slightest quiver of fear. I chalked it up to the dampness from the water and having an extraordinarily unordinary day. I walked back to the warmth of the fire.

It was nothing more than fear of the unknown.

CHAPTER FIVE

Naira and I were finally able to pull Sekou from the party after we reminded him he had ferry tours early the next day. His uncle James owned the fleet and would be pissed if he showed up late.

We piled into Sekou's cart, waving goodbye to those who weren't ready for the party to end. Naira was in the back, with me riding shotgun. I had spent the whole night without bringing up the elephant in the room: *Luuuuke*. But I couldn't wait any longer.

"So, this Luke," I began, nodding at her phone. "Who is he?"

Sekou chimed in, checking her in the rearview as we bumped along the road. "Yeah, who's the frat boy?"

I said, "She was slobbing him down at concessions."

Naira grimaced.

"Yeah," I said. "Not only that, but you introduced him to, like, everybody. It'll be all over the Isle by tomorrow if it isn't already that you have some secret boyfriend." I crossed my arms over my chest, settling back in my seat.

"Real talk," Sekou added. "It's one thing if it's a dude from the

Isle. Even one from Cal or right across the way at Hilton Head or someplace we know. But this guy? What do you really know about him? Where'd he come from, Naira? Thought we didn't keep any secrets from each other."

Well, almost no secrets.

Naira sighed. "I already said we met during my hybrid class with the Endowment."

"You met online," I countered.

"Everything happens online," she returned.

Sekou asked, "What's so special about this Endowment Research Company?"

"Endowment Research *Lab*," Naira corrected.

Sekou shrugged.

"The Endowment has been primarily focused on recovering, restoring, and returning lost cultural artifacts," she said. "You know how I've been working with Nana Ama on chronicling the history of the Kinfolk and tracing back our lineage in case any of the Kin wants to return to their motherlands to see where they came from? Other groups along the coast, like the Gullah people, have retained their African roots even though they were captured and enslaved like our ancestors. All of these cultures have artifacts from their lands that have been lost or stolen over time. When the Endowment gets a lead on a find, they dig it up, determine where it came from, restore it, and return it. Luke was in the class too and reached out to me after I presented about helping Nana Ama chronicle our history, and we've been talking ever since."

If it was daylight, I bet I'd see Naira blushing right now, the way she hid her smile behind her hand and turned away.

"So, he slid in your class's version of a DM? Nice," I cracked. Sekou cleared his throat in warning.

"Then I mentioned Nana's ceremonial cuffs and how they tie into our culture and ancestry and tradition when we started talking about family," Naira continued as if I hadn't said a thing.

The mention of the thick gold-and-cobalt cuffs that had been passed down in my family made my shoulders tense. They were so old even Nana couldn't say when they were created, and she only wore them during our most sacred and private Kin occasions.

Sekou looked at me nervously while I began a slow simmer. "You shouldn't have done that, Naira."

There were a lot of things Naira shouldn't have been doing.

"You know we don't talk about our ways here. How the island is kinda . . ." He trailed off, whirling his hands around in a pantomime of thoughts. "Special," he whispered. "And Nana is"—the hands again—"also special."

She could heal people was what he wanted to say aloud, but didn't.

"While Ada is . . ." He looked at me with a pained expression.

Not so special. Because I was supposed to be able to heal too, but couldn't. Was supposed to be able to do a lot of things, but couldn't. When I dug my hands into the Isle's earth, I felt its energy, all the spirits and life force Nana had infused with it there, but I couldn't use it to do anything. Not like Nana.

"I didn't tell him any of that," Naira said defensively. "I just said we kept our traditions since slavery, same as the Gullah Geechee up and down the coast. I just mentioned she had African heirlooms passed down in her family and hidden by her ancestors when they were stolen and brought here."

"Still . . ." Sekou shot quick glances my way like he was checking my temperature.

It was rising, the slow simmer beginning to bubble.

I brushed a loose coil of hair from my face, looking out at the homes lined along the street and the banyan trees looming overhead, their leaves low enough to practically touch. And just beyond them, marshes and ravines, massive trees, creeks and lakes, a nature preserve. Remnants of tabby cabins, some of the first homes the founding families built when they'd come to this place.

Talking about the cuffs was *my* family's business, not Naira's. And that she was spilling to not only some rando, but a mainlander rando was way too much—I didn't care how much she liked him. Her loyalty should have been to me, to Nana.

Naira continued. "Luke was talking about some artifacts the research lab at the school uncovered in Virginia under the statue of Robert E. Lee. There was a necklace, and when Luke described that it had blue gems, it made me think of Nana's. So, I mentioned that she had something with blue gems. And he was like, what if they were related."

"Oh, he said that, did he?" I said.

Naira's nostrils flared. She could be frustrated all she wanted, but it wasn't *us* yakking to strangers about Isle shit, much less Nana Ama's heirlooms.

"Y'all, it wasn't even like that! It was a two-second conversation!"

I turned to her, accusation coating my words. "Did you show him any of the drawings you and Nana did?"

Her eyes went from shock to hurt. "What? No! No, I would never show anyone our work. I would never tell anyone about how special Golden Isle is, the Kinfolk, and about you and Nana Ama."

Nana Ama spent countless hours detailing the history in intricate drawings of maps and family trees and scenes of gods, goddesses, and battles she had envisioned from the writings of Kin throughout the time, especially drawings of Anansi the spider god, Nyame the supreme god, and his twin goddess daughters who tragically ended up being the vampires of West Africa.

The adze, Nana Ama began long ago, as she showed me the drawing of two African goddesses, daughters of Nyame the Sky God and his queen, Asase Yaa, draped in rows of cowries and gold as they seemed to peer out through the drawing and right into me.

They were first created to help mankind cure disease, but over time their story and purpose have become convoluted. Our people needed a reason for where illness had started coming from. The adze sisters could move with Light, becoming fireflies, often at night, to help the sick. However, over time and due to the fear of the unknown diseases brought in from enslavers and colonizers, ravaging our people, the legend and true purpose of the adze became convoluted superstition, and one of nightmares. That's why we honor the sisters on Golden Isle, a land of fireflies. They guided us to this land, protecting us as they always intended to do.

Naira might not have told Luke everything, but she still told him about things she didn't truly understand. Nana Ama cast incantations over the land, protecting it from those who would do it harm, using its bloody history when the First Peoples who owned and roamed it were massacred by the British in the 1700s to help fortify the protections.

As Sekou pulled to a stop in front of her house, Naira leaned in close, her voice barely above a whisper, warm breath tickling my ear. “I think I might leave Golden Isle.”

CHAPTER SIX

What. The. Hell.

Slowly, I faced Naira, hoping I hadn't heard right. She looked back at me with her luminous brown eyes, waiting for me to say something. Her fingers twisted around one another in her lap.

"You mean you're going to leave on this research trip?"

Naira swallowed, slow to speak, like she was weighing her words. "Well, yeah. But I mean after that." The skinny gold bangles covering Naira's slender arm nearly to her elbow jingled from her movement.

"Just say what you're going to say," I muttered, already feeling the heat building behind my eyes.

She took a deep breath. "So, I've been thinking about applying to U of Charleston for the fall if I can get in. If I go on the research trip, it won't just be to kick around. It'll be to check out the school and make a final decision."

The last word she said real low, ducking her head down in shame like she shouldn't have been telling me this bullshit news.

She shrugged. "I mean, that's what I've been thinking. The weekend will help me figure it out."

The hell was she talking about? There was no way Naira had been thinking about leaving the island and me and Sekou.

The words rolled around in my head. Naira said *leaving*. She meant *leaving*, leaving.

"You're screwing with us, right?" There was a piece of me warning to be cool, but it was a teeny-tiny piece. Being cool wasn't really my style.

"I'm dead serious."

The burning in my eyes increased, and I bit my lip to hold back the tears and words I knew would get me in trouble.

I knew what this meant. I knew it when I saw Luke with Naira. I knew it when I woke up this morning to my grandma in a weird trance. And now, I knew that I was losing my best friend. That she would leave me behind.

My place would always be here on the Isle, where I would one day take over Nana Ama's role. Naira had promised she would be right there with me.

Sekou pursed his lips like he was trying to figure out how we got here. That made two of us. It was like Naira was tossing us to the side and didn't give a damn about it.

I heard myself asking, "Are you, like, for real?"

"The realest," she said. "Can Charleston really be considered 'going away'? And if I did want to go farther, why not? Honestly, I think you're making a bigger deal of this than necessary."

"The difference," I said, "is that you're talking about living there. Like, with mainlanders."

"For school. I'll be back some weekends. And on holidays. And for the summer."

"I just always thought . . ." I was at a loss for words. What did I think? I hadn't. I thought the Isle and working on it, living on it, was enough. I didn't think Naira would want to live like a mainlander. She'd be *away,* away. Not commuting like we'd been doing for high school. Not even going to the community college right across the way. But living there.

"You thought everything would stay the same." She snorted. "Life isn't like that, Ada. It might be for you. But not so much for me."

I waited for Sekou to step in, to tap me out like a tag team wrestling duo. But he kept quiet.

"Kinfolk leave all the time. They come and go. Live abroad and return home." Naira stepped out of the cart, her tone cool as ice.

"But—but . . . we're different. This is our home, and we swore we'd stick together. Hold this place down. How can we do that when you're"—I waved my hands into the void—"out there."

"Then come with," she said suddenly, like it was the best idea in the world. "Me, you, and Se away at school."

I flinched, her words like stabs.

At the same time, Sekou said, "You know Ada can't just up and leave the Isle whenever she wants."

Naira turned to him. "Why can't she?"

It sounded like a dare and an insult to me and my grandmother. She knew Nana's fear of traveling far distances across the sea and her unwavering belief that crossing the sea always meant one wouldn't return. That the most Nana would occasionally do is venture the few miles over the waterway to Hilton Head or towns along the coast when she needed to step out. Because of all this, Naira knew I was just as oathbound to the Golden Isle as my grandmother. She knew we had to stay to protect ourselves and the land we owned. I opened myself up to feel. Naira's vibe was different. Resentful. Fearful. Chilled. Feelings from her that were new to me, and terrifying. Confrontation was her enemy. She was supposed to be the sensible one. Sekou, the playful one. Me, the hothead. We balanced one another out, but now we were out of whack.

"What's the problem? That I want to see the world?" she scoffed. "It's not even the world, it's like a microcosm of the world." Her thumb and forefinger nearly touched for emphasis. "It's just Charleston for god's sake. What's wrong with going, huh? With knowing what's out there? With knowing *who's* out there?"

And there it was. The real reason why Naira wanted off our rock. School my ass. This "change of mind" was all about god-damn Luke.

Sekou finally said, "It's a surprise, Naira, you know? Just the other day you were talking about what we were gonna put on the grill for the Fourth. You and me were looking at online schools just last week. It's been us three since we could talk, so, I mean, we need a minute. To process all of this."

Naira said, "Know what I think?"

I didn't want to know, but Naira was going to enlighten me any damn way.

Sekou whispered, "Don't do it."

"I think you're really mad about the thought of me and Sekou finally getting out from up under you. I think you like that we follow you around like little birdies. It's the Ada Show all the time, we're just the sidekicks. And we play into it every fucking time because it's your family who runs all of this." She took a deep breath like she was preparing to say something big. Then she delivered. "You think you own us."

I felt heat flush my cheeks.

"Naira, what?" Sekou said, shocked.

Naira couldn't unsay what she just said. And I couldn't unhear it.

I clenched my fist and tried to keep in all the rage and hurt I wanted to unleash. I'd tried up until now to keep quiet, tried to hold myself back from lashing out because I knew how sensitive she was.

I really tried, but Naira had made it impossible.

Sekou slung an arm across the back of the seat, the tips of his fingers grazing my shoulder like he was going to comfort me or rein me in. I moved out of reach, not wanting to be touched. I didn't want to be here with Naira, who wanted to leave, and Sekou, who seemed fine with it all.

I got out of the cart.

I wanted to say the most hurtful things possible. I wanted to cry.

"We can talk about it tomorrow when everyone's had a moment, you know? Not say things we'll regret in the morning," Sekou suggested.

What was he saying? It was better to be the one leaving than the one being left.

"Ada, wait," Naira called out as I increased the distance between us. It was enough to accuse me of wanting to keep her down by keeping her here. It was enough to spring a new plan different than what we'd talked about for years, to not trust us enough to discuss it. And now she wanted me to *wait*. For what?

"Ada," she said again while Sekou looked back and forth as if he was unsure which side of the rope to land on. Well, I'd make the choice for him.

"You're a liar, Naira," I told her.

"What?" she squeaked.

"A liar. You signed up for this research trip for your college class. Fine. But then you say you want to go away to find yourself or see what's out there or some shit. I think there's nothing, but whatever. But now I know why you're really leaving for that trip tomorrow. I know 'what's out there.' A boy. A boring, entitled, ignorant, rich mainlander prep you barely even know."

Sekou groaned as his head dropped in his hand as if I was the one who'd broken our pact. But it wasn't me. It was Naira who'd flipped on me, on him and the Isle, on our friendship.

"Jesus, Ada," Sekou muttered.

My body trembled, but I held myself together, just for a little bit longer. "So, go be with that boy and leave me the hell alone. For good." I turned on my heel and began walking.

"Ada!" Sekou called from behind me. "What the hell? How you gonna . . . What about your ride?"

I kept walking.

I SPENT ALL NIGHT TOSSING AND TURNING, WONDERING HOW I could have done or said things differently. But in the end, Naira had said enough and I guess I had too. I tried brushing off Naira's accusation that I wanted to control them, to keep them here and content on the Isle like I was. But a part of me feared she was right. I'd never want to trap someone where they didn't want to be. Nana's number one rule was clear: Everyone deserved the freedom to choose their own path. Naira had made hers, and I knew that meant she would probably leave the Isle. This trip was just the beginning. And as much as it gutted me, I couldn't stand in her way.

I couldn't wave goodbye either. And I couldn't stand to see Sekou's disappointed face that I'd handled Naira all wrong. What was I supposed to do, baby her? What about me?

When I woke up the next morning, nightmare and earthquake-free, all the feelings from the night before rushed at me at once when I remembered what Naira had said. What Sekou didn't say because I had said enough.

. . . Leave me the hell alone. For good.

That part I hadn't meant. As angry and hurt as I was by Naira, I couldn't send her off with what I'd said.

From the top of the pier at the private marina on the Kin side of the Isle, I watched as the boat Naira was on backed up farther and farther from the dock, curving into a turn, and began its way up the two-hour trek to Charleston Harbor.

My phone buzzed in my back pocket and I fished it out, seeing the text from Naira pop up. *I'm sorry.*

My anger and pride might have kept me from answering her

sorry or the string of messages that followed, but at least I'd still shown up for her, though she didn't know it. She wouldn't know I stayed on the pier, watching the boat's wake eventually subside to light ripples as it moved farther away. She wouldn't know I remained long after everyone else left to go about their day's business. Long after the boat was barely a speck, and then when it was no longer there.

CHAPTER SEVEN

Sekou and I walked along the reedy shores of the fisherman's dock a few days later, looking for oysters to collect for lunch. I'd helped with his Isle tour runs after his older brother Ahmad couldn't make it. The dock was pretty empty, most of the boats out to get their catch. We talked about everything except the elephant in the room, him waiting for me to ask and me hoping he wouldn't bring Naira up. I wasn't so lucky.

"Saw you on the pier when we pushed off the other day," he said. He'd been the one to run them to Charleston on one of his family's boats. "You should have come. They were saying some crazy shit about a few people disappearing all of a sudden."

"I had to help Nana make herbal remedies in her cabin," I said, knowing damn well I'd gone back home to watch YouTube vids and wallow in self-pity.

The smell hit Sekou first. "Something reeks." He gagged, his face bunched up, and his hand flew to cover his nose. He was thigh-deep in the reeds, behind me and heading toward a new section of shallow water we hadn't checked yet. We didn't need more, our buckets nearly overflowing with oysters.

"Could be something washed up," Sekou said.

That wasn't the smell of washed-up marine life. It wasn't an animal that had gotten too close to the water's edge and had been caught by a gator. It was a smell of decay that infiltrated every fiber of my being and made my stomach wretch something fierce, bile climbing my throat.

"God, what is that?" he asked, barely able to contain himself.

I didn't answer, seeing the sandy mound washed up in the reeds of low tide salt water. As I got closer, I waved away the thick swarm of black flies crawling on it as the breeze pushed a waft of stink and rot at me.

I put my hand up to my nose and mouth, not wanting to taste the stench. But it was too late, and the smell quickly coated my insides, sickening me. The rot was at war with me, making my blood race. Yet, there was a trace of familiarity and repulsion. The smell was wrong. It smelled of disease.

"What is it?" Sekou asked quietly from behind me.

I moved closer, hoping my suspicions were wrong. The mound began to take shape as the tide washed over it. Two legs, one booted, one showing a decaying foot caked with sand and dried blood. Torn plastic fisherman's overalls. I moved closer to see the face, staggering back when recognition hit.

Behind me, Sekou turned and threw up all the breakfast he'd had, and then some.

Nana's words rushed at me.

... became a disease.

Then the flash of the shadow with its two red dots staring back at me. I remained still, unable to tear my eyes from the old man I'd waved goodbye to not so long ago.

Not in Florida visiting family where I wished to Nyame he had been.

Mr. Gilbert. With his throat ripped out.

On the Isle, there was no murder, no real crime beyond the occasional drunken fight between friends who'd make up the next day after a good shaming by the rest.

There wasn't an official police force here. With a population of just under four hundred, we were too small; only a quarter of us were actual Kinfolk natives and the rest were transplants who'd relocated to the Isle after getting Nana Ama's permission.

We were good at sorting out our own issues. We didn't need anyone on the mainland telling us how to act. That's what our elders—led by Nana Ama—were for. But private island or not, we were still in the US, and that meant we still followed the mainland laws. We paid taxes and voted, and someone still had to make sure we remained law-abiding citizens. The bi-monthly visits from Sheriff Lyle, Kinfolk formerly of the Golden Isle now living on the mainland, used to be enough. But after finding poor Elder Gilbert . . . I didn't know if anything would ever be enough again.

Word had traveled like wildfire on a dry day. "Thank Nyame he didn't wash up at Freeman's Port," Nana Ama said, standing next to Lyle as he peered down at the body. Her words shocked me.

Nana seemed more worried about the tourists finding out than the dead man lying at her feet. Farther up on the embankment, the crowd of islanders was growing, sounds of cries and disbelief coming from them in waves. I wished I had my earbuds handy. The growing noise was becoming too distracting, even here where I could normally keep the buzz back. I wondered where I'd last left them. Had they dropped in the water's edge while I was trying to calm Sekou enough from freaking out so we could get help? I was freakishly calm, more concerned with what had happened to Mr. Gilbert than at having seen his wrecked body. Maybe once the adrenaline died, I'd be as bad off as Sekou was.

Nana Ama seemed to remember eyes were on her. She tightened her wrap around her thin shoulders and raised a hand for silence.

"Please, let us give Sheriff Lyle and the authorities time to conduct their case." She paused when someone from the crowed cried out. "Yes, I know. It is a deeply sad day for all of us. Please make way and we'll update you." She called on the Kinfolk specifically. "We will hold a town hall this evening. Prepare yourselves. And to all, please do not let this become fodder for gossip, especially to the tourists. We need their continued revenue, yes? Sheriff and I will keep everyone informed of this tragedy." Her eyes, clouded with emotion I couldn't read, swept the group. "Nyame be with you all."

This time, my grandmother's words sounded more like an ominous prayer than her normally casual send-off.

Death wasn't new to me. The old ones died on the Isle when their time came, and whenever it did, it would be Nana Ama and me giving Homegoing rites over the bodies. The dead would be welcomed peacefully in the spirit world of the Asamando, and would remain there until their time came to walk the world again, when the veil between the Asamando and our mortal world of the Asase was lifted. Our Harvest Festival was one of those days, held on Thursday. The day of the week when the veil was always at its thinnest.

"Nana Ama," I said shakily, stepping away from Sekou, who sat in the warm sand, staring listlessly at the ground, as if he'd never move again. Behind us, the crowd began to slowly trickle away, our fellow Kin starting a slow hymn song in Mr. Gilbert's honor. Poor Mr. Gilbert. My eyes burned. I wanted to cry, but the hardness in Nana's voice, mixed with something else I couldn't read, kept any tears at bay. If I cried, she'd think I was a child. She'd never let me in and let me help her.

She turned slowly to me. "Hmm?"

I went to her. I didn't want to go toward the body again, not like that, but I went anyway. "That's not a boating accident," I whispered. I didn't know what it was, but boats didn't just take out the neck and leave everything else.

"Luckily no one else has seen what has become of Elder Gilbert except us." She held me firmly by both sides of my face, searching my eyes until she was sure I was paying attention. "And no one should. We don't want to scare anyone unnecessarily."

I didn't even know what she meant by that.

"But . . . I'm already scared." I gestured at Sekou, who hadn't moved. "And he's sure as hel—" I swallowed. "He might actually be stuck that way forever. He's very scared."

Sheriff Lyle said, "I'm going to have to call in the folks. Helicopter in. Get him to the medical examiner on Mainland."

Nana turned from me sharply. "You know he can't go there. You don't know what caused that. Better to burn him."

"Burn him?" Sheriff Lyle and I said at the same time, both of us appalled.

I stepped back, unsure who this was in front of me. "Nana, you can't just burn a body without proper procedures. Even here on the Isle. You know that."

"And I can't leave him to be taken to Mainland," she said. "Not for an autopsy. Not for his family to deal with. He needs to be taken care of now. Please, Kambrell."

Hmm. Always thought Sheriff Lyle's first name was . . . well, Sheriff.

Nana got close to Lyle, gently laying a hand on his arm. Her voice lowered to a murmur. "You haven't called it in yet. We'll take him to the cabin and deal with it there. We're doing it for his sake."

The way she spoke to him was so intimate, close, as if they had been more than just matriarch and Kin.

I opened my mouth to protest. To ask for an explanation, but Nana remembered I was there, and Sekou was just beyond. "Ada, take Sekou home. Take care of him."

"But, Nana, why are you bur—"

"Addae, be quick." She offered me a small smile that was meant to be reassuring but failed at its job. "In due time you will know what you must know. But right now, I must do what is needed."

CHAPTER EIGHT

It was dusk by the time I found my way to the Gathering Tree, where everything of meaning happened in Kin's Landing: our celebrations, our concerns posed about the community, Isle, or whatever else, and the decisions we'd make collectively under Nana's guidance. Our meetings and ceremonies here were just for Kin, and it was the Kin Nana wanted to speak to first.

Tonight, there were no djembe drums sounding their rhythmic beats. There were no melodies or discussions of Homegoing rites for Elder Gilbert. There was only Nana Ama standing in front of her stool.

The majestic, sprawling Gathering Tree was the oldest live oak on the island, believed to have been here since as far back as the Revolutionary War and since our founding families inhabited the land. They had nurtured it and let it flourish until its limbs reached nearly across the expanse of Kin's Landing to the west and east. The tree was the reason why the Kin built their cluster of community here, at the northmost point of the island. It was thought to have the most earthly spiritual power from those who were here before the Kin.

I usually felt inspired beneath the mighty tree, but tonight I felt a weight on my chest and an unease in my skin. I had so many unanswered questions.

Was this what Nana had meant when she said, *She is gathering*? Was Elder Gilbert a victim of the gathering? And what could Nana do beyond the protective barriers of the Isle?

Protective barriers. My stomach lurched. Wherever Elder Gilbert had died, whatever had taken him, it was like the Isle had brought his body home to be taken care of properly. Nana's enchantments would call forth a guide for lost Kin. And yet, Nana wanted his body burned, rushed, without proper rites and recognition. What could he have done to bring that kind of fate?

I wished this night was like all the others, that Naira was at our house as Nana's apprentice, assisting Nana with dressing and accompanying her over to where Nana usually sat in her wide-backed Marimba wicker chair with many intricate handwoven designs. Nana was small, but her aura towered over everyone like an African queen sitting in the midst of her people. Flickering fire torches would surround our ever-growing square, casting shapes all around. And fireflies would dance around us, blinking in and out in their infinite beauty. It was a breathtaking scene, nights like those.

Usually, Nana liked to dress the part when she "held court," decked out in amulets of golden squares and ivory cowrie shells, with her hair wrapped up in a headdress of multicolored woven African cloth. Tonight, Nana was simple in flowing white linen.

Her circlet of cowrie shells draped over the crown of her head, tucked in the folds of the top bun of half of her gathered locs. On her wrists were the gold-and-cobalt cuffs.

My breath hitched at the sight of them, filling me with a twitchy mix of longing and dread as they always did. A part of me wanted to wear those cuffs one day and feel their power.

Another part was terrified of the day I would.

If she was wearing the cuffs, this was serious.

"Brother Gilbert will receive his proper Homegoing," my grandmother said after the Kin had quieted down. She always left Nyame's stool unseated for the time when he decided to sit among us.

Sekou slipped down in the seat beside me, his eyes red rimmed and face puffy. I gave him the most comforting smile I could, and a squeeze, knowing it probably wouldn't count for much.

"It is as we initially believed, a tragic accident at sea while he was out fishing. His boat was recovered, capsized. He's been out there for days and succumbed to boats out at sea. The medical examiner has him on the mainland, and when he is cremated, with permission from his family, we will hold a Homegoing for him and commit him to the Asamando."

The crowd spoke in whispers around me, their heaviness lifting, comforted by Nana's reasonable explanation. The sea was the sea, and anyone who ventured out on it could be claimed, they rationalized.

Nana continued. "But for the meantime, be vigilant out there beyond the protective links of the Isle. Comfort one another here. Stay close to home so we can grieve."

Stay close to home to grieve? Sounded more like she didn't want us out there because it was unsafe. And if it was unsafe out there, then what about—

"The kids," Sister Michael asked from within the crowd. "The kids at the other Sea Islands have been gone for days. Maybe we should bring them home?"

Nana Ama shook her head. "They are fine. Sheriff Lyle called to check on them and we, the teachers here, conduct routine checks on them. No need to alarm them. They'll be home soon and we can move forward."

Nana's words were strong and assured. They'd make any of the islanders feel safe and like Elder Gilbert's death was just a freak accident. But I knew her better. I remembered her lesson that sometimes with responsibility, the truth did not always set people free. That sometimes it could be too much for them. Was this one of those untruthful moments?

I caught up to Nana on her way to the cabin, nestled farther back in Kin's Landing. I waited until she managed to pull away from the normal crowd that gravitated to her after a meeting.

"I'll text you later," I told Sekou when he gave me a look like he had no plans to separate. He still looked a little green from earlier, and I felt sorry for him. "I need to catch up with Nana. Text Naira, huh? See if she's okay?"

He barely gave a nod before I was off, jogging to catch up with Nana, who was walking pretty briskly for an older lady. She veered off the sidewalk and onto the path that didn't take her directly to our house, but beyond it, to her cabin and her space. I called her a few times before she finally slowed her pace enough for me to catch up.

"Nana Ama," I panted.

"Not now, I have things to take care of."

"Like Elder Gilbert's body?"

She spun on her heels to face me, grabbing my elbow and pulling me close. The gold in her eyes flashed. "You don't know what you're talking about."

"How'd you get the sheriff to give you the body? That's against the law. That could cost him his position." Wanting to keep this on the low as much as my grandmother did, we moved farther away.

She said, "Go home, Addae. I'll be there shortly."

I whispered, urgency rising in me, though I was unsure why, "Call Naira and the group back. This doesn't feel right."

She studied me. "Why? Do you sense something?"

I assessed our surroundings. "No but—"

"Then they're fine and will be back soon. No need to alarm them, or the rest of the island."

"But why do you need to burn the body tonight? What will happen if you don't?"

She looked away. "It's nothing. A precaution."

I couldn't believe she was saying this. "A precaution when you can just let the cops follow procedure, especially if you think his death is suspicious." I stepped in closer. "It's suspicious, right? His death isn't right, Nana."

She looked around, pausing to listen, ensuring we were still in relative privacy. "You have something to say." It was a statement instead of a question. She pulled me closer to her. "Go home and when I get a moment you can tell me what you have to say."

"Tell me what you're thinking, Nana," I pushed, willing her to let me in.

"Child, you forget your place," she snapped.

I reeled back, stung, unsure what to say or do next. My place had always been by her side, to learn how to create protection links, the elixir, and her blessings and incantations she constantly supplied for the Kin when they needed them. She'd never slammed the door between us before.

"I need you to give me a little time," she said. "I can't deal with Elder Gilbert and calm nerves and protect the Isle and look out for you at the same time. I need you to do your part."

"Does this have anything to do with the other morning when I found you in the grove? You said someone was gathering. You said something about the heavens, the spirit world, and the earth clashing together. What does all of that mean?"

"Who said that?" It was the first time Nana's armor cracked. She stepped back from me, looking alarmed and like I'd wounded her.

"Why haven't you mentioned this before? I said what?" Her hands rubbed on each golden cuff as I repeated what I'd seen.

It was her turn to look as sick as Sekou had been down at the dock. She remained silent, her fingers rubbing against themselves. Each second of her confusion was an increase to my anxiety.

"And a mountain with the Adinkra symbols circling it?" She looked at me skeptically. "Truly?"

"In gold." I nodded. I was starting to second-guess myself. I should have said something earlier and maybe not here, even though we were covered by trees and far enough down the path where we could no longer be seen well from the square, but the argument with Naira had thrown me off and it was easier to brush that other stuff away because that wasn't real, not like Naira. Those were just dreams and the Isle playing tricks on me.

She breathed. "In gold. And I sounded like a man?"

I nodded again. "More like a mix of you and I guess a man. It was your voice but deep. I've never seen a spirit take you over, if that's what it was."

"That's because spirits cannot take you and I over. Not like they might everyone else. And so if it wasn't a spirit from the Isle, then what?" Again, she said this more to herself than to me.

"It was a shadow with a bunch of arms sticking out on either side." I searched my mind for a connection. "To be honest, it kinda looked like Anansi. From your stories."

She inhaled sharply, making me jump. She put a hand to her forehead as she attempted to get herself together.

She whispered to herself, not me, "I wonder . . ."

She trailed off.

I was getting worried. My normally rock-solid grandmother was crumbling right in front of me, and I had no idea how to help her. She wouldn't let me.

"Have you rested? Have you had more than just palm oil and coconut water? That's not enough, Nana."

Nana Ama had never been a big eater. She was always so picky and careful because whatever she had could affect her gifts. Still, she needed to eat, and I was positive she wasn't doing what she needed to do for herself.

She was quiet for what seemed like an eternity. She finally moved, holding her hands out at me, palms down, as if I should take them. I placed mine just beneath hers, not touching, an inch of space between our hovering hands.

"I've been staying in on the Isle for longer than I normally do, tending to it, and perhaps I have tired myself and need to rest and replenish. But what you think you heard . . . Addae . . ."

The air in the space between our palms began to stir, the energy emanating from the Isle accumulating there, taking up space, becoming as physical and solid as Nana and I were. Her eyes settled on our hands and the growing heat between them, the low hum that sounded like insects and electricity buzzing. The space began to brighten as Light formed. Nana's Light coming from her to me.

"Didn't come to me. Came to you." She sounded wistful. "Through me. After so long? Could it be you're to have visions?" The energy surged between our hands, growing warmer. My hands trembled from the intensity of it. I had to hold on, a little longer. Maybe this was it, without the big ceremony or any pomp and circumstance. Maybe now I'd finally Light and get my gifts full force, not all these bits and pieces like scattered thoughts and warning signals of if a person was for real or not. If something was safe or not. All these things switched on and off without rhyme or reason. I couldn't control them. But maybe now. Maybe this was it and I'd finally be able to control what had been our family's legacy.

"Tell me what it means," I said. "I am ready."

My hands were shaking now. Nana widened the gap between

us, creating more space, becoming denser. On her wrists, the cuffs gleamed.

"Try it now," she said, hope edging in. The energy was so heavy, too heavy, like a megaton ball I couldn't hold. "Take the Light. Accept it fully. Receive it."

I hesitated for a moment, fear beating back every other emotion.

Do it here? Where anyone could walk up on us? And once I Lighted, accepted the heaven-given gifts Nana's been waiting for me to have, who would I be? Still me? Or someone entirely different? Sometimes I didn't want to assume the responsibility of the Golden Isle when Nana Ama stepped down. Sometimes I didn't want the few gifts I had . . . sensing people's emotions, which could get so loud I could lose myself; the little bit of energy I could muster up to heal—as spotty as it is; the sight; knowing once I Lighted and assumed the full scope of my legacy and all that came with it. Would I be able to handle that? Did I even want it?

How could I lead people if I couldn't even lead myself to make the right decisions? The responsibility was too much. The weight was too much. All of it was just too much.

"Addae," she sighed disappointedly. "Another time."

I couldn't accept another defeat, not when victory was right there. At my fingertips. Everything I'd been asking for, waiting for since I hit puberty. All I had to do was grab ahold and accept it.

But we always had a choice of what we'd become and the cross we had to bear.

And just like that, the heat, the Light, the energy between

and around us dissipated, leaving me with nothing but a sense of loss and rejection.

My grandmother's shoulders sagged as she drew her hands from me. "You are not ready."

"I am," I shot back. At least, I thought I was. I wanted it. I was supposed to want it.

She looked at me, pitying.

I swallowed, feeling like I was being kicked when I was already down, and by the person who I needed the most acceptance from. "Well, maybe I . . ."

"Do you want to know why your gifts won't be fully realized? Why you can't Light? It's because you haven't chosen it. You cannot obtain what you cannot accept. The Light only comes when it's truly and wholeheartedly accepted—the good it brings and the bad, because with these gifts you will have the power to heal as I do, or to cause great harm." I had no idea what she meant. I'd never seen Nana cause anyone harm. Not really. She sighed tiredly. "Go home, child. Perhaps it is not to be your calling, and that is okay. Perhaps you are meant for something else."

"Grandma," I whispered, devastated that I had disappointed her once again. I knew how high the stakes were. I am Nana Ama's only descendant. The protection of this island and the Kinfolk on it depended on me.

For the past six years I had tried to Light, and each failure was worse than the last. I was her only direct descendant left, the only one who could carry on her legacy from our ancestors.

But I couldn't do it. Or, it wouldn't come. Maybe there was something wrong with my body or my mind, or maybe I was just born weak. Or maybe, I just wasn't worthy of it. No matter the reason, not being able to fulfill my birthright filled me with immense shame.

I wished she would rage and rant rather than look at me the way she was through watery eyes, like I had crushed all of her hopes and dreams. In this moment, my grandmother, who always appeared ageless, looked every bit of her years as she realized that maybe her only grandchild would be just that and nothing more.

CHAPTER NINE

The next day, I got a text from Sekou. *Head over to Naira's.* I frowned, wondering why he was telling me to go there when she wasn't back yet. Last night, after I'd returned home, the only person I wanted to talk to was Naira. Had she been here, I'd have gone to her house instead of to my empty one. I'd have climbed up the tree by her bedroom window—centuries younger than our Gathering Tree at the center of Kin's Landing town square—and let myself into her room, like I'd done all our years growing up and vice versa. But she wasn't here, and instead, I sent a text.

naira u gud?

I had waited for the three pulsing dots. None came. Minutes had passed, each one making me more anxious than the one before.

look sry 4 being an ass. cud u answr? pls? need to knw ur good

shits happened here

I fell asleep waiting for the dots. I woke up the next morning, forcing myself to go to work at the golf cart rental at Freeman's Port. The Mast General Store was still closed, but I shrugged it off. Maybe they were running late because it was still early. Maybe Naira had been partying late last night and was sleeping it off. Or she was annoyed that up until now I hadn't answered her back? Whatever the reason, she wasn't answering. Then Sekou texted.

"Cover for me?"

My question came out more a statement as I handed my coworker Rita my clipboard and redirected the customers coming at me with their thousand and one questions to her. Rita didn't have a chance to say no because I was already hopping in my cart and zooming off to Naira's house to see what was up.

The surprise was on me because not only did I see Sekou's cart parked on the curb, but Nana's cart was parked in the driveway of the Russells' big beachfront home. She rarely if ever took it out since someone was always on hand to drive her where she needed. The sight of her cart was the first signal that something wasn't right.

I recognized Sheriff Lyle's official truck parked among the carts. Usually he kept it at the municipal building closer to the public port. Usually he rode around in carts as we normally did. The truck meant he had to get somewhere quickly. I wondered if this had anything to do with Elder Gilbert.

A bunch of ppl r at ur house. What's up?

I waited for the gray dots letting me know Naira was replying. Nothing. I sent another message, this time to Sekou.

Se, what's the deal?

There were dots pulsating. Then they stopped. They started again and then Sekou's reply came.

Come in

Now that I was here, I wasn't sure I wanted to know what was on the other side of that door. The familiar feeling when I woke up from the earthquake, that a shoe was hovering ready to drop, was back and I wasn't ready for it to slam into me.

The vibe was like the humidity: heavy, sticky, and suffocating. It smacked me in the face and clung to me like glue. The vibe here was all wrong.

Eventually I got out. If I hadn't, Sekou would have come to get me. I focused on what was on the other side of the front door. When I went inside, the house was full of people, but it was as quiet as a tomb. There wasn't the usual Russell family commotion—a blaring TV or Alexa playing Mr. and Mrs. Russell's favorite jams, the four younger kids screaming and running around with Naira's parents yelling at them to settle down.

Through the hall and in the great room, I spotted a few elders standing around. Some wiping their eyes. Some mumbling what sounded like prayers under their breaths. Others patting backs and looking like the world had ended. One of them was humming, a long solemn melody of the Lord working in mysterious ways. No one said much to me, as if they were trying to avoid me. I counted one brother and all three of Naira's sisters. All present and accounted for. Whatever this was, it wasn't about any of them. I swallowed hard, but the lump in my throat wouldn't go away.

Sekou was there. He'd squeezed himself in a corner near the doorway I'd entered. His eyes were vacant, lost. Seeing him there made me slow my step. My stomach triple-flipped. The way Sekou looked, hell, the way they all looked—turning in unison to watch me walk in, conversation suddenly halting like some kind of screwed-up movie—had me wanting to turn around and go back the way I'd come. My knees jellied and I could barely keep myself upright.

There was Nana, bending over Naira's mother, rubbing gentle circles on the woman's back with the soft palm of her hand. I couldn't see Auntie Janet's face—her head was buried in a blue striped dish towel in her hands. Her aching moans chipped away at the affirmations I'd told myself before coming in that whatever was going on wasn't too bad.

Uncle Kofi, Naira's spitting image with eyes like hers—gentle and kind and inquisitive—leaned heavily against one of the eggshell-colored walls, his feet crossed at the ankles. He had both his hands shoved into the pockets of his pants. His eyes weren't the usual warm with a hint of comedy that had comforted me all my life. Now, they were glazed, hollowed out and unseeing as he stared off to a space over everyone's heads. He didn't seem to register anyone, even as Elders Andrew and Edu sandwiched him in, taking turns murmuring in low rumbling tones, speaking words I couldn't decipher and didn't know if I wanted to.

In the middle of the room was Sheriff Lyle, looking grimmer

than I'd ever seen him. I'd take his usual aloofness to the way his face was closed in, looking as if the world had ended.

Beside him was a cop I didn't recognize in a military-style buzz cut, with small ice-blue eyes that held not an inch of warmth, and *DNR* etched on the lapel of his uniform. The DNR caught my attention. Like, *do not resuscitate*? From the way his eyes shifted from face to face and then to the wide, pretty room we all stood in, I could tell the guy wasn't used to being in a room where he was the minority, a shock of white in a sea of black and brown. But I didn't have time to dig into the irony of his situation because his being here with Lyle was suspicious. The way he and Lyle gripped their hats in their hands looking like a couple of grim reapers had wild thoughts beating at my mind's door, and I only caught the last part of what he was saying.

". . . with me from the Department of Natural Resources and they are doing everything in their power to locate her."

Locate?

"Who?" I asked, since no one seemed to want to clue me in.

No one said anything.

I turned to Sekou. If the adults weren't going to answer me, then at least he would. But it was as if he were trying to get inside the wall, as stuffed into the corner as he was. And his eyes were glassy.

"Se?"

The only people who existed in this moment were me and Sekou. Me asking him the question and him trembling as his will to keep himself strong crumbled in front of me. The tears pooling in his eyes began to leak, and all he could do was shake his head, his lips smashed in a firm line as if he were fighting to keep them from spilling whatever news he had.

Sheriff Lyle cleared his throat and, in a voice filled with regret and without any of the humor and easy drawl he normally had, said, "Well, there's been an accident."

He hesitated and Nana prompted, "G'awn, Sheriff."

Nana pulled away from Naira's mother with one final pat of the shoulder, taking a few steps toward me. She didn't reach for me, knowing her granddaughter more than anyone else. I didn't need coddling right now, not in front of all of these people. I needed the truth.

He stepped forward, shoulders sagging and face full of pity. "Naira and a classmate were out boating during the night, and there was an accident. We think the boat may have run aground on some rocks in one of the inlets around Charleston and . . ." Lyle swallowed, casting a worried look at Naira's parents, who were too dazed to be paying attention.

"We're out looking for them, but they haven't been found. Neither Naira or—"

"Luke." His name choked up in my throat, bitter and vile.

Lyle nodded and surveyed the room, holding his hat out. "We are still looking, y'all. It's not over."

"Is this related at all to Brother Gilbert?" Elder Mabel asked from the back corner of the room.

Yes, Elder Gilbert. My head twisted to Nana Ama, whose face remained serene. I turned to Sheriff Lyle. He cleared his throat as DNR looked at him, confused.

"I'm sorry?" DNR said. "Who?"

"An island matter," Nana Ama said smoothly, her tone commanding and ending that topic. "Continue."

"The location of the boat, however, was pretty far out. It would have been nearly impossible for anyone to swim back in those conditions."

It was like the DNR guy wasn't talking about someone's loved ones, like he was talking about a busted-up boat that didn't have two people in it. Like he thought of Naira as a statistic. Another irresponsible kid. His lack of empathy had me seeing red. He was talking to us like we were a bunch of country bumpkins.

Lyle had to have caught the death stare I launched at Officer Buzz Cut because he cut in. "It's still a rescue, everyone, okay? Let's not get ahead of ourselves. Coast Guard is still out, and we need to let them do their jobs. We're still looking. You know the coast is filled with inlets, and when the tide goes out, new patches of land emerge."

"Only to be submerged again when the tide comes back in, though," Buzz Cut returned. "Again, with the type of damage the boat sustained, and the fact they were so far out . . ."

The lump that had been in my throat had moved down, getting bigger and bigger. It had gone from a pebble to a stone to a boulder. There was so much damn anger. I let out something like a laugh and a sob, slapping my hand over my mouth to keep my emotions in check. *Not here.* I couldn't unleash it here, in front of these people who were watching me. I swallowed it all down until there was nothing but dullness.

"You should check harder," I said, because there was no way he was going to give up that quick. Holding myself was so hard. I was supposed to be like Nana, calm and rational. Solution-oriented when all I wanted to do was destroy everything.

"She's not about to be another missing Black girl that you just write off."

I could imagine the stories he'd heard about the Isle. I could practically hear how they described us when there wasn't anyone around to stop them. How they spouted stories of us practicing voodoo (an actual religion they wouldn't even understand), or worse, devil worshipping, and running around like we were uncultured heathens. Like we were wild, how they thought of people from Africa. How they worked so hard to take all of this from us, couldn't believe this Black family had managed to take and retain an entire island for their own use, and then built a world within a world on it. Thinking we had been the ones to steal, forgetting that if it hadn't been for them and their greed, we would have never been here. They acted as if we didn't know hard work. As if we hadn't suffered. As if we weren't suffering this very moment.

"It's not about . . ." He tried explaining to a crowd who wouldn't give him an inch, not even Lyle. "In the dark, it's hard to tell the distance from water to land. And if one, or both of them, was injured and the other was trying to tow them in . . . with the currents and especially after a freak storm. There is practically no chance they could have swum to shore."

Screw what he was saying. Naira could have made it. She could have made it back to land.

"We live on an island," I said. "Grew up in the water. Naira is one of the best swimmers around."

"Miss, swimming around an island's shallow waters is a little different than swimming in pitch black in the middle of the Atlantic. There are too many factors they'd be up against. They could swallow so much seawater that it affects mental capacity. Exhaustion. Trauma from the accident. Marine life—"

The way he talked down to me stirred the monster in me. It threatened to come out, to tear the smug look off his face.

Buzz Cut continued, "It is easy to get turned around."

Three sharp raps on the floor, hard and like thunder, startled the both of us back to our corners.

"That's enough," Nana Ama barked, sending a glare that could melt metal at DNR so he melted back in line with Sheriff Lyle. She gave the reddening man a long and hard stare until he wilted beneath her. A five-foot woman able to make a man double her size cower in complete fear.

She returned her gaze to me, the hardness in her eyes melting away as my breathing hitched and I attempted to lock the monster back in the cage.

Naira wasn't dead. Maybe she was out there floating in some high reedy inlet or passed out on a sandy beach in some area where people didn't usually roam. But she wasn't dead.

I thought about explaining, but Nana's sharp head shake and quick flick of the wrist silenced me as it had done the officer who came with Lyle. Not here. Not in front of Naira's parents. Her eyes shifted toward Naira's mother, working through a fresh wave of tears, the other four kids gathering around her.

The last thing I'd done was walk away from her. She left thinking I never wanted to speak to her again. And for the past few days

I'd doubled down on that thought, ignoring her messages. The thought of how I'd acted over something as minor as going away to college was concrete gloves slamming into me so hard, I stumbled back toward the door. I had to leave. Had to get out of the room where everyone wanted me to believe my best friend was dead.

There was no air in this place. Everything became a blur. I spun on my heel and charged forward, pushing the people who'd gathered behind me, bottlenecking the doorway.

I pushed past them, unable to stand the way the house suddenly felt like it was closing in on me. There were too many eyes on me, watching for my reaction like I was on some show. The Ada Show, just like Naira had accused me of wanting.

I couldn't think about putting her to rest.

The things we say, we speak into existence.

I managed to make it to my golf cart before my heart started racing. I clawed at my throat, unable to breathe in the thick humidity. I was falling, throwing out a hand to stop myself when an arm grabbed me by the waist, steadying me. Through blurry eyes I made out Sekou, hovering over me like a hanging rubber tree plant. I fell into him, letting him swallow me up in his arms.

It took him a moment to work up the ability to speak. Watching him try almost made me burst. "It's okay. They'll find her and we'll be able to say goodbye . . ." He swallowed like he was taking down an impossible pill. It was impossible. Impossible to believe any of this was reality. "It'll be okay."

Except it wasn't okay. It never would be.

I snatched myself away, looking at him with new eyes. "You think like they do? Like she's *gone,* gone?" How could he ever think Naira was dead?

His face was slick with tears. He reached out to me, but each time I staggered back.

"Get away from me," I said between heaves.

"Who doesn't know the sea better than me?" he choked out. "And what it can do. God, look what it did to Elder Gilbert. I know it's unbelievable, but don't we gotta face facts?"

"I don't gotta do shit," I seethed.

Sekou was speaking nonsense. I wished he'd go back to his non-speaking self instead of telling me all of this. He grabbed at my arms, attempted to pull me into him.

I slapped him away. If he believed them, then Sekou could stay with the rest of them. I turned away, stumbling down the street like I'd downed a huge pitcher of the Garvey Brothers' moonshine. I pushed past the people showing up to find out what'd happened, the news about Naira spreading through Golden Isle like wildfire that one of ours was lost.

She was lost because *I* made it that way. Nana always said that words spoken on the Isle held power. I should have known better. I'd seen Nana in action, walking the circumference of the island, chanting to fortify the protective links that made her feel safe, boiling poultices for the sick or wounded, and whispering blessings for those who asked, only to see them fully healed days later. Words held meaning, power here. And the last thing I'd said to Naira was to stay gone.

Now she was.

CHAPTER TEN

No one would listen to me. Not Lyle, who wanted to do things by the book since so many agencies and another family were involved. Not Nana Ama, who refused to connect Elder Gilbert's death with Naira going missing. Not even Sekou, who couldn't believe there was some sort of conspiracy or weird shit happening that Nana Ama and the elders didn't want us to know.

Days had passed and there had been no word. Then a week, then two, then three. I was about to combust. Each night, another piece of hope chipped away. Each morning meant less chance of finding her alive. Each week meant the move from search to recovery to nothing.

"The longer we wait, the harder it'll be to find her. She's out there," I told Sekou as we walked back to the Landing from the fishing dock where we'd found Elder Gilbert. I wanted to look for clues. Didn't find any. Only thing there was a memorial built for him.

I held out because Sekou begged to give the cops a chance to find her and reminded me that Nana said that we were not to leave the Isle. The rest of Naira's research group had returned and we had to remain on the island. At least Naira's death was still uncertain and not being mourned. Not yet.

"You really gotta chill, bro," Sekou said under his breath. "They're doing all they can."

I kicked at the pebbles, wanting to do much more damage than that. "Are they? Because it looks to me like everyone's given up on her." Tears stung the backs of my eyes. "Some Kin we are. Just because Gilbert is gone doesn't mean Naira is. Naira has a chance."

Sekou threw a branch of palm with a grunt. "That's not fair, Ada. Think of how you're acting looks to her family. When you're out there coming at Lyle being all pissed, you're making it worse for them. You'd know that if you'd been by to see them. You know, like folks who were her best friends should."

Were, past tense. I could only shake my head at him, not trusting my words to be nice.

I hadn't been by the Russells' to see how they were holding up. Sekou thought I was being selfish, but the truth was that if I went over there to see them, it meant accepting that Naira was in the past tense. She wasn't past tense to me. She was still very much in the present.

I couldn't stand the looks of pity because they thought I wasn't coping well, wasn't accepting what they thought were "facts." Even Nana told me to let it go. To her, to all of them, even my remaining best friend, Naira had been caught in a storm. And it pissed me off that they could give up so easily.

"Nana Ama," I asked for what felt like the hundredth time as I watched her meticulously stirring the pot of bubbling elixir. It was later that evening and she was preparing for our upcoming Harvest Festival, held biannually, where our tradition was to honor and pay tribute to Nyame, the god supreme, lesser gods of the pantheon, and the land-dwelling deities who protected, guided, and helped us to prosper.

I noted the rows of small glass vials she would use to offer to the Kin in appreciation and in exchange for the continued promise of their loyalty and commitment to safeguarding of the Golden Isle and fellow Kinfolk. If only they knew how much my grandmother sacrificed to keep them healthy and strong and a cut above everyone else. They would never know, but I did.

"You may not go," Nana Ama said, also for the hundredth time.

I sighed.

"Then you go," I said. "You can check into it for me. She's alive out there, I just know it. We can't leave family out there alone."

Nana's shoulders flinched like I had struck her. "You don't know what you're talking about. Our place is here on Golden. If I left every time someone was in trouble, land developers would take our home. The Kin would dissolve to parts unknown, and what would happen to Golden Isle? It entrusted itself to our family's care. It saved us."

"But don't you think it would want us to save others too? Save our own? It's not like I'm asking you to be out there like one of the Avengers saving the world. I just want you to save Naira."

Nana sighed, placing her thick wooden ladle in the holder. She turned to me as if the world were on her shoulders, looking older than I'd ever seen her. "I don't feel her, my child. Like Gilbert, she is gone. All we can do for her is send her off in honor with our traditions so she is well in her afterlife and prepared for the next."

Screw that was what I really wanted to say. Forget sending Naira to another life when there was still this one.

But I kept these thoughts to myself. We might be able to sense our other Kin, but my grandmother never entered others' thoughts, finding that intrusive and a misuse of her gifts. *A person's mind,* she said, *as their choices, are their own. Who am I to intrude just because I can?* It was my hope that when I finally Lighted, I'd never be able to fully read thoughts; the sensing was loud enough and just barely contained when I drowned it out in earbud noise. Plus, I could never get a sense from her like I could others. Maybe it was because I was a descendant of hers.

Nana thought she'd given her final decision and I'd obey as always. What she didn't know was my mind was already made up.

"We will have her Homegoing right before the Harvest Festival. It can't be helped," she said, checking me for any protest.

"Timing is horrible, but we must give thanks, the Kin for their good year, and you and I for being allowed to be with them."

Sending Naira off to the spirit world Asamando would be the end of Naira's story here on Earth, and it was the last thing I wanted to think about, let alone be a part of.

She continued, "It'll be good for us to release Naira and then welcome her the following day with the rest of the spirits when they walk," Nana Ama said. "We will spend extra time with her." Tears fringed Nana's eyelashes, and I knew they were real. I just couldn't deal with them. "If that's what's gotta happen." I handed her a warm glass of coconut water and palm oil, watching as she drank deeply.

"You and I need to be strong, Addae. The Kin look to us for strength and guidance."

Don't I know it. I tried to see it from Nana's point of view. I'd never seen her break. I guess this was what being a leader meant, not letting everyone see you break and be vulnerable. But what about when something happened to someone you loved? Nana barely flinched when Mom died. She'd just bucked up for the rest of us. I didn't think I could be that kind of leader. I didn't think I *wanted* to be.

When I thought of saying goodbye to Naira once again, this time for her journey into the World of Spirits, I felt all of my sadness and regret and rage rise up like a wave and roll through me, threatening to pull me under.

Nana wanted me to be like her and move on from the pain for the rest of the Kin. And if that was the kind of leader Nana wanted me to be, then I'd have to disappoint her.

"The—the—" I had to force the words out, my will overcoming my need for self-preservation. "Right before graduation . . . you said a storm was coming. You said—"

"Nothing you should be worrying yourself sick over. Whatever you think you heard and this tragedy are not connected," Nana Ama said briskly, waving her arms as if shooing away my concerns. Her golden cuffs etched in intricate designs glinted against the brown of her skin, making her glow.

"Okay." I let it go as quickly as I brought it up.

"You've had a hard day. A hard few weeks, my girl. Why don't you get some rest, hmm?" She smiled, back to her warm self, and I nearly bought it. But I hadn't spent eighteen years studying her every move for nothing.

She was hiding something from me.

She looked down at her precious elixir. "I'll need to go out tonight. The elixir takes a lot from me." She pulled off her cuffs and wiped them down before placing them in their deep purple velvet-lined box, closing and locking it. She wanted me to accept that the conversation was over, like I always did . . . following her rules to a T. But I couldn't this time. I couldn't just keep silent.

Nana's warning held on and wouldn't go away. Someone gathering. A secret boyfriend who was Naira's real reason to go on the research trip. Then Gilbert washed up on shore. Finally, Naira disappeared. If all of this was a coincidence, then we had the worst luck in all the world. It had to be something else.

If only I could talk to Naira. If she were here, she would help me solve the mystery. She'd always been my partner in crime, my fellow schemer, coming up with practical jokes on Sekou and adventures on the Isle that made our island feel a little bigger than it was.

I had scrolled through Naira's texts too many times to count, searching for any clue that would tell me something. There was nothing but some fuzzy, dark picture her phone probably snapped by accident.

A thought struck me. What about Naira's journal? Did she take it with her? Or leave it behind figuring she'd have no time to write in it? If she left it, then I knew exactly where she hid it in her room. I'd never read it, but hopefully Naira would understand that I was invading her privacy for a good reason. For her.

Besides, if my grandmother wasn't going to give me answers or help me find my friend, I was going to have to do it myself.

CHAPTER ELEVEN

It was easier to move on foot, taking the lesser-known routes to get from my house and the most northern point of the island to Naira's house in the more populated area of the Landing. I didn't want to be seen. It was the middle of the day and the Russell house looked empty from what I could see from my hideout among the trees.

It didn't matter much because I knew how to get in without being seen. I'd been doing it for as long as I could remember. When we were young, Naira and I snuck into each other's rooms to get away from our lives for just a little bit. For that reason, we didn't leave our windows locked. I hoped Naira still kept up with that. I hoped more that her parents hadn't been to her room to clean and found the window latch undone, locking it.

The room still smelled like her as soon as I opened the window and climbed in. I looked around as if it were my first time inside, lingering on all the Broadway show posters like *Hamilton*, *Rent*, and *West Side Story*. Shows she'd wanted to see in real life but happily watched when they came on TV. Had she been able to take in at least one when she'd gone to Charleston? I hoped so.

Naira wanted to see the world. And let the world see her.

Naira's dresser was littered with junk. I never understood how she functioned with all the stuff on top of it. Tubes of lipstick of all shades scattered on their sides. Mascara. Cotton balls. Her favorite bottle of Dusty Rose polish. I touched the top of it, thinking of how she begged me to put some on the last time we were here, even though my preference was clear. She needed to come back so I could be her nail polish guinea pig again. Whatever would make her happy.

Stuck to the inside edge of the mirror to Naira's vanity were various snapshots of us. Those hurt to see. My heart thumped hard as I stared down at the photos of Naira—cheek to cheek next to me, at the General Store, at a Harvest Festival, striking a pose with the other dancers. There was a much older photo of three kids in matching white with magnolia-and-leaf-woven crowns on their heads. Two girls on either side of the boy. Beaming. The boy had his arms around their shoulders, already standing many inches above them. Best friends for life. Brother and sisters, closer than blood. Naira. Sekou. And me.

My heart panged hard in my chest. What I really wanted to do was stay in the comfort of Naira's room where the world couldn't get to me and get lost in the memories of us. All we had and things I could do hadn't been enough to keep my friend safe.

I wiped away the tears, reminding myself I came here for a reason and crying over memories wasn't it. If I was going to make new ones, it meant I needed to force myself to hunt clues. That thin little thread that I was missing something trembled ever so lightly, plucked like the line on a spider's web.

I checked under her mattress for the journal. Nothing. Rifled through the drawer of her nightstand with the pink lamp on top. Nothing there either. Perhaps she'd moved it to keep it away from her siblings.

I went to her closet and felt around on the shelf above the rack. I finally caught a break, pulling Naira's journal from under the pile of folded sweaters. I almost let out a laugh, shocked that she'd left one of her most sacred things. I flipped to the last few pages, to the last notes Naira wrote about Luke Hall and her weekend plans with him.

A Word—

When I go, I'll put highlights of the trip on my phone because I don't want to overpack and there's barely enough room for everything I want to wear let alone this big ole thing. It was a big-ass, hardbound notebook. *Plus, with Davis, Maris, and them I don't know who might come sniffing around and find it. Last thing I need is anyone reading you and knowing. Luke's got it all planned. I'll ditch Ms. Cabel and the group before dinner and tell them I'm sick or have cramps. Luke will come get me and has planned to take me on a private tour of the Endowment and meet his uncle Simon—the big boss. Maybe I'll get to see the amulet in person. Maybe even hold it. Imagine!* Amulet . . . *Then a romantic dinner on his boat for just us and a big surprise he says he has. Boats are nothing, but it hits a little different when it's with your guy. OMG. My guy!!! I have one for real! Eeeeek! Tbc . . .*

Tbc? Someone's initials? But another second and no more entries made me realize she meant *to be continued.*

I sat there for a moment, rereading her last entry through blurring eyes. Naira had been so happy, so excited, and I squashed it all, and for what? Because I'd been jealous that she knew what she wanted and was going for it while I stayed in the same exact spot. Not moving forward, or back, just unbelievably the same.

My eyes landed on *amulet*. There was a connection I hadn't made yet. I slid to the floor and pulled up my messages for another look. I skimmed through Naira's last messages and the pictures. I'd sent a billion since her last one, hoping this time there'd finally be an answer. There wasn't. I checked again, thinking there might be a clue in her messages that I could use.

This time, opening her messages again felt like opening up Pandora's box.

I took a deep breath and began to scroll again.

I landed on that picture I'd blown off earlier, thinking it was an accident. But after reading the journal, what if it wasn't taken or sent accidentally? I looked closer. Real hazy and dark. Rain and the rim of what I made out to be the helm of a boat just like Naira had mentioned. I sucked in a breath. Luke's boat maybe. This was her final message before *it* happened. I looked away, gripping the phone so I wouldn't toss it. I had to keep going.

I forced myself to look again, harder this time. I sat up straighter, something catching my eye. I leaned closer to the screen, squinting.

With the murky background, it was hard to make out what I was seeing. The light could have been playing tricks on me. The picture wasn't clear, and where I was sitting wasn't brightly lit. I stared harder. No, it was definitely an outline of something—of someone? But couldn't be. It was hard to tell and I was getting more and more frustrated with each passing second. What could possibly be looming over the water like that? Like UFOs that Sekou swore were real and this would be his proof. The shape in the dark was an unidentified flying object.

Only it wasn't a UFO.

Those tiny yellowish flecks.

A glint of gold and flash of blue that were way too familiar.

I scrolled up the stream of unanswered texts, swallowing the guilt like a bad pill until I came to another picture she'd taken while on the campus tour when they'd visited the Endowment Research Lab.

I thought back to Naira's story of the uncovered artifacts in Virginia. The invitation from Luke to look at them up close and personal since she liked old stuff.

The snap was blurry, and the artifacts were still dirt encrusted. But all that dirt and muck couldn't hide the gem nestled within its golden necklace that was etched in Adinkra signs. A gem that shone the deepest of blues that I'd seen before. Signs I knew the meanings of, lived by every day. Drew them on my body during ceremonies. They were the same as the ones engraved in the arm cuffs tucked away in the box locked in Nana Ama's drawer. And centered in each cuff, two deep blue gems.

As blue as the flash in the picture Naira took before her boat disintegrated into a million and one pieces in the Atlantic. The screen faded to black as a bunch of loose threads began knitting together into something ugly. Nana's warning, the storm, Naira missing . . . and whatever happened to her was definitely connected to the Isle and to me.

CHAPTER TWELVE

I made one stop before I left. Elder James opened his front door, glowering at me and then pointedly at the watch on his wrist. I apologized for the time, praying he wouldn't send me packing. I could have asked Sekou to meet me, but it was easier and quicker to make the surprise stop and hope he wasn't out.

Elder James let me in with a wary look and a warning to make it quick. I apologized, rushing up the stairs to Sekou's room.

"Ada?" He was startled and just out of the shower, a towel wrapped around his long torso and another around his neck, which he used to dry his freshly cut temp fade. He craned his neck through the doorway at the stairs. "Uncle James let you in?"

"I told him I'd be quick," I said. I eyed him. "Do you mind?" I gestured to his towel and went back to the living room while he got dressed. When he came back out, dressed in gray jogger sweatpants and a pink tee, I gave him the quick rundown of what I was planning.

"What the hell?" His voice was like a foghorn.

I slammed my hand over his mouth. "Shhhh, your uncle is down there!"

Sekou peeled my fingers off his face. "This is the worst idea. You can't be over there alone. Nana Ama . . . I don't even want to think about the bricks she'll shit." His whole vibe was one big, blaring stop sign. "I get the news about Naira is hard. Hell, I don't even want to believe it, but the cops couldn't find anything. So how will you?"

"I'll figure it out," I said. "I have my ways."

He scoffed. "What ways? It's not the Isle. It's Charleston. You know, big city, lots of crowds and noise. Plus, you don't know what's out there." He hesitated. "Can't you just talk to her?"

And tell her I was on the hunt for the truth behind Naira? That I thought Nana had something to do with it?

"That's a no. She'll keep me from going."

"Not a bad idea," he grumbled. He switched to plan B. "Then I'm coming with. Naira's my friend too."

I shook my head. "No. One of us needs to be here when shit hits the fan and they realize I'm gone. You can tell them I had to deal with her loss on my own before her Homegoing. They'll believe you. You gotta stay here."

Because I can't lose you too, I didn't finish.

I held up an envelope, and he took it. And then he grabbed me up and pulled me in. I'd never felt as vulnerable and as strong as I felt the moment Sekou hugged me. And when I felt wet drops soaking through my shirt, I was undone, completely. Entirely. We stayed like that until Elder James said it was time for me to go home.

The next day, when I knew Nana was distracted with Isle business and then working in her shed, I left my island home. The weight of what I was doing, the stand I was making against my grandmother wasn't lost on me. I was going against my grandmother's wishes. I was leaving a place that had been my safe haven.

I didn't know what was waiting for me, but I was taking a leap of faith, reversing the course my ancestors took when they fled their captors. They'd seen the beacon of light from the Isle and they'd used it to find their way. I had no light guiding me as I sped away.

Even if I came back empty-handed, having learned nothing new about my best friend, knowing that I hadn't given up on her would be enough for me. I had tried, even when the weight of it all felt too much to bear.

CHAPTER THIRTEEN

As soon as my feet hit sidewalk, I began walking away from the pier and into the city.

With the Homegoing happening in days, I didn't have a lot of time. The first thing I needed to do was find Luke's sister, Hailey. From Naira's journal, I knew that Hailey and Luke lived together.

I plugged her address in my phone, which I'd found in one of Naira's earlier entries from a Valentine's day gift Naira had sent to their house, and began my walk away from the Old Slave Mart.

As many times as I'd been to Charleston to drop off and pick up ferry passengers, this was the first time I'd really walked the city.

Charleston had been one of the largest markets of enslaved people. It wasn't so long ago when our ancestors walked these same uneven cobblestone sidewalks and passed mansions behind wrought iron gates. Churches and ancient cemeteries punctuated the city, where you could walk through and read the carved tombstones and mausoleums dating family lineages going back centuries . . . All of it was beautiful. And yet, so much ugly history created this beauty. Golden Isle was a place of freedom and light. Charleston was the opposite.

I had time to kill, and after getting a kick out of watching tourists explore Charleston on carriages with huge horses clomping through the streets, the blinding white building of the Mother Emanuel AMEC rose before me, forcing my steps to a stop. Without thinking, I had come here like a ship to a beacon in the night. I let out a slow breath looking up at one of the two staircases to the front door, and all complaints about the overcrowded city and the drain on me fell away. As if pulled by some invisible force, I began up the steps. A strange hum rose in my chest as if it recognized something in me as I did in it. It refilled my depleting well. The door creaked opened and a warm energy flowed from it. The energy was attuned with my own, like the same kind of transference I had with Nana Ama. The oneness I shared with this place confused me, having never deeply considered other religions and belief systems than what I'd been taught and practiced. This was more refined, whereas mine was older and of the land. I was practically at the door when a small elderly lady with graying dark hair twisted in a bun and warm eyes appeared, opening the door, and the energy within it, wider. She noticed my hesitation and gave me a serene smile. Like she knew.

"No matter what you believe, child, you are welcome here." She answered my unspoken question. "Everything God, gods—whatever names we bestow on them—see the same light in us."

"But I'm not—"

"You don't need to be. Beliefs are only variations of one

another depending on the cultures and places. Don't fear this place because it's unlike your own. Welcome it." She stepped back as if to beckon me in, and I almost took her up on it, the pressure of energy building in my chest. "Come in from the cold."

It wasn't cold, it was late summer, but instantly I knew what she meant. A flicker, a cool wisp of air tickled the fine hairs on my arms and the feeling that aside from me, the lady, and the few people passing by, something else was there. Something out here was very wrong.

I turned sharply, my arm out, ready to protect the lady from whatever harm was coming our way.

Nothing.

The moment slipping away like smoke and a trace of that diseased smell from the corpse on the Isle, broke the spell and reminded me of my purpose. I almost laughed. I was spooking myself. I returned to the woman, who was watching where I had been looking, her eyebrow arched in defiance. I thanked her for her kindness, saying I had somewhere to be.

She hesitated, studying me, then nodded her understanding. "If you must. Another time, maybe."

I trudged down the steps and turned to give one more look at the powerful church and felt as at ease there as I was on the Isle.

"Maybe."

I ended up on Rainbow Row in the Historic District. I couldn't fully appreciate the multicolored homes that made this street so famous because recognizing Luke and Hailey's turquoise-blue row home made my anxiety flare. I was on unfamiliar turf among strangers; my only hope was that Hailey, or one of her neighbors, wouldn't call the cops on me.

There was a bright-red Camaro in the home's short driveway but my unanswered knock at her front door meant no one was home. I didn't want to miss Hailey's return, so I decided to hang around for a little while. Maybe I'd get lucky. At least the street was relatively quiet, except for the few tourists staring at the homes and the occasional resident taking their dog out, or riding a bike, or walking themselves. Each time one passed by, they threw guarded glances my way. As a Black person, I was triggered, and my knee-jerk reaction was for me to automatically go *there* and think their side-eye had to do with my skin color.

Soon, it started to get dark. I needed to find a hotel where I could stay for the night and come up with a plan B. I had no idea when she'd be back.

Poor planning, girl. You should know better.

I should have also planned for a place to stay. I pulled my phone from the pocket of my hoodie, finally gathering enough courage to look at my messages. I had a bunch from Sekou checking in on me.

I answered Sekou's last message, telling him I was fine. I reminded him that I wasn't coming back until I found answers or Naira. Or both.

Take care of Nana 4 me pls

If she wanted to, Nana could swoop over here and bring me home, but with all the "choice" she touted, I was banking on her staying true to that and humoring me, if only for a minute. She had, however, left me a voicemail.

Nana's message was short. *"At least you thought to leave a note. Do what you think will help you deal with Naira's death. A reservation is waiting for you at the Francis Marion. You may have two days before you must return for Naira's Homegoing. And then, Addae, life must continue."*

Life must continue.

I was a big old ball of confusion and guilt. Second-guessing if I was making the right choice or if I was being reckless for sitting on the sidewalk of a girl I'd only met once. Guilty for adding to a heavy load I knew my grandmother already had. Was I being selfish, like Naira had said? Thinking only about myself when life was supposed to continue?

But how could it without Naira?

Hailey was apparently going to be a no-show tonight. I pushed up from the curb, shrugging on the straps of my backpack. It was time to head to the Francis Marion on King. There I could figure out a game plan for tomorrow and where to go first. I had two days to find out what happened to Naira. Or make my peace with never knowing.

The skittering behind me, like nails scraping on cement, started off low, barely there. It was coming from an alley in between the houses I had been hanging in front of all evening. I froze, sensing danger. I ran the sound through, trying to give its owner a name. Maybe a rat. Too big. Could be a cat?

The old-fashioned streetlamps had blinked on, casting hazy

swatches of light down on the street. The sky was a dark purple. The alley was extra dark. The Isle got dark, especially deep in the forest and swamp, but this extra black was something else. From the corner of my eye, the pitch black seemed to swirl into solid mass, into something like a body. My heart jumped. Not possible. I'd been in this spot for a while and no one had come or gone into the alley. It led to a dead end. What the hell kind of tricks was my mind playing on me? I backed up a step.

Earlier at the church, hadn't I felt something off, something lurking? There one moment and gone the next? I played it off then, but it wasn't as easy to do now.

One of the straps of my backpack slipped down my shoulder and I tugged it back on, twisting around to get a better look as I put more space between me and the alley. I didn't scare easy, but I wasn't totally senseless. I didn't know this place. It was unknown terrain.

The skittering started up again. My eyesight was great, but the light cast off from the streetlamps made it hard to see through the darkness to the wall at the end of the alley. I struggled to tell dark nothing from something in that alley. The noise got louder, like it was coming closer. I tried to pinpoint its location. Didn't seem to come from directly in front of me on the ground, but around, on the walls of the houses on either side of it. Coming closer toward me as I shuffled backward, step by step. I looked both ways down the street for someone. Just a minute ago there had been people on the street, checking their mail or on an evening stroll. Now there were none. Like right out of some freaking movie.

Another sound came after that, the low, guttural growl of

something about to pounce. My head snapped back, facing the alley, and for a second there were spots of lights close together like eyes, zooming in closer to me while I kept backing up, one foot, then another, not looking where I was going, only looking at the two iridescent lights homing in on me.

Until the shrill of a car horn screeched and a car swerved past me in a blast of wind, narrowly missing me.

"Whoa! Are you okay?"

The noise snapped me out of my daze. I jumped, disoriented, the red brake lights from the car that nearly pummeled me glaring at me angrily as if it meant more than braking to a stop. It felt like a warning to turn back, pinning me in its lights until the SUV made a right at the end of the street and was gone.

"I—um—" My mind jumbled as I tried to adjust and understand what was happening. The world around me started to clear. I realized there was a hand on my arm, and I looked over to find a familiar face. Hailey's skin wasn't a block of ice like when we'd met at my graduation. It was warm, and her grip was strong.

"Something's in there." I pointed at the alley's dark entrance. I wasn't easily spooked, but for some reason this got me. My pounding heart wouldn't slow and whatever breath I had was gone. *Pull it together*, I told myself, not wanting anyone to see me like this.

She craned her neck to see around me, tiny wrinkle lines of worry stretched across her forehead. "It's only a stray," Hailey said lightly, the worry lines smoothing out. "Hey. Cat."

I looked back at the alley where there were no swirling shadows or hovering lights of dull red with specks of gold coming at me to devour me whole. Out of the darkness popped a dusty gray cat. In the lamplight, its eyes shimmered iridescent.

It let out an annoyed meow, unhappy its evening hunt had been interrupted. It gave me one last withering look and ran off, tail high and straight in the air. I felt stupid knowing now I'd been terrified of a cat. But that dark in the alley . . . it had left me so unnerved . . . It couldn't have just been a cat. Right?

"You were nearly hit," Hailey stated.

The sudden absence of warmth let me know she'd pulled her hand away. I shivered—from the sudden cold spot, from the sudden case of willies. I wasn't sure.

"It's a street, you know. You can't just jump out into oncoming traffic." She cracked a wry smile.

My face flushed. "I didn't mean to. I thought I saw . . ." I didn't finish, not trying to sound like a baby. It was only a cat. If I kept repeating it to myself, then maybe I'd actually start believing it.

I took a cleansing breath. "I lost my balance." I could run barefoot in the swamps and marshes over razor-sharp reeds grinding into my heels in a single breath, but she didn't know that.

"We'll be sure to watch out for you then."

The back of my neck became incredibly itchy as embarrassment flooded my system. I rubbed at it, looking everywhere else but at her.

She wasn't alone. The Camaro's owner had returned and brought with her two friends who looked as fashionable as she did. I straightened my wrinkled T-shirt and jean shorts as if that would make any difference. This wasn't a good start. First the cat in the alley, nearly getting hit, and now looking run-down (pun intended) in front of people obviously dressed to go out. I hated how appearances bothered me in front of these mainlanders when I'd never cared about it before. Pulled up behind Hailey's car was another, a black four-door. The driver drummed black–nail polished fingers on the steering wheel to the beat of Paramore thumping from the speakers. The volume went down a couple notches as the car waited.

"Doesn't that dumbass driver know this is a residential?" a Black girl who could be a model complained after having left the car to see what was going on. She wore pearls and rocked an all-leather jumpsuit that hugged every inch of her beautiful curves—not that I was looking. Many couldn't pull off all leather, but she did with perfection.

"Anyway, you know the line gets long fast and though I"—she gestured to herself—"in all my wonderfulness can get us right in with no wait, we still don't want to push it. The club's in North Charleston."

"Is she alright?" the driver asked. I was unable to appreciate the full look for the night except the sunglasses on top of gelled hair and possibly suspenders over a white button-down shirt.

Hailey eyed me like she wanted to call me on my BS. "*Are* you all right?"

"Yeah. I should get back to . . ." I had to think for a minute because I hadn't expected her to . . . care. I rattled off a hotel, volunteering all sorts of info to someone I didn't know, whose brother I didn't trust. I had to keep telling myself that despite the sense that she was okay. Senses could be off, and we already knew mine came and went as they pleased.

"Hails, go grab the thing you said you desperately needed and let's go. You can even bring your new friend. Hello, new friend. See? We're all friends now. Can we go?" The driver's smile was genuine and kind. I returned with my own and included a wave.

Hailey made quick introductions, pointing everyone out. "Karlie and Flex. Addae." She remembered. To her friends: "Go ahead without me."

Karlie had already rolled her eyes, heading back to the passenger side before Hailey could finish.

Hailey still watched me, her voice like a melody. I met her gaze and refused to back down as she practically analyzed me. Hell, I was doing the same. Sizing her up, trying to figure out what it was about this girl and why she wasn't freaked out that I'd shown up on her doorstep.

Flex groaned. "I knew she'd do that. Guess it's the two of us. Again."

"Right?!" Karlie complained loudly from inside the car. "A day will come when we stop inviting your ass places if you keep flaking out."

Hailey lowered her voice, whispering, "I always do that when I have better options for the night."

Better options. It got warmer. I tugged at my shirt collar, trying to get some air on my body.

Flex suggested, the peacemaker among the three, "Maybe tomorrow after the welcome on campus then. We could come over, hang out."

"It's your last chance," Karlie called out as they drove away.

Hailey turned on her heel, heading toward her house. She called over her her shoulder, "Coming?"

"You're letting me in?" I asked, a little shocked that she'd be so open to a stranger.

"I guess. Or would you rather stay out here with the cat?"

I found the cat watching me, daring me to even try it. Behind it, in the dark alley, I swear I saw movement in the shadows once again.

I quickly followed Hailey inside.

CHAPTER FOURTEEN

Cool, crisp air-conditioning greeted me when I entered Hailey's home and took in my new surroundings. The house looked bigger on the inside, with a wide-screen TV and sound system and pristine kitchen that looked like no one had cooked in it in years. I bet the trash can was full of take-out containers . . . unless Hailey and Luke had a chef. I wouldn't be surprised.

Most of the homes on the Isle were laid-back, bohemian, or beach style. Hailey's place smelled like a hotel, one of the upscale ones that piped in the expensive scents. I always felt uncomfortable in places like this, as if even the furniture wondered what I was doing here.

"Does it meet your standards?"

I shrugged. "It's alright." I turned around, finding Hailey right behind me and in my personal space. I didn't like how she could creep up on me without me knowing she was coming. It was something no one had ever really been able to do.

I shook off my unease, noticing like I had the first time how pretty her eyes were. And her lips, they looked like the top of a heart, perfectly covered in red lipstick—

I shuddered. What was I doing getting distracted when I was here on a mission? I must have been tired.

She raised an eyebrow, her red lips curving in a smirk like she knew what I'd been thinking. Heat flushed my cheeks.

Her eyes narrowed like she was using her bullshit detector. "Don't let my mom catch you saying that. The amount she dropped on this place." Hailey sighed resignedly. "It's repulsive."

"And yet, here you live." I put a hand on my hip, twisting my lips at her to let her know I was calling bullshit too.

Her eye twitched. I hit a nerve, and I had to admit it felt good to give it a little to someone after everything that had been going on.

I shook my head and mumbled that she should forget it and moved past her to the row of family pictures on the walls and the mantel of her fireplace in the living room. Her and Luke at various stages of their lives, together and always laughing. With their parents and looking so formal, very blond magazine-cover perfect, the four of them.

"I got tired of blond," she said when she noticed me looking at the photo.

And then another photo with an extra guy added in. I leaned in. He looked like Hailey's mom, with a sharp nose, thin lips, and a stare that could freeze water.

Hailey studied him too. "My uncle Simon; my mom's younger brother. He runs the Endowment."

"He looks intense," I said.

Hailey's lips pursed, her gaze growing distant. "He can be." She came back from wherever her mind had taken her, refocusing on me. She mustered up a smile. "Make yourself at home."

I sat down stiffly on the edge of the cream-colored settee, beating down the sudden onset of homesickness. It came out of nowhere. But I had spent hours alone in Charleston, something I'd never done before even though the city wasn't that far away, as wild as that sounded. It would be too easy to say *screw it* and go back home where Nana would take care of everything.

Hailey sat opposite me, looking just as uncomfortable as I felt. "I guess you got the news about the search."

The homesickness went away. I nodded.

She mimicked me, her hands sliding up and down her thighs like she was nervous. "Why are you here?"

"It was one of the places Naira visited when she was here, and I want to know what happened. And why."

Hailey blew out a slow breath. Her eyes flickered toward the windows, like she'd done when we were outside. I turned, thinking again that something might be there, but there was nothing in the dark on the other side of the glass.

"Don't do that to yourself," she whispered me. "She's gone. Luke's . . . gone. They called the search off."

"Don't you want to know what happened?"

"Their boat crashed and sank. It's been three weeks, Addae." I hated how she looked at me, like she felt sorry for me.

"Because life must go on, right?" I snapped. She was just another person who wanted to move on like nothing happened, like they didn't even exist.

"What's that supposed to mean?"

"Don't you want to know what happened to your brother? Don't you want to at least try?"

She ran her hands over her legs as she shifted, looking out the window again. Maybe that's what she did when she needed to think.

"Of course I want to know, but is it worth it at this point? My parents went back to Boston because my mom couldn't handle being down here with all the reminders of Luke. It's been hell."

Story of my life. If Hailey had given up, fine. But I needed her to tell me everything she knew about that last day, and then I could go and investigate by myself.

Hailey's phone went off, the music like doom and gloom was calling. *Duh, duh, duh, duhhhhhh.* Judging by Hailey's expression, she knew exactly who was calling.

Hailey pulled out her phone. A display of emotions crossed her face like she was going through stages of grief. I wondered who in her world had the power cause that kind of reaction.

"Give me a sec," she said, jumping up and accepting the call.

Hailey's voice lowered to a murmur as she walked toward the kitchen, while I went the opposite way to the closed French doors that apparently led to a gated backyard patio. I walked to the doors, peering through one of the small square panels. I got up close, nose nearly touching the cool glass. Behind me, I heard snatches of Hailey's conversation. From the sound of it, it wasn't going well.

I traced my finger over the smooth surface, wondering how much I could trust Hailey. I was in her house, pretty much at her mercy if she got the drop on me. But I was hoping there were holes she'd be able to fill. Maybe if this was really all some intricate plan to run away devised by Naira and Luke, Hailey would clue me in since I was obviously the last to know. I'd come here ready to figure things out. But I hadn't thought about how alone I'd feel, how othered I'd be in this city where no one was like me.

I pulled back from the surface. There was something on the other side of the door. Something out there in the dark, hiding in the shadows, watching me. The light behind me made it hard to make out anything concrete. My hand hovered over the door handle.

From the other room, Hailey said: "Yeah, it was a surprise to me too." A long pause followed. "No. Give me a little time. Let me do it my way." Another pause. "It's not like that." Hailey's voice was strained.

Pitch-black was on the other side of those doors, darker than it should be in a neighborhood with plenty of lights. Not even one firefly pierced the dark. If someone was trying to scare me—

She is gathering.

—I wouldn't make things so easy for them. I moved away from the doors, from my thoughts, distracting myself with the conversation Hailey was having in the other room. Whoever was on the other line made Hailey shrink into herself until she was a ball. Tiny sounds came from her and I realized she was crying. Seeing her like this made my wall against her crack a little, letting compassion seep through.

When Hailey and I first met at my graduation, when I touched her ice-cold hand and sensed nothing from her, it threw me off. Made me think she was some weird entity. But now whatever barriers she had up were gone, making way for her sudden surge of emotions.

No matter how much contempt I had for her being a mainlander, being unreadable, or for her brother getting my friend in this horrible mess, I realized that in this regard, Hailey was no different from me. Her loss was like mine. She let me in her house when she didn't have to, and despite my conclusions about her brother and if he had something to do with all of this mess, Hailey was the best shot I had. Now if only I could convince her that I was hers too.

"Sounded like a bad call in there," I said when she reentered the room and sat back down.

She sniffed, looking like a strong gust of wind would blow her over. "My family has strong opinions on how I should be dealing with Luke and all this." She searched for the words. "And I, um, was trying to explain how I needed to go through my own . . . process."

Nodding, I said, "I know the feeling. To really believe the truth is out there."

Hailey's head tilted. "Which of us is Mulder and which is Scully?"

Silence.

"*X-Files?* You've never seen it?"

I shook my head.

She tutted. "Poor, depraved soul."

I prepared myself for my pitch, hoping this time around I'd get her approval. She had every reason to say no. The recent call was clear evidence. "Look, Hailey, I don't know your situation, but I would do anything to figure out what happened to Naira, and I think you'd do the same for your brother. Do you really believe Luke is dead?"

"Why wouldn't I?" she cut in sharply. "Believe he's dead?"

I was shocked. "That easily? You don't hold out any hope that maybe they could have made it?"

She snorted, whispering, "Hope." She shook her head at me.

Again, she looked out of her French doors. I followed her gaze. Again, I saw nothing. "I think if we trace some of their steps, go where they went and ask around, something might come up." I shrugged. "And even if nothing shakes out, we can move on knowing we tried the best we could, you know?"

Hailey studied me for a moment, lost in her thoughts. "You really think this is all worth it?"

If it meant getting to the places where Naira had last been, hell yeah it was worth it, even if I still wasn't sure about Hailey's angle in this.

I nodded.

She seemed to debate something to herself before finally saying, "It's late, and if you want, there's a guest room that you can stay in while you're here. Save some money."

"I have money," I said quickly, embarrassment and anger sweeping through me. "I don't need handouts."

"I know," she said just as quickly, as if she'd realized her mistake. She held up her hands to appease me. "I'm sorry, I just meant if you stayed, it would be easier for us to talk if you're only right down the hall instead of across town. Plus, I wouldn't mind the company. Since Luke's been gone . . ." She stopped herself, swallowing hard and sending any remnants of my anger down the drain.

CHAPTER FIFTEEN

The next morning, I stepped out onto the already busy streets thinking that in the bright of day, the city was pretty. The row of rainbow-colored homes along with the horse-drawn carriages clopping along was like a dip into another time.

"They're nice, huh?" Hailey asked, coming up behind me on the steps. "I can't believe you have me up this early." It was 8:00 A.M. I almost ran down the list of all I would have done by now, but that didn't seem helpful. She yawned, covering her mouth. Ultra-dark sunglasses so large they nearly took up half her face. She used a hand to block her face from the sun, turning slightly away from it. The sounds of hooves *clop, clop, clopping* on cobblestone streets echoed between the buildings.

"When Luke brought Naira here, the horse-and-carriage tour was one of the things she wanted to do most of all. She was so excited," Hailey said. "They didn't get a chance before . . . all of this happened."

She let her words hang in the air, the rest unnecessary.

I appreciated that she didn't say Naira had died, whether she truly believed it or not.

"When I walked here from the marina—"

Hailey grimaced. "You walked all the way from there?" She made it sound like I'd said I trekked across the country.

I nodded, following her down the steps with my backpack slung over one shoulder. Her lips were bright red, her hair hung in perfect short curls, and a tiny designer backpack dangled from her hand. She moved fast, bouncing down the stairs to the sidewalk.

She went around to the driver's side of her car with three jagged claw marks painted over the headlight. She opened the door and almost got in until she saw me still standing on the sidewalk.

"What's the holdup? Get in."

I eyed her car, remembering how she peeled out of the stadium parking lot at my graduation. "Do we have to . . . Maybe we can walk? It's not that far."

She made a face. "Yeah, I don't walk. Plus, I need Starbucks. Get in the car."

Still feeling like Hailey behind the wheel was a bad idea, I forced myself in.

"Okay." She dropped her key fob in the middle console, a smooth, rose-gold egg-shaped contraption attached to the key ring.

I pointed at it. "What's that?"

She briefly glanced at what I was pointing to. "A panic button. If I'm ever in trouble, I can push it and nearby security will be notified. You live in the city, you learn to never leave home without something."

"Noted," I said, hoping I'd never have to hear it.

She started the car. "What's the itinerary?"

I only had two places on the list. Hopefully they wouldn't lead to dead ends.

"Let's start with the marina where Naira and your brother took off."

We passed another church in the historic district Hailey lived in. It was huge, with Gothic architecture and stained glass windows glinting sunlight off of them.

"The Cathedral of St. John the Baptist," I read as we passed. "I heard there's a crypt somewhere in there. That true?"

"Wouldn't know."

"But you live right—"

"I don't step foot in churches." Hailey cut in. Her eyes remained straight ahead, her speed accelerating.

"Why not?" I asked, curious about this new vibe from her. Cool. Barriers slammed back up.

How was she able to do that?

Again, "Why?"

"Not my thing." Which ended the conversation whether I wanted to or not.

Hailey was the worst driver I ever had the bad luck to ride with. She rode people's bumpers. She blew her horn and muttered curses at innocent people who weren't moving fast enough for her. She blew through yellows and I think a red while I clutched on to my seat belt and door handle for dear life. I was pretty sure nail marks were embedded in the leather.

"Could we please maybe slow down?" I flip-flopped between

squealing in fear and sending up every prayer imaginable. "You don't have to drive so faaaasst!" The last part just came out in a screech as Hailey floored it and cut off a Challenger to get in the left turn lane. All of my years passed before my eyes.

She didn't hear me, or maybe she ignored me. Finally, we came to a squealing stop at the marina. We nearly hit the fence post in the process.

"You're a terrible, horrible, no-good driver," I informed her.

"Yeah, well, you're welcome," she returned, reveling in my trauma way too much.

She gripped her Grande coffee while she led me along the docks where rows and rows of boats bobbed happily in the water. We ended up in front of an empty space. Several wreaths of various colors looped over the thick, round wooden post that marked Luke's empty docking space like a ring toss. Hailey stood solemnly in front of the memorial, pushing her large glasses flat against her face. I couldn't see her eyes, but her whole vibe told me she was struggling.

I was about to say something nice because that's what a decent person was supposed to do in times like this. But Hailey started talking.

"Going out on the water was his favorite thing, and he loved coming to this marina and talking sailing with everyone here. He'd been planning this night for so long for Naira. Like since the moment they started talking. I think he fell for her the minute he saw her."

Hailey was probably the last person to see Luke and Naira. It must have weighed a ton on her. At least she got to see Naira happy. The last time I saw her, I'd basically told her to go to hell.

"Before he met Naira, Luke would just go to class, work with our uncle on the artifacts they found in excavations for the Endowment. Sail around on his boat. He didn't have many friends." Hailey snuck a look at me, and I could barely make out the outline of her eyes. She wiped at her nose with the back of her hand. "Did you know he took one of those tour ferries to your island?"

I stopped moving. I hadn't. "I thought our graduation was the first meetup."

"No," Hailey said, pushing her glasses up so they sat atop her head. "He surprised her and came over. He said the island felt like it was made of magic. I always thought it was bullshit and that he was just saying that because he was so into her. Later, he told me the island was like heaven. You should have seen how excited he was when he got home. He couldn't wait to tell me. Our uncle even made a comment that he'd never seen Luke look as happy as that before."

Must have been nice hearing all that in real time. Naira kept her real first meet-cute from me. He came all the way to Golden Isle and Naira never said a word.

I pushed down the remorse. It was distracting me from what mattered. Hailey said Luke had been working with the Endowment's artifacts. They were the ones owned by the lab where the artifacts were being restored, like from the picture Naira had sent me.

"You said your uncle and Luke work for the Endowment?"

"Our family is the main benefactor. My uncle Simon was an archaeologist and led a lot of the excavations. Now he oversees the entire program. Luke helped out a lot; he was pretty into that kind of thing, like Naira. They used to debate about stealing and appropriating artifacts from other cultures. But I'm not involved in looking for the artifacts. Digging in dirt isn't my thing." She held up her clawlike red nails and smiled.

I sighed. I knew Hailey meant well, but hearing about this side of Naira that I knew so little about just made me feel worse. If only she'd told me. But if she had, would I have acted different? Or would I have been the same ass I'd been that night?

"What is the lab for?"

"Research. Where we work with the artifacts uncovered in digs."

"Stolen stuff you all appropriate and then try to pawn off as discovered and give back to the true owners like you did them a huge favor." I rolled my eyes. "You're only doing what you should be doing in returning those artifacts. You're not, like, doing some humanitarian service to the world. You won't win the Nobel Peace Prize or some shit for doing what you already should." Come to think about how big business worked, they probably would.

The jaw muscles worked under Hailey's skin. I side-eyed her as she licked her lips while I braced myself for whatever she had coming.

"That's fair. It's what happens, right? Throughout history."

She didn't have to tell me about it. I knew the history. I *lived* the history.

"Maybe we should try to find someone who might have been here that night," I said.

As we walked to the dock office, a voice blared from nearby.

"Another discovery of a mutilated body . . . awaiting the medical examiner's report, but sources say the body appeared to have been ravaged by animals . . ."

The news report broadcasted from a radio on a cerulean yacht, *Sleeping Bluety*. I tuned into the broadcast, listening closely.

". . . the body count steadily rising in the last several months, not including the recent disappearances. Unconfirmed sources say the disappearances may be connected and the work of a serial killer, though police are not yet labeling it as the work of one."

"How's it not a serial killer?" I asked. "That many people dead?"

"Haven't you been following the news lately?"

I hadn't.

"There have been a bunch of unexplained attacks and missing people up and down the coast," Hailey answered. "But they're scattered so I guess no one's alarmed, but it's weird."

That's right, Sekou had mentioned something about missing people, but I had dismissed it with bigger things on my mind. Now I wished I'd paid attention. Then I could have asked Nana Ama what she thought and if she sensed anything whenever she stepped out to clear the haze building in her, which wasn't very often.

"Don't forget the sick folks who go into the hospital and then go missing," a voice said from behind us. Hailey and I turned to see a ruddy-faced man wearing a white hat with a blue sail insignia on it stepping off the yacht. His face was sun blasted, and he was wiping his hands on a grease-stained towel.

I said, "What sick folks?"

He shrugged. "That's what they won't tell you on the news. How they up and walk from their hospital bed. There one minute, gone the next. I'm retired janitorial services from one of the local hospitals. Still have friends there." He grinned. "Who like beer and cards."

Hailey returned his grin. "Who doesn't like beer and cards?" she said easily, finding the connection between them.

He stuck out a relatively clean hand toward us. I stared at it, debating if I wanted to take it when Hailey grabbed it, having better manners than me. I followed her lead.

"Barry, right?" she asked. "My brother's mentioned you."

I caught how she still referred to Luke in the present. So maybe she was with me on the two of them still being alive for real and not just to humor me.

Barry looked over at the wreaths we'd been looking at, realization washing over him.

"Hey, you're the sister. Hannah."

"Hailey."

"Sure, he used to talk about you a lot." Barry looked at the empty space of water sloshing against the pier and boats. I guess he didn't talk about Hailey enough for Barry to know her name wasn't Hannah.

"Terrible thing happened to him and his friend. I met her the evening they were setting off for their date. They were pretty excited. Cute couple."

He looked at me when he said *friend,* like I'd know who that was. Guess he assumed we all knew one another. Usually, I'd get all in my feelings like, *Not all Black people know each other, bud.* But since he might have had something I needed, I let it slide. This time. Plus, Nana always said you get more flies with honey. And old Barry here definitely liked to buzz around shit.

Hailey thanked him for his condolences. "Between what's on the news and the boat accident . . ." The corners of Barry's mouth fell. "Damnedest thing. Real tragedy. I was out there when the weather went bad. The storm was unreal. So sudden. So weird." Barry shivered.

"Why was it weird?" I was thinking of the dream I had that night and of how I still felt its cold effects. I forced my body not to shiver with him.

"Because it just came up on us, and there was only a little patch of it. I could see it raging over yonder, but I didn't even get wet. Storms strong enough to break up good-sized new boats like Luke's, you get notice they're coming. But this squall or whatever they wanna call it, no warning. Real fast. And barely made a tickle over here where the rest of us were wrapping up. They weren't even that far off! Not much farther than the sound."

A freak storm that only seemed to hit Luke's boat? Ravaged bodies? Missing people? This news hadn't made it to the Isle—at least not that I knew of.

Barry tucked the towel in his back pocket. "Where you from?"

I sensed Hailey's curiosity growing as she waited for my answer. Hell, I was waiting for me too.

"From farther down," I said, preparing for what came next. "Golden Isle."

Barry's eyes grew round. His lips puckered up, and he let out a low whistle as his eyebrows disappeared beneath the rim of his hat.

"Y'all are supposed to be some hedonistic island of hippies, left-wingers, and African witches."

He said it so earnestly that I laughed. Something loud and sudden that felt good to release. But Hailey must have misread because she cleared her throat, and if stony looks could kill, there would be a report on the local news about Barry.

Barry must have realized how he sounded because he tried cleaning up.

"What I meant was—"

"It's okay, Barry. We hear that stuff all the time." Then I added for good measure, "I heard you mainlanders are nothing but a bunch of soft, greedy, stuck-up children who don't know how to take care of themselves."

Barry waggled a finger at me. "Ah, you got me there—"

"Ada."

He considered it. "Ada. Beautiful name. Good boat name."

"I know," I huffed out, swallowing the surge of annoyance. "I have one."

Hailey cut in, likely sensing danger . . . not for me, but him. "Barry," she said, her voice high and loud as she gave me a pointed look that I returned with one of my own. "Did you notice anything else the night of the storm?"

"The whole evening was off. Now that I find out your friend—"

"Naira."

"—is from the Isle, the freakiness of the whole thing, and the lady showing up makes more sense."

Wait. What?

Hailey and I shared a look. Barry's words had hit center target.

"There was this woman standing at the end of the dock wearing this long cloak like the one Little Red Riding Hood would wear. Only this one was black."

In my mind, something began dislodging itself.

"I called out to her because she was right at the edge, not moving, but she could have fallen, you know."

Coils of snakes constricted and unwound themselves in my gut, and I pulled off my backpack, unzipping it, digging in.

"I said, 'Hey, ma'am, you might wanna back away from there.' And I started walking to her, like so, thinking maybe she needed help or something. My mother, bless her soul, used to do that when her memory got too bad. Wander off and get into predicaments until we had to put her in a home. She's passed on now."

"I'm sorry." Hailey ducked her head all respectful like, activating me to nod in sympathetic solidarity.

Barry's words triggered something I'd seen and I pulled my phone out. Unlocked it. I was fumbling with shaky fingers to where I'd last seen the shots from Naira.

"But the lady turned real fast on me. Looked at me and, swear to god, her eyes glowed like rubies. And her teeth. Two long ones. Like a tiger. Big! Like a saber-tooth."

His eyes were saucers, growing larger until they were nearly all white as he recalled the moment. His voice lowered to a near whisper. He moved in closer. Barry wasn't bullshitting either. He was scared. I could tell.

"I mean, it—she stopped me cold. I'm not ashamed to say I didn't think much 'bout saving her at that point. Next thing I knew, this voice from nowhere was warding me off, but I wasn't sure if I'd heard it inside or out of my head. You know what I'm saying?"

I didn't know, but I could imagine. Barry's story put Naira and Luke here, and my excitement grew. Not only them, but now there was a mysterious woman with saber-tooth fangs. I'd found them. I pulled up the selfie of Luke and Naira on the boat.

"I blinked. I swear that's all I did. Felt a gust of air. And the next second she was gone. Like she was never there." He let out a slow breath. He checked if we believed him. I did. Hailey's face was a blank slate. I had no idea what she was thinking.

"Haven't told a soul," Barry continued. "I'd been drinking that night. I don't want to believe what I saw. It'll give you nightmares. But I been thinking, those murders and disappearances all over the news. Then fang lady. Gotta be something. Don't you think?"

I held my phone screen out to him and showed him the picture. "Is this like what you saw?"

Hailey craned her neck, angling for a better view. Barry's eyebrows furrowed in concentration.

"It's blurry." I sounded apologetic, wishing there was a clear shot. A clear confirmation of what was out there with Naira and Luke.

With his thumb and pointer finger, he zoomed in on the picture, peering closely at the two red dots. "Right there. Those dots. That's what her eyes looked like."

His voice was shaky. His hand, shakier, as he swiped to the second picture of the necklace in the exhibit. All bravado erased, the tremor in his voice was clear.

"And that gold . . . I saw some gold on her arm. Right before she disappeared into thin air."

CHAPTER SIXTEEN

"WANT TO EXPLAIN ALL THAT?" HAILEY STARTED UP AS SOON as we got back in the Camaro. "Where'd you get those pictures? Can I see them?"

Her questions were rapid-fire. I settled in my seat and handed my phone over. "From Naira. They're the last thing she ever sent me."

Hailey turned the phone every which way, pinching her fingers, then expanding them just like Barry had done. We'd left him back on the docks worse than how we'd met him. It was like I'd confirmed UFOs were real. Now any story he told about the Isle would be backed by the strange woman he'd encountered on the boat ramp.

"I think I've seen this necklace before. At the Endowment Research Lab."

"I think we should go there next." I buckled up, tightening the strap as I thought about our drive here. She handed back the phone and pressed the ignition button, making the engine roar to life.

Hailey's eyes met mine. "I agree. But we might have a problem."

"What kind of problem?"

"You'll see."

THE CAMPUS WAS BUSY WITH ACTIVITY. THE QUAD WAS DECOrated with school paraphernalia, and in the center stood a large stack of wood pyres with a huge papier-mâché lion on top. There were too many people, sending my senses into overdrive. I quickly stuffed my earbuds in to help mute the noise.

Hailey tapped her ear, and I pulled a bud out to hear her. "Start of the school year is coming up so they're having a new student–orientation kickoff," Hailey informed me as we walked through the maze of students on the lawn, sprawled out on blankets and playing games like Frisbee, beer pong, and horseshoes.

"They have all this on your magical island?" Hailey smirked. I hoped my straight face let her know how very unfunny she was.

We entered the newly built facility, where I noticed the security was pretty tight with guards posted up at the entrance. I brought it up to Hailey as we got in an elevator and she scanned her ID badge. The button for LL lit up.

"Everything's pretty valuable. It's underground because the researchers and restorers don't want a lot of light deteriorating the stuff before they have a chance to study them and prepare to return them to their rightful owners."

"But what if their rightful owners aren't around anymore?"

Hailey shrugged. "Then we donate it to a museum specializing in that particular culture, if there is one."

The temperature in the lower level was ten degrees cooler, and she undid the tied sleeves of her plaid sweater, shrugging it over her shoulders. I did the same with the sweatshirt I'd stuffed in my backpack.

We walked down a lit hall lined with several empty labs, each displaying different artifacts on large steel tables that we could see through the bay windows. Only a couple of labs had people working in lab coats, masks, and white gloves, holding a variety of tools.

We stopped at the end of the hall, where a young South Asian woman stood taking notes on the clipboard she held.

"Dr. Patel."

The woman looked up, mildly annoyed at the interruption, but then smiled when she saw who was speaking.

Hailey peered in the darkened room through the glass. She frowned. "Still no word about Dr. Franco? Nothing from the investigators? Or my uncle?"

Dr. Patel mimicked the frown, twisting her lips back in annoyance. "No. Seems like I'm the only one who comes to work these days."

"Who's Dr. Franco?" I asked, peering around them to try to see for myself.

Dr. Patel's frown remained, her expression saying it all. *Who the hell is this?*

"This is my—" Hailey turned to shoot me a quizzical look. She didn't know what to call us. We definitely weren't friends. Acquaintances? But in this short amount of time, we had shifted into some kind of alliance on our quest to figuring out what happened to Naira and Luke.

"This is Ada. She's from the Golden Isle. Born and raised. Dr. Patel, one of our researchers."

Dr. Patel studied me with renewed interest. Her eyes moving over me like I was a specimen in a petri dish. I tried not to take it personal. "We have been trying to interview a native to the island for the longest time, the woman who owns the land especially."

"She's my grandmother."

Hailey wasn't surprised. Either Luke had clued her in, or he hadn't been the only person Naira had been chatty with.

"Remarkable." Patel looked like she'd won the information lottery.

"We can trust her," Hailey said, reassuring me, though I intended to come to my own conclusions.

"A few days ago, our lead researcher, Dr. Franco, took the amulet from the lab, and we haven't seen him since," Dr. Patel explained. "It's the archaeological find of the year, and probably the century, and we didn't even get a chance to carbon date it, let alone run enough testing to determine its origins."

She paused when a guy who'd stepped off the elevator, pushing a cart stacked with folders, approached us. "Excuse me for a moment," she said.

I stared into the room as if the amulet would magically appear from thin air. "How's this not on the news?"

"How's it not on the news? My uncle would never let the public know an Endowment employee walked off the premises with not only a priceless ancient amulet, but a priceless ancient amulet that was likely stolen from African people and brought here."

Patel returned, holding a bundle of mail to her chest. "You know, there was another young lady touring the lab with . . ." She trailed off. Her eyes shot to Hailey, whose head ducked away.

"She's my best friend," I said, ignoring the way my stomach twisted whenever Naira was referenced.

"I'm sorry for your loss as well," Patel said, followed by those awkward seconds of silence when no one knew what to say next.

"We'd love to talk to your grandmother. We've been speaking to members of the Gullah people on some of the other islands and here in town. It's amazing, the way you all have retained your culture. It helps build a complete story around the artifacts we find. Do you think she would speak to us?"

Patel was saying all the right things, but I couldn't forget she wanted something I had, information on the Isle.

"The island was founded long before my ancestors arrived. Several Indigenous tribes were there first." That was history I wasn't sure was common knowledge. "Then they were either massacred or run off by the Spanish armies who were trying to colonize," I said matter-of-factly. Hailey kept quiet. Dr. Patel nodded sagely.

Hailey walked the length of the long table, which held various old-looking items under glass casing. A Bible, some coins, other stuff. But one of the cases was empty. It was the biggest case, and the blanket that the artifact was supposed to be on was empty.

"This is what I wanted to show you," Hailey said, directing my attention to the empty glass box protecting nothing but air inside of it. Next to the box was a photo of what should have been there. All the items on the table had photos beside them.

I leaned in to look at the photo of the mysterious amulet. This picture was clearer than the one Naira had sent me, and I could finally study it properly. I'd never seen anything like it before, with its rows of draping golden chains that all connected to the central precious gem. I'd never seen it before, and yet, it was undeniably familiar.

This missing artifact belonged to my grandmother's people, to mine. It wasn't just an artifact to us, but a piece of who we were, of the land we were taken from.

This amulet was a vessel of my ancestors' power.

CHAPTER SEVENTEEN

I KEPT QUIET ABOUT THE AMULET'S CONNECTION TO NANA Ama's cuffs, not ready to share until I knew more. Dr. Patel, while nice enough, was still a researcher employed by the Endowment. That's why she was looking at me like I was a snack she wanted to dig into. She reminded me of the land developers who chased Nana incessantly with nothing but dollar signs in their eyes, wanting to make our home another vacation destination.

As for Hailey? While we shared Naira and Luke, her family still owned the Endowment, and the Endowment had ulterior motives. I needed to remember that. From the photos, I asked if we could check the cameras, prepared to be stonewalled at this point. But Hailey, once again, readily agreed, leaving me both curious and confused about her fluctuating moods and her willingness to give me access to her family's company.

"Who's he talking to?" I pointed to the screen where Franco's head angled and his steps halted, like he didn't have complete control of his legs. He shook his head as if trying to get himself alert. Or shake something loose.

"His lips are moving. Every few seconds it's like he's speaking. Then he stops." I was a sports broadcaster calling out shots as Franco performed them. "He dips his head as if he's listening to something. Kinda strains like he can't hear it well. Then he replies. There's no volume on this thing?" I twisted in my seat to meet Patel's eyes.

She firmed her lips. "Unfortunately not." She shook her head. "All we've done, and here Franco waltzes right in, in the dead of night, and takes maybe the most valuable religious artifact we have. Certainly the oldest, if my guess is correct."

The oldest, I repeated to myself. Like how old were we talking? I thought about Nana's cuffs and how they looked so similar, and my stomach lurched. How much longer before the Endowment was on the Isle and learning everything they shouldn't about Nana and me?

"Simon employed lip-reading experts to parse out what he's saying, but to no avail," Patel said.

"What do you mean?"

Hailey had been typing furiously on her phone. Whatever was going on between her and whoever was on the other end wasn't good. She answered, "They said he was mumbling something unintelligible, so it was hard to figure out what he said."

Patel shot a troubled glance Hailey's way, her mouth opening and then snapping shut. I could tell there was more she wanted to say. Her brown eyes darkened with an internal debate I wanted very badly to eavesdrop in on. But Nana Ama taught me better than that. If someone wanted me to know something, they'd tell me.

Patel's irritation won out over her need to let me in on what was really in her mind, and she snapped, "Every time I watch this feed, I get angry all over again. We're entrusted with these artifacts. We're charged with the responsibility to restore these items as best we can and return them where they belong."

I switched my attention back to the screen. If you ignored the strange movements, Dr. Franco looked like a pretty average guy. "What was Dr. Franco like before he stole the amulet? Had something happened that would lead him to do this?"

Patel's anger transitioned to sadness. "Dr. Franco was a great colleague. A little depressed, maybe. He was going through a divorce. He was a good guy, and a wonderful scientist. Very generous with his findings."

"I didn't know him well," Hailey said. "But he and Luke were close. He took him under his wing, even though they hadn't planned for him to be in the lab. Luke was supposed to attend a school up north when he graduated high school. But instead, he followed me here. You know, we have always been close like that. Which is why he followed me here. Followed me to his—"

Some words shouldn't be spoken into existence.

I whispered, "Don't you dare say what you almost said."

I knew the power of words.

But I also knew the power of misguided guilt. Like the guilt Hailey felt, thinking maybe she should move on like her parents did. Neither of those things were true.

And I realized that now.

I reached my hand out before I realized what I was doing and took Hailey's hand into mine, squeezing it.

Patel cleared her throat, reminding us that we weren't alone.

The awkward silence that followed made Hailey suggest we get going.

I started to follow Hailey out, but her phone rang just as we were about to leave. "It's my uncle," she said. "Be right back."

This left me alone with Dr. Patel, who seemed lost in the frozen video feed of Dr. Franco with the amulet clutched in his hand, gleaming brighter than it should have been in the lighting. I was staring at it too.

Who did it belong to? Why did he take it? Where was it now? And how did it connect to my grandmother?

"I really wish I knew what he was muttering," I said quietly.

Patel broke her daze, turning to me. She dropped her voice. "They actually did make out one word. It was an old language. Ancient. We sent it to an expert we trusted would be discreet even though we didn't give much context beyond asking what this word was."

"What was it?" I asked, even though I wasn't sure I wanted to know.

"I don't know if I'm even saying it right." She hesitated. "Ah-wu-rah. I always get tripped up."

I knew the word, and it wasn't as ancient as Patel's experts thought. It was an honorific still used by the Akans, one of the groups from the West African region, for women of high rank and prestige. It was a title my grandmother was also called in formal settings.

It meant *Lady*.

CHAPTER EIGHTEEN

As we rode the elevator, I wondered why Hailey lied about the lip-reading experts' discovery. *What could she be hiding?* Until I had it figured out, I needed to stay close. But the moment we stepped out of the building, we were hit with noise and music; I temporarily forgot about what went on downstairs and took in the scenery. Seeing college events on TV was different than real life. Hell, high school couldn't touch the amount of people spending a summer night partying on the campus.

I followed Hailey, checking out the scene. All the people laughing and enjoying themselves, spread across the lawn, reminding me of the Isle when the Kinfolk would dance to the drums and our chants, celebrating Nyame's golden stool and the gods who protected us and spirits who helped us take care of our land.

This was a different kind of celebration. A moment ago, Hailey had been edgy after her heated conversation with her uncle. But walking out onto campus and toward the quad, away from the heavy responsibilities and toward freeness, she began bobbing to the beat of the music blaring from huge speakers.

"This looks like our celebrations on Golden Isle," I said.

"Mainlanders—that's what you call us right? We like to let loose sometimes too." Hailey inclined her head. "You could join them . . ."

I didn't reply, instead popping in my earbuds to dial down the noise as I took in the crowd, thinking this wasn't so bad. The last party I'd attended felt a hundred years ago instead of only weeks. So much had happened. Too much. Ours hadn't been nearly as big as this one, just a handful of us on our boats and catamarans, celebrating finally being freed from high school. I thought of all that waited for me back at the Isle—so many responsibilities and surely more failure, and always the pressure to put on a brave and happy face. There, I was always on. Here, I didn't have to be. The thought was freeing. Each moment here, I began to understand more and more why Naira had wanted to experience life beyond the Isle. Maybe one day, I could be like these students, dancing as if they didn't have the weight of responsibility on their shoulders.

In the meantime, I had to remain focused as my time here counted down. I would leave with way more questions than I arrived with. Questions only Nana Ama could answer.

"Well?" Hailey asked, swaying in time to the music like she was trying to suck me in. "All work and no play . . . ever heard that before?"

It was tempting. I yearned to toss everything aside and go out there with her, to feel unrestrained even if only for a few moments. But then I started thinking about Naira. I'd run from home for something specific and this wasn't it. Wherever they were with that lady from the photo, they weren't partying.

"It's not my thing," I said over the noise.

Hailey pouted. It was cute. A little too cute. *Focus, Ada. You came here on a mission. Stick to it.*

"You sure?" Hailey asked, still swaying. This time her fingers motioned me to join her.

I smiled. "We need to figure out our next step."

Hailey groaned before following me to the parking lot where her red death trap awaited us.

Hailey and I moved away from the dense heat of the college crowd, the cooler air reenergizing me.

I sensed movement around us, not a bunch of college kids heading to the quad, but something familiar and not in a good way. It was the same feeling I'd had when I was sitting in front of the alley outside her home. Only moments ago, I swear there were people in the lot with us, which was suddenly deserted except us and a growing buzz like a swarm of locusts in a wheat field, signaling that something, or some *things*, much worse than that were coming.

CHAPTER NINETEEN

THE SOUND, LIKE A MILLION NAILS SCRAPING ACROSS CONCRETE and cement, came first and from all around. Then a hollow moaning sound of torturous agony. My body came alive, sensing that danger was close. Hailey was too busy assessing her drink situation to notice right away. It wasn't until I grabbed her wrist, not realizing my strength until she flinched, snatched her hand away, and stopped what she was doing. Confusion wrinkled her brows as our eyes met and she opened her mouth to protest. Until she heard them too.

The blue lights from the emergency call boxes were a call for help that would not come, and from us. The streetlights cast an eerie, yellowish glow. A *whoosh* sounded above us, dimming one of the lights, as if something had swallowed its light. Then another. I tried locating the source but was too slow to catch whatever had made that enormous shade. Shadows swirled and reshaped themselves around us, becoming a tight net of black, closing in on us.

"What is happening?" Hailey breathed, her once-confident tone replaced by fear. She pressed her back against mine, her hand finding mine. No electricity this time. Just pure, unadulterated fear shared between us.

There was a heavy thump as whatever had been flying dropped to the ground. And then more thumps as shadows with tiny, gleaming specks dropped in ones and twos from the trees, scampered out from beneath parked cars, and emerged from the darkness between the buildings.

The shadows merged and then sheared from one another, becoming distinct shapes. The bodies with the shining, speckly eyes stood there, facing us, surrounding us, tilting forward with their arms extending at their sides, elbows bent outward like prehistoric humans. But these things around us weren't human. Their fingers spread apart, and when they began advancing, emitting moans and high-pitched wails, I could see the thick, dark curving lines running the entire length of their bodies, all the way to their faces. Their veins showed through the color of their ashen skin—it didn't matter if they were white or Black, or different races. Tonight, they were one singular being, moving in sync, getting closer and closer to us, their veins and whatever was coursing through them shining like thick black permanent marker.

"Oh my god, oh my god," Hailey repeated. I had never seen anything like this. Had never known anything like these things with their eyes that were tiny, red-rimmed pinpricks of light. Their mouths dropped open, gaping, and drooling down their chins, down to the ground.

My mind raced. What should I do? I would go down fighting. But with what? And fighting against what? Nothing Nana Ama had taught me prepared me for these—these creatures with their torn dirty clothes, as if they'd been rolling round in the dirt and mud. The smell of them hit me hard. Of sickeningly sweet disease. Of putrid flesh. Of old blood and filth. What had happened to them? They were close enough now that I could see one was dressed in a suit. Another was in a ripped maxi dress cinched by a Louis Vuitton belt.

They were right over us. One of them struck out, grabbing ahold of Hailey's arm. She screamed, short and high. It was enough to give the thing pause for only a second before the creature yanked Hailey toward it. Hailey's screams echoed in the wind.

Let her go!

I called on whatever parts of my spotty gifts that would work for me now and save us. My strength, despite my fear, bubbled up in me, and I did a half turn. I brought my hand down hard on the creature's lower arm, breaking it and Hailey's physical connection. Hailey screamed again from the force of it, but the thing said nothing. Its limp arm swung uselessly back and forth.

I needed space. I needed air. I needed the deafening drone of their noise to cease. I didn't know enough, wasn't strong enough. I wasn't in control of myself enough to fight one of these things off, let alone the horde a hair's breadth away from us. I only had my will and my anger to drive me.

Another one of them reached its pockmarked arm out at us. The arm was covered in bite marks and gashes. We dropped to a crouch. Hailey shrank back, trying to get away from it, but the thing suddenly stopped, frozen. The creatures loomed over us, a stinking humanoid tent, as if they were of one mind. Then the one directly in front of me focused in on me, its large, onyx eyes catching me in their sight line. It watched me with vacant eyes that were a one-way mirror where someone or something could see me, but I couldn't see them. I tried to get a sense of its thoughts, but its mind, an impenetrable vault, was occupied by something else.

The thing's mouth unhinged to a length I hadn't thought possible for a human. The jaw popped and cracked from the effort. A low hum emitted from deep within it.

"Ahhh-bennn-niiiiiii." The word came out in a low, wet whisper from deep within the thing, from the other side of that one-way mirror. Its lips did not move.

I froze.

Abeni. My mother's name.

There was no way this woman-thing could have known who my mother was. Only people of the Golden Isle knew her name. Only Nana Ama. Only me.

I didn't answer.

The creature spoke again. "Who . . . are . . . you?" The words came out garbled, gravelly, like it was trying to talk through a mouthful of sharp stones. Like it was trying the words out for size. Its eyes, bright like fireflies, were rimmed in red. The deep grooves of poisoned veins carved in its face were too close, way too close.

"Who . . . are . . . you?"

Only this time it wasn't just this creature talking to me. All of the creatures' mouths had disengaged, with thick ropes of saliva dripping down, nearly touching me. I looked at each of them. All of their eyes were fixed on me. All of them mirrors. I was in a house of mirrors and couldn't find my way out.

All of the things spoke in unison. Speaking to . . . me.

Again, they asked, "Who are you?" Intoning the question over and over until whatever held them in its thrall began to consume me too.

They were drawing me in and I couldn't think of anything else. I had to push through, fight back, protect myself, protect Hailey.

The woman-thing stirred. Her arm extended toward me, fingers curled, clawlike, reaching for my face, closer and closer still. She meant to touch me.

My mind thundered. *Stay back!*

My body finally cooperated, and a swell of burning energy I could only guess to be from the Light unfurled within me and burst out, propelling the thing backward and into the rest of them. Just beyond them, back toward the streetlamp, stood a tall figure. She looked impossibly tall, and I realized it was because her feet were not on the ground but hovering above it. She was wrapped from head to toe in a dark cloak fastened at the neckline. Through the slivered opening at the nape of her neck, an object gleamed against her chest, illuminating her face in an eerie glow. For just a flash, I caught sight of her. My mind must have been playing tricks because she looked no older than me. But before I could get a better look, she turned her head away, hiding herself and the object back in shadows. The ethereal being canted her head slightly as she studied me intently, her telepathic fingers probing my mind for information about who I was, how she could control me, and how I was able to break the connection to these monsters.

I was trying to figure that one out myself.

Beside her, a smallish man, whose feet were firmly on the ground, turned the adoring gaze with which he looked at her to me. I sensed nothing but rage and resentment emanating from him. He was different from her, from the others, but also unlike me or Hailey.

The break, the discombobulation of the monsters, was enough to jump-start action. I flipped around on my hands and knees, scuttling past Hailey, who was staring at them, as petrified as the fossils her family dug up. I got to my feet, reaching down.

"Now. Now. NOW!" I yelled. We had to move while they were confused. While the floating lady was contemplating, or whatever. "Let's go. Now!"

I grabbed the top of Hailey's shirt, bunching it in my hand, and yanked her to her feet like she weighed nothing.

She stammered, "That's not how . . . Wait. Luke—"

There was no time for waiting.

"Now!"

Hailey got her life together, stumbling along, trying to match my speed. Together we pushed through the remains of the horde, expecting them to follow and attack again. This time I wouldn't be able to fend them off. Whatever element of surprise I delivered earlier had evaporated.

But there weren't dozens of feet pounding behind us. There weren't disjointed limbs reaching to grab us. The horde groaning and snapping their teeth didn't close in. The floating woman wasn't suddenly hovering above. I did the one thing I knew you should never do. I chanced a look behind me.

The man at the woman's side remained there. Hailey and I fought our way out. The gangly things tumbled into each other as they, as one, fell back and let us through.

We ran to Hailey's car saying nothing, our breaths coming out ragged, our fear driving us forward. She unlocked her car as we approached it and we jumped in, locking it as soon as the doors slammed shut. As she gunned the engine and careened out of the student parking lot, I dared to look back. The spot where at least twenty of those things had attacked us was now empty. It was as if nothing had happened.

But my racing heart and shaking hands told a different story. Something was coming for us, and it wouldn't stop until it'd ripped us apart.

CHAPTER TWENTY

Hailey and I didn't speak the entire ride back to her house. What had happened was too unbelievable to grasp and too terrifying to say out loud. Hailey didn't have a chance to cancel with Karlie and Flex, and we were compelled to hang out with no reasonable excuse not to. If she was feeling anything like I was feeling after what we'd just been through, she probably didn't want to be alone. Not with whatever was lurking out there.

Karlie and Flex brought a buffet of food, a welcome distraction and hidden gift. The adrenaline from earlier, the energy I'd spent calling forth that elusive burst of Light had exhausted me. Their spread of junk and desserts were the things available to help me get by, even if only for a little, until I made it back to the Isle. Hailey hadn't flaked out this time, but we weren't good company. And we weren't able to tell them what happened, so Karlie and Flex left early and we were alone.

On the other side of the room, Hailey remained quiet. She sat unmoving, staring into the flames of the gas fireplace. Her expression was unreadable.

"Should we talk about earlier?" I felt I needed to ask.

Hailey pulled her legs to her chest, wrapping her arms around them. "What is there to say? We were attacked by . . . things that came real close to being zombies."

Things that said *my* mother's name.

Hailey went to run a hand through her hair, but her hands shook so much that she clasped them back together again. "I just need a moment, okay? Like, what if they come here? I don't think I can deal with this."

"They're not, or else they wouldn't have let us go to begin with," I said. "Something stopped them."

What I didn't want to say or consider was that it seemed like the woman knew me, knew my mother. She had stopped those things. But why, when they clearly came to attack?

"What if they don't stop the next time? And who was that lady? Did you see her?" Hailey asked.

I couldn't unsee her.

Hailey's voice rose. "She was hovering over the ground, Ada. People don't do *that*."

"I know," I replied, because it was the only thing I could say.

Hailey couldn't be still, fidgeting anxiously. She was making it harder for me to think.

"What if she sends them after us?" She suddenly rushed to her alarm panel and activated it. I didn't have the heart to tell her that if those things really wanted in, her home security system wasn't going to keep them out.

I had no answers, only more questions and even more frustration. Just when I thought I was getting somewhere. I had found evidence to show Nana that Naira was alive and she'd finally do something to bring Naira home. Then this. Attacked by ghouls.

She is gathering.

My body shuddered involuntarily. Gathering ghouls. This was more than I bargained for. It hit me that Nana Ama might have suspected this and tried to keep me on the Isle. I should have listened to her.

"Let's just stay here together tonight. Tomorrow we'll think of something," I said, hoping I sounded like I knew what I was saying.

Before I settled down in the blankets I made into a sleeping bag, I sent Sekou a text.

Can u come get me tmrw

He answered me back in an instant with a thumbs-up. Then he asked what happened.

The story I had to tell could only be told in person.

Sleep was wishful thinking. I was on high alert with visions of the vacant eyes of the ghoul things, black lines all over them, chasing me, and thoughts of how they would have eviscerated Hailey and me if they hadn't been stopped by the cloaked woman hovering over the ground.

I was alone in the living room, the remains of the sleepover we'd had evident from the crumpled blankets and pillows and the mounds of empty and half-finished take-out containers. I was already fully dressed and pacing a hole in the floor, my decision made.

Hailey had been in the shower and came downstairs, still drying her hair with her towel. "Once I have some coffee, then we can figure out what comes next," she said. She rattled around in the kitchen. I followed her, leaning over the center island as she dropped a K-Cup in her Keurig.

"I'm going home," I announced.

Her movements slowed as the words sank in. Then she started back up again. "Okay. Sure, of course. Go back to the safety of your island and leave me here with those—those zombie ghoulie things."

I was about to make a huge mistake, and I had to say it fast before I had a chance to think it through, and by the time I'd realized I should have thought it through a little more, the words couldn't be called back.

"I think you should come with. It's not safe here with those 'zombie ghoulie things,' and until we figure out what they are, who that woman is, and what's going on, maybe you should come with me. At least until after Naira's Homegoing. Then my grandmother could maybe help us figure out what to do."

I was already thinking of the excuses I'd make to Nana so she wouldn't be pissed I was bringing a mainlander to stay without permission first. When I had the chance to talk to Nana directly and tell her everything, she'd understand. She'd want to help. She'd know what to do.

"I'll just explain the whole situation and that Naira was your friend. I think she'd understand that."

She probably wouldn't. I'd probably be disowned. But Nana wouldn't turn her back on someone in danger. Not after I told her what came after us.

"Seriously?"

"Yeah," I said, the idea gaining traction. I could tell Nana that Hailey was releasing Luke's light too. That this was what Naira would have wanted. That would settle Nana down. "I think it'll work." It was more reassurance to me than to her.

Hailey rushed me, swooping me up into a hug and thanking me repeatedly. I inhaled the scent of her citrus shampoo, lingered in the feel of her.

"Thank you, Ada," she said, squeezing me, her words muffled.

She let me go, and I plastered on a Kool-Aid smile. "No big deal."

All the while I was thinking, *Addae, you're in some deep shit now.*

CHAPTER TWENTY-ONE

"WHAT THE HELL, ADA?" SEKOU LOUD-WHISPERED AS HE steered his boat heading back to the Isle. "Here you go again making decisions without giving anyone a heads-up. Not me or your grandmother. Do you really think anyone wants this white chick on the Isle, let alone at Naira's Homegoing?"

"White chicks live on the Isle," I reminded him. "Matter of fact, you've messed with a couple there. Remember that? Or is this selective amnesia?"

His nostrils flared. "I meant mainlander. Scratch that, a complete stranger."

He had me there. Bringing a mainlander was one thing, especially one we barely knew. But this was different. Naira trusted her, and she and I had been through some shit. That had to be worth a temporary pass.

"Don't you think she deserves some closure too? She lost someone who Naira cared about. Her family is all the way up north, and she only has an asshole of an uncle who's around. We could help. Luke and Naira were together when they . . ." I still couldn't bring myself to say the words.

Sekou glowered at Hailey again as we cut through the water heading toward the Isle. She'd left her life on the mainland. We'd said bye to Flex and Karlie, and made them promise to go nowhere alone, although they didn't understand why.

"See there," Sekou had whispered when they said their good-byes at the pier. "Those two have sense. They know when to decline a polite invitation."

I hadn't told him the other part. My offer to Hailey hadn't only been a polite invitation or even not wanting her to face that woman and her things alone. There was curiosity from the moment she picked up my grad cap. Then she let me in her home. Let me take her around the city playing detective. She nearly got killed because I'd dragged her around. Was this how it started with Naira about Luke?

"There's more to why I didn't want to leave her behind," I explained. I ran through everything that had happened from the marina to right now. I was out of breath when I finished.

"Are you sure you all didn't catch a contact high from some weed or something? Because what you're saying is some high shit."

"I know it."

Sekou banged a beat only he could hear on the boat wheel, trying to make the irregular shapes of my story fit right like in Minecraft. Finally, he burst out laughing, loud and abrasive. He waggled a finger at me.

"You almost got me on that one. Glowing red eyes, drooling

zombies, serial killers, and amulets that look like Nana Ama's one-of-a-kind cuffs. Ooookay."

I grabbed his arm, shushing him. "Not so loud," I said.

"Let's say you weren't tripping off a bad batch. You really think the Isle is the best place for her to be?"

I nodded.

"They didn't attack y'all at her house," he said. "Maybe they moved on. And they said your mom's name? Then they don't want her, and she doesn't have to be on this boat. Until we figure out what to do about those things.

"Let me just repeat that this is a bad idea so when shit hits the fan, I'm gonna say a big ole 'I told ya so.' Trust me on this."

It was the only thing I could trust right about now.

From the public marina, Nana Ama waited with Elder James beside her, his face already screwed up to let me know how disappointed he was in my recent behavior. He watched Hailey step gingerly on the inclined walk from the boat to the pier, likely thinking I'd done it this time, invited a stranger to the Isle not only for a private Homegoing ceremony, but during our most sacred time, the Harvest Festival. He kept sneaking peeks at Nana Ama and tutting disapprovingly, like he was trying to rile her up, but next to him my grandmother remained cool and unreadable.

Nana Ama watched Hailey carefully as well, her eyes swiftly moving from top to bottom, taking her in, waiting for any sign that Hailey was not welcome here. I held my breath, waiting for the same. Waiting for any hint that Hailey would not be welcomed on the island. But Hailey was all smiles, commenting about everything she saw in Freeman's Port.

When we finally made it in front of Nana Ama, she settled her intense glare on me, her blank face never cracking. I had so much to discuss with her, so much to ask. There was a whole conversation in her look, one that promised I'd be held to account later and that showed she wasn't pleased with Hailey's presence without her permission. But she would never be outwardly rude to Hailey. It wasn't her way.

She let out a resigned sigh, turning her attention to my guest.

"Seems the Golden Isle welcomes you, Hailey. As do I," Nana Ama said.

Hailey refocused on Nana Ama, even performing an awkward curtsy-kind-of-bow-combo thing that was cute but totally unnecessary. But I got it—Nana Ama had that effect on people.

Nana Ama said, "Oh ho, that is much too formal for this little island. We're all family here."

Nana's laugh peeled away the anxiety that had built up, and everyone visibly relaxed. Elder James looked from me to Nana Ama with a mix of caution and curiosity, it being the first time he'd known someone to go against one of the biggest rules we had.

"Why don't we show you to our guest accommodations? They're located right here at the port, so there is plenty to keep you entertained while you're here and my granddaughter is unavailable."

Unavailable could mean a lot of things, and the implications were making me uneasy.

I avoided Nana's eyes when they landed on me. "And then hopefully we can get to know each other a little better before Naira's Homegoing."

CHAPTER TWENTY-TWO

"This is true, what you've just told me?" Nana Ama asked, looking from me to Hailey and back to me again. She sat at the small table in Hailey's guest house, which was a tiny one-room cabin the size of a hotel room with a teeny bathroom included. It wasn't meant to be occupied for long stretches of time and was used mostly for emergencies or the rare tourist or two who didn't mind small spaces. Hailey and I were sat at the foot of her bed. Nana Ama sat in the only chair in the room, considering us with an unreadable expression.

"Describe the beings that attacked you again."

We did, and with each word, Nana looked more and more troubled.

"And the woman," she said carefully. "You didn't recognize her?"

"I didn't except from the blurry screenshot Naira sent." I wanted to add how she knew my mother's name, but since Hailey was there, I kept that to myself.

Nana turned to Hailey. "Were you harmed? Scratched? Bitten?"

"I'm okay. Just terrified." Hailey asked, "What were those things?"

Nana stood up abruptly. "I'll call Sheriff Lyle." She paused, looking unsure of her next move for the first time.

I got up too, worried that I'd made a mistake. Maybe we should have waited until after Naira's Homegoing before laying this on her.

"I need to get my thoughts together," she said. She walked toward the door, her steps heavy, her mood heavier. Hailey and I looked at each other.

None of this was good.

Nana opened the door, and Elder James and Sekou were right outside, and they looked like they were in the midst of their own heated conversation. Elder James cleared his throat. He peered in the cabin, finding Hailey, regarding her with the same kind of suspicious expression Sekou had on.

It was as if Nana remembered we were still there. That's how deep in thought she was, and I was dying to know what she was thinking. But I couldn't. She turned back to us.

"You're safe on Golden Isle," she said. She spoke to us, but her mind was somewhere else. "Let's get through Naira's Homegoing."

"But those things," Hailey said, sounding tense. "What if they come here?"

Nana stepped over the threshold. "Nothing gets on or off the Isle unless the Isle wills it. And if I'm here, they cannot come."

Hailey's face crumpled and she made a move to speak, but I grabbed her hand, shaking my head. She snapped her mouth shut. Now was not the time for questions.

CHAPTER TWENTY-THREE

Golden Isle held Naira's Homegoing and released her light at the edge of the beach at dusk.

It was beautiful in spite of the pain of the occasion, all of us in variations of white for purity, from traditional wear to modern. I was dressed in the same outfit as Nana Ama, in a white gauzy cloth wrapped around my chest like a bandeau and a long white cloth around my waist, cowrie beads adorning my head and wrists.

It wasn't just the Kin who attended, but the locals as well, anyone who knew Naira well and wanted to share in her special moment. I watched her family, who stood stoically and welcomed all the well-wishers with a smile, though the smiles weren't as bright as they used to be. I listened to the soft beats as Sekou hit the djembes with the other drummers. And then they quieted down so Nana Ama could give her blessings and release Naira into the light, bending at the water's edge to place a circlet of white flowers with deep green leaves and a tiny tea light flickering in the soft breeze, into the water to float to sea. Naira's family did the same, each with their own circlets.

As I watched them slip toward the horizon, something receded inside me as well. I had never lost hope that Naira was still alive, never lost the sense that she was still out there, somewhere. But now I could feel her presence disappearing, her spirit drifting toward the horizon along with the crowns.

I had thought I wouldn't go through with it, but now I bent down and set a large bloomed magnolia flower in the water, its wide cup cradling the tiny fire in the middle that would accompany Naira on her journey into the Asamando and her next life, where I wished to the gods she'd have an even better life and that we'd meet again.

As the magnolia joined with the flowers released by others and melted into the horizon, I felt the final wisp of Naira's spirit leave me.

She was truly gone, and I was alone. My chest heaved, and I willed myself not to double over in pain. Instead, I stood there stoically, allowing the pain to rage inside me. This was how a leader said goodbye.

As dusk settled, the lights danced on the sea like little fireflies. Homegoings were supposed to be happy, a send-off to our loved ones now on their journey of peace to the spirit realm and to watch over those of us still here. But how could Naira be at peace after what might have happened to her? Or even Luke? Hailey was beside me and slipped her hand in mine after she'd sent off two lighted flowers, one for Naira and one for Luke. Whether she understood the significance of Light and our ways, her reverence to my traditions shook something loose in me. Something warm and curious.

"I never could have imagined something so beautiful," she said. She squeezed my hand. "Thank you, Ada. What you all have here . . . is a gift."

I broke away from the sea, staring into her tear-filled eyes, and wished I could shed some myself, but the anger wouldn't let me. Hailey tried to say more but couldn't, and that was okay. Sometimes it was better to say nothing at all. She tipped her head to mine, and I let myself melt into the moment, serene on the outside. At war on the inside. I watched the floating lighted flowers move farther away, while the music and singing went on around us.

Homegoing was supposed to be about celebrating one's life, but this one felt like a fraud.

How were we sending Naira off in peace? Or Luke, for that matter? There were too many unanswered questions.

Even if Naira was gone I wouldn't stop looking for answers.

Nana said I never achieved the Light because I didn't really want it. I never accepted it. That was why it was more important than ever that I become strong and Lighted, so that I could find Naira's killer and make them pay.

THURSDAY, THE DAY OF OUR HARVEST FESTIVAL, HIT DIFFERent this year. It was nearly 11:00 A.M. and Hailey was probably still asleep. But an idea had made its way into my mind and wouldn't let go. I jumped out of bed, more excited than I'd felt in forever, and quickly got dressed. The weather was supposed to be great for an early August day, and the water may be a little cool, but it would still be nice. I slipped into my swimsuit, then pulled on a pair of cutoffs, a loose-fitting peasant shirt, and flip-flops.

I bumped along the skinny network of dirt paths crisscrossing from my house in the private area of the island where the Kin lived, past the Gathering Tree, and through our front gates. I turned onto the public roads toward the marina, running through my mental checklist of good hosting. Yesterday, I showed Hailey around the public areas of the island and around Freeman's Port where the day visitors came and went. Today, I'd make it more of a private tour with just Hailey and me. So she could see some parts of what made the Isle so special and beautiful. And I had to admit to myself that I kind of wanted her all to myself for a little bit before tonight, when we wouldn't be together at all.

I knocked on the door to Hailey's guest cabin. It took her a few minutes to answer. When she finally did open the door, I jumped a little because Hailey looked like hell warmed over. Her dark hair and bangs were all over the place, and her makeup was smeared like thick stage makeup. I guess after our late night, she didn't have the energy to wash her face.

She jumped, too, when she saw my reaction. Her hand flew to her face.

"Don't look at me!" she squealed in an octave higher than I expected. It actually stung in my eardrum a little, like when there was really bad feedback from a mic being too close to an amp.

I averted my eyes on command, looking down at the dusty

rose-pink nail polish on my toes. I'd applied a fresh coat yesterday before the ceremony, in Naira's honor.

"Sorry! I just came so we can have a picnic." I pointed in the general area of my parked cart, where a huge wicker basket sat in the back seat with a blanket and towels . . . and necessary sunscreen, because skin health and all.

Hailey craned her neck around me as if she didn't believe it was really daytime already. Her hands rubbed her face, creating raccoon eyes from her leftover makeup. I tried not to laugh.

"Really?"

"Really. So go get dressed already."

Hailey abandoned the front door, her long legs sticking out of a long black shirt. She slammed the bathroom door behind her, rattling the tiny cabin.

I called through the closed door, "Swimsuit too, if you brought one!"

For someone who wasn't a morning person, Hailey dressed fast, and we were soon in my cart, bumping along the trails to one of my favorite places on the island, one of several inlets off the Calibogue Sound. It was in one of the private areas, deep within the forest and away from gen pop, or the island's general population of locals and tourists. It was also a quiet spot that the other Kin didn't visit much either, which was fine by me when I needed to just get away and be me without a bunch of eyes and their expectations on me.

When we got there, it was empty. None of the fishermen had made it up this way to get catch that wasn't already run through by others. If they'd been there, it was before dawn, as that was the prime time to get your catch for the day.

I liked the way the inlet curved into a U and how the beach was so far below sea level that the cliffs towered over on either side, making it like an open cavern of lush landscape beneath a perfect light blue sky. The long, lazy S of the waterway opened out into the expanse of sea, making me feel like a little fish in a large pond instead of the other way around.

"This is beautiful," Hailey said. She slid her dark glasses down the bridge of her nose, taking it all in. She had spent the last twenty minutes complaining about the bugs and the animals rustling too close for her comfort, but now she looked around her, overwhelmed. "I mean the whole island is beautiful, but this place is . . ." She didn't need to finish because I knew what she meant.

"I know," I said.

We set up under the line of trees, just before they ended and the beach began. It was shady with dappled sunlight filtering through the open pockets between the branches and leaves. A breeze coming in from the sea and the heat rising from the sun-baked sand made a perfect mixture to keep the bugs Hailey was worried about, and the heat that would melt her, at bay—and soon she and I were leaned back, stuffed from an assortment of charcuterie I put together along with other stuff I found in our fridge: a small container of Nana Ama's mac and cheese that still tasted delicious even though it wasn't bubbly hot, and Ms. Mae's famous homemade cake, so moist I suspected it came from a box. To top it off, I pulled out my very own bottle of the Garvey Brothers' peach moonshine.

I laughed at Hailey as she took a deep swallow of the moonshine, thinking she could handle it because she'd been to all the clubs along the coast and up north. Tell that to the coughing and sputtering that ensued after only one gulp.

"I thought you could 'handle your liquor,'" I mimicked when my laughter died down—though the giggles remained, and every time I looked at her watering eyes, I nearly erupted in them.

"This isn't liquor," she said, holding the bottle out in front of her so she could inspect it with one narrowed eye. "This is something radioactive."

"Told you it would put you on your ass."

She handed the clear bottle back to me, looking at me through her lashes. "I like knowing you're thinking of my ass."

I'd been taking a small sip of the moonshine and choked when she said it. I blinked at her, wondering if she was for real or if it was the 'shine talking. I'd brought the not-for-public-consumption version and she'd taken a big hit of it.

"Yeah right," I mumbled, playing off the way my stomach flip-flopped every time we made eye contact. Maybe I'd had too much 'shine myself. I was feeling lightheaded, I think. Or something. I let the bottle down, stretching out on the blanket to lie on my back with my hands folded behind my head.

"I like you this way." Hailey's voiced lowered and she scooched toward me. She propped her head up in her hand as she faced me, looking down at me. "You're different here. Not on a mission like in Charleston. And not on duty like you are here. In this moment, you're totally relaxed. You look totally different."

I smirked. "If you mean cute, just say it."

"You've always been cute." She turned away as if suddenly shy, and I did the same, my stomach fluttering.

"I know it's only been a few days, but—" She hesitated. "I sound ridiculous, right? God, how embarrassing."

We didn't need to be embarrassed. We were in this beautiful place, finally able to take a breath after a day of hell and a day sending off the people we cared about the most. When I looked back up, Hailey was watching me intensely, and I immediately felt shy, something I wasn't familiar with. I got lost in her eyes and how the sun didn't seem to reflect in them. I took in the light curve of Hailey's lips that looked so pronounced when she wore her red lipstick.

"I can get used to this side of you." She nudged me and I nudged her back, feeling the warmth radiating from her body.

The butterflies again. I was finding it hard to keep looking at her because every time I did, I was afraid I was smiling too hard when I wanted to play it cool.

"What's that?"

"The soft side."

That was a first. "I have many sides."

"I think I'd like to get to know them. Is that weird?"

Not weird. But maybe not possible either. I didn't think it was possible to know all of someone else. But I would have said yes to just about anything Hailey asked, the way she was staring me down, hovering over me with her hypnotic eyes. I took a hand and brushed back the lock of long, brown bang covering her face because I wanted to see it clearly.

"It's easier to be this way around you," I told her, meaning it.

"You don't expect things of me. I don't have to be on all the time with you. I can just chill."

She trailed a finger in the sand, making large loops of it.

"I know the feeling," she said. "Being part of my family feels like I'm always running a gauntlet. They loved my brother because to them he was perfect."

"And you?"

"And I was," she said, sighing, "the rebel. I moved down here when they wanted me to stay in Martha's Vineyard. I tried to fight working at the Endowment. Always being 'on the job' is exhausting. But what was I gonna tell my uncle and parents, *no*?"

I nodded, finding it hard to pay attention to what she was saying. Her lips were distracting and I could only think about wanting to kiss them.

She brightened. "What about if we make a pact to always be 'off' with each other. Deal?"

Her hand stopped playing with my shirt and she held it out to me. I considered her offered hand as it waited for me.

"Pacts mean something here," I said. "It's not a joke to make a promise to someone. It's for real."

She laughed. "What? Does it mean we're married?" Her laugh trickled off when she saw I was serious. "I'm joking . . . about being married," she said when she saw I wasn't. "Not about the pact. I always want to be real with you."

We were a people built on ceremony and tradition. We didn't bind ourselves to others so easily. But something about Hailey made me see her in a different light and give in. Just this once. Even though everything about me said not to.

I took her hand, tugging it toward me, throwing her off balance so her eyes rounded. She crashed into me and I crashed my lips into hers, finally able to do the thing I'd desperately wanted to do all afternoon, all day. Her lips were incredibly soft and she tasted like peach moonshine. Her feathery soft hair curtained us, putting us in this tiny private space of just her and me. The feel of Hailey's body alongside mine, the growing heat as we kissed, was exactly what I'd been needing. To get away. To think of nothing else for just a few minutes. No responsibilities or expectations. No monsters. No death.

Just her.

CHAPTER TWENTY-FOUR

Their voices carried as I approached Hailey's room later that evening, and I recognized them immediately: Sekou's deep growl, with occasional squeaks when he was shocked or adamant, and Hailey's low tone that seemed to rise a notch with each passing second.

I burst in without knocking, and they both spun around to face me, standing in the open doorway.

"What are you doing here?" I asked Sekou.

The air in the room crackled with tension I couldn't figure out. Sekou, tall and lanky and practically towering over Hailey, glowered down at her, his lips set so firmly in a line that they were nearly nonexistent. I didn't think I'd ever seen him this mad. Not even after my big blowout with Naira the night before . . . and the day . . . she'd left. He practically hulked over Hailey, who stared back at him, her eyes speaking volumes I couldn't understand.

She looked, I don't know, worried. Pissed even. Her eyes flashed as she stood up to him.

I switched back and forth between them. What had I walked in on? Why was Sekou even here when he'd spent the last two days skulking around, throwing all sorts of shade at Hailey and making her feel pretty damn unwelcome?

Hailey lost her brother. Same as we'd lost our sister. We should have all been able to come together, grieve, and release Naira's light in her Homegoing without any drama. But here we were, my best friend and my . . . what the hell was Hailey to me now? *Get it together, Ada.* I couldn't think about any of that right now.

I stepped into the tiny room, sliding in between them.

"What the hell is going on?" I asked Sekou, my voice laced with a sharp edge. "Why are you here instead of getting ready?"

His shoulders slumped and he shot a quick look at Hailey. "I came to tell her to head out." His eyes zeroed in as he stared at me, talking to me as they blazed with intensity. "It's not right for her to be here now that the Homegoing is over."

Hailey snorted. "You can't tell me where I belong. Ada invited me here."

"You know why she can't go back yet," I said. "I don't know what this is, but I need to talk to Hailey."

"We can ask one of the locals to run her back to the mainland. Get Sheriff Lyle to pick her up and help get her where she needs to be," he suggested.

It was too late to ask anyone to make a round trip at this time of night.

"Can you give us a minute?" I said.

He shook his head again, then raised his hands up in defeat.

"She could be a spy," he said. "Ever think about that? It's weird that the same 'research' facility that has been trying to get on the island to see Nana Ama all this time happens to be owned by the family of the guy who cozied up to Naira to pump her for information.

"Hear me out," Sekou said when I started to interrupt.

"He got sweet, innocent Naira to spill. Now Luke's out the picture and suddenly his sister is here and has made it to the Isle. All the way in. Infiltrated. Like the next phase of their evil plan." He punctuated the last word. "Tell me she's not a spy. Or a mole. She gonna run back to Mainland and tell her uncle shit they could maybe use to snatch the land from under us. It happens all the time!"

Hailey crossed her arms over her chest. "You watch way too much TV," she said flatly. Then she muttered, "Asshole." She turned to me. "And you're buying his load of bullshit? After everything we've been through? You came to me, remember? Not the other way around."

She had me there. I had basically come knocking at her door.

If looks could kill, there would be two more Homegoings tonight.

Sekou's family was a founding. His ancestors had been here since the beginning, along with my family as they boated to the mysterious Golden Isle guided by the light of fireflies. I trusted him like blood and to me he was that, so his voice carried weight with me. If he had doubts about Hailey Hall, I couldn't ignore them, no matter my own feelings and how much I wanted to believe otherwise—wanted to believe that the attraction between us was more than an immature crush. Sekou had as much stake in the Isle as I did. Hailey had wanted to find her brother safely as I had Naira. Together we grieved losing a brother and sister. One minute I'd wonder if this was a trick and I was being played. The next, I'd think about those things and how her expression mirrored my feelings: tired, scared, and confused. Like me, Hailey was trying to make it day by day.

"You remember I went to Hailey first, right? I asked her to help me," I said.

He huffed.

"She had no idea I was coming. And she helped me out. Plus, there was the attack, which is the reason I asked her to come here. I told you I couldn't leave her alone out there and that we needed Nana Ama to help us. So how does that all figure in?"

"Right," Hailey snapped. "How the hell would I know I'd be invited here? I was minding my own business when she showed up."

Sekou sucked his teeth. "I don't trust her, Ada," he said. "She may have not planned this, but she can definitely take advantage of it. She knows about the Isle from whatever her uncle and the Endowment have put together on us. Something's not right."

I shot a quick glance at Hailey, who glared back, daring me to join in with Sekou. There wasn't time for this. There was a festival to get to.

I had to Light tonight. It was a matter of life or death.

"Gimme a minute," I asked Sekou. "I'll be right behind you."

His nostrils flared as he waited a beat. His lips twisted and he glanced over at Hailey. "She's leaving tomorrow. First thing."

I spun him around by his shoulder and pushed him to the door. "And she can't come to the festi—"

"I know," I growled against his back, shoving him out the door one final time. He turned around on the step, his mouth opened to say something else.

"Right behind you," I said, shutting the door.

I faced her. I took a gamble bringing Hailey to Golden Isle. I'd gone a step further than Naira had. At least when Luke came, it was under the pretense of a tourist. I had brought Hailey around the Kin. She'd been inside Kin's Landing.

"Listen," I began when I turned back into the cabin. Hailey and I needed to set some things straight. "You can't be here starting stuff up with my friends or anyone on this island."

Hailey gawked at me. "Last I checked, he came to my bungalow and started with me."

"You're a . . . guest," I almost said *outsider*, but I stopped myself in time.

Hailey paced the floor, activated with anger at Sekou and now at me for standing up for him.

She flushed red and her eyes smoldered as she pinned me with a stare.

"He's right about one part, though," I said. "You can't attend the festival. It's for family only." I willed her to understand and not put up a fight. There was no room for argument, and if Hailey and I were going to explore anything more between us, she'd have to understand that there were some things I wouldn't share with her. The Isle's private traditions were one of them.

Hailey's pacing slowed, then stopped as she turned to me incredulously. "I really can't go?"

I shook my head. "You can't. It's private."

Her eyes narrowed and her voice came out clipped as if she were talking to a child. "Then why the hell did you bring me here?"

I snorted. "To keep you safe? Because we were chased by monsters? To attend the Homegoing? Pick a reason."

"A festival is festive. It's for the public to attend and enjoy. What's so special about what you all are doing?"

I bristled. I got that she was pissed. I got she didn't understand, but she wasn't going to speak about me or our traditions any kind of way either, no matter how mad she was.

"You don't need to understand our traditions, but you need to respect them, especially if you want to be my friend."

She hesitated, the light coming on that maybe she'd gone a step too far. "I didn't mean it like that," she said. "I'm not here for anything other than to pay my respects to Naira and for my brother."

I read truth in her eyes. Or what I thought was truth. It was hard to stay clear when she was around.

"So, you'll hang tight?" I stepped in the direction of the door, thinking all was clear. "I'll see you in the morning?"

I had no more time to waste because things were already going to get started. Already in the background the steady drumming of the djembe had begun.

"Ada, can you wait a minute?" Hailey said. "Can we talk about the whole Endowment thing? It's not at all like what your friend was saying."

"Tomorrow morning," I said, opening the front door. I really had to go. I was cutting it close as it was.

"Ada—"

But I couldn't delay any longer. I cut her off, shutting the door. I rushed back to the Landing, not wanting to be late. The drumbeats quickened, calling us to the Gathering Tree.

I would drink the Light tonight.

CHAPTER TWENTY-FIVE

By the time I made it back within our gates, the sky was black with twinkling dots in it. The trees cast shadows all around and would have been terrifying if I hadn't lived here all my life. The rhythmic drumbeats beckoned me and the rest of the Kinfolk to "ready ourselves and come" to where we were all supposed to assemble at the Gathering Tree.

Thursdays had always been my favorite day of the week. But the festival on a Thursday night was an added bonus because it was like a perfect alignment. And Naira wasn't here to experience it. She wasn't going to experience anything anymore.

Get it together, Addae.

Tonight wasn't the night to be wallowing in sadness. I had to focus.

Preparing for the ceremony took a lot of work. You had to get your head in the right state of mind. There were the clothes. There were the traditional dances and incantations to call upon the gods and goddesses, the spirits that protected us and watched the island, protected the island. There would be singing songs of glory and rejoicing of three good months and paying homage to those spirits that helped us achieve it. And there would be prayers for three more months of good fortune and blessings that Nana Ama would call to the gods to bestow on because she always carried the responsibility for others, whether they were Kin or not.

The drumbeats filtered through my open window. I studied my image in the mirror behind my door, making sure my traditional dress was on properly. The red bandeau top around my chest, the layers of multicolored beads, accentuated with bright blue ones that looked similar to the blue gems embedded in Nana Ama's thick golden cuffs.

I tied the band of white cowrie beads around the back of my head, adjusting them so they aligned perfectly over my forehead. Rows of multicolored beads wrapped in layers around my waist and hips and covered the beaded belly chain I'd worn since I was little, which wouldn't come off until I married, if I ever did. The ceremonial beaded belts hung in loose scallops over the underwrap I wore, after I tied them at my lower back.

Draped over my front and rear, two long swaths of thick African print cloth of deep gold with a pattern of black and blue shapes throughout. The gold respresented the gold of Nyame and the fireflies sent as guides. The blue symbolized the blue gems in Nana Ama's cuffs. Elder Haniah, one of the best seamstresses in all the Low Country, made our traditional clothes using the formulas from the old days and spent most of her days creating the designs for our outfits for whenever we needed them, and for tourists who wanted a piece of the Golden Isle to take back home.

In our culture, ornate displays of jewelry, cloth, and accessories were a significant part of our lives. The beading, the intricate designs held meaning and played a part in everything we did . . . every ceremony and blessing, every dance and honoring. We decked ourselves out when celebrating or when at war, when we worked or when at peace, when our lights were released at our Homegoing. I completed my look by pulling a leather cowrie-covered band up each of my legs until they sat right above my calves. I pulled several thin gold bands along my arms until they stretched over my biceps. I was ready to serve as the granddaughter of the Lady of the Golden Isle.

I couldn't see Nana Ama's tiny cabin from the house, but I could sense she was close by, getting herself in the right state of mind. We'd left so many things unsaid between us, and I could feel the heaviness of whatever she was keeping from me. I could feel the guilt of what I hadn't fully told her either. I hated being like this, distracted when our minds were supposed to be clear.

But soon the heavy thoughts and worry evaporated, and I was drawn to the pounding drumbeats, getting louder and louder as I walked the winding pathway between my house and the Gathering Tree with little yellowish-white lights flashing on and off, one second here and another there. Our path was a direct vein from our home to it. It was the only path to that tree, a tree that had been here since the moment the runaways washed ashore. The tree had grown and thrived. It was the heartbeat of Golden Isle, from which we drew our strength and our unity. I could hear its heart, calling steadily to the beats of those drums.

Thump. Thump. Thump.

Come. Come. Come.

Singing its siren to me and all the other Kinfolk who lived within our gated community.

The sky was alight with the light of the fires, and when I joined everyone already there, dressed in their own ceremonial uniforms of beads, cloth, bone, and golden bands, I saw Nana Ama already seated at the base of the Gathering Tree. She was perched in her fanned-out, high-backed chair made of ornately carved wood. To her left was James, always at her side, her counsel. To Nana's right, between her and the seat that I would occupy momentarily, was the golden stool. The stool of Nyame, tall and wide and empty.

No one ever sat in that chair, another of our rules. To do that would be a desecration, an abomination. It was the throne of the king of all gods. It was left for Nyame to come and take his seat to watch the ceremony and be honored as he and all gods and goddesses and spiritual beings he created in the world were supposed to be every day, but especially tonight.

Harvest Festival was the time when the threshold between this world and the one above was thin. The spirits walked among us to survey the land and make sure we were doing right by it.

Sekou was already at his drums, looking serene as if we hadn't just had it out, and creating the rhythms the dancers would move to in their circles before Nana Ama. Two circles, one inner and one outer. The drummers rimmed the outer, bare-chested or wearing bandeau tops with their own intricate layers of roped beads draped in regal beauty all over their bodies. I weaved in sync through the moving bodies and to my seat on the other side of Nyame's stool.

The music started to really settle in deep, and my body swayed to it as the two circles of people within the ring of torches started singing and did their own dances, the outer circle and inner. I moved in time with the ones in the outer circle, following along with their intricate foot and hand movements, in sync, as they kicked their feet out left foot, right foot. They moved their hips side to side, clapping with the *thump, thump* of the drums, their claps so precise they sounded thunderous in duet with the drums.

The ones in the middle, the nine Diviners made of priests and priestesses, posed with thick, polished black staffs that stood over six feet in the air. The thumping beats grew deeper and slower, and the dancers moved clockwise around them, humming and singing a chorus to the Diviners as they called to the ancestors.

One of the Diviners let out a high-pitched yell that pierced the air, sending off a flutter of wings from the treetops. He lifted his staff above his head and the noise ceased.

"We call to our ancestors. We welcome you to come down. To walk the earth and walk among us. To see what we've done and how we honor you. To take what you will and give your blessings upon blessings." He struck his staff hard to the earth, and with it the bass drum sounded.

Boom! Like thunder.

And the outer circle of dancers clapped, their sound deep and resounding.

Crack! Like lightning.

Their bare feet stomped the earth, the little bells attached to the bands around their ankles chiming in.

"We bless the Golden Isle." *Boom. Crack.*

"The Kinfolk of those who fled." *Boom. Crack.*

"The people who first lived on this land and had it stolen." *Boom. Crack.*

"We bless Nana Ama, our lady and guardian of the *See-kah-kaw-kaw Shoo-paw*."

Golden Isle spoken in a native dialect of the Akans resonated to my core on nights like tonight.

"She is the keeper of the stories. Sankofa." *Boom. Crack.*

Nana Ama bowed her head deeply, acknowledging their tribute.

"We bless Addae, descendant of the first, guardian, and future awuraa and keeper of the stories." *Boom. Crack.*

Hearing those words, my chest pounded with the beat, bursting with excitement, but also dread.

For what was to come.

CHAPTER TWENTY-SIX

THE YOUNGER KIDS ZIGZAGGED THROUGH THE CIRCLES, HOLDing trays of tiny shot glass–sized cups filled with a thick, dark liquid that everyone took. They downed the shots of liquid and returned the glasses to the trays. Nana Ama's elixir, one she ground in her asanka, the earthenware grinding pot with rounds and rounds of ridges lining the inside walls against which she used a tapoli, a wooden masher, to mix ingredients for tinctures and medicines she provided whenever someone was ill or sought Nana Ama's spiritual guidance or to start the elixir she gifted at every festival.

The distribution of the blessing, or Nana Ama's elixir, was done with efficiency, barely putting a hiccup in the dancing and chanting, singing and praising. I plucked one of the shot glasses from the wide trays when it was offered to me, though I didn't need it. I liked being able to do what everyone else was doing when they took a shot.

If I was on the outside looking in, I guess Nana's elixir was like taking Communion. Only instead of a thin wafer and wine, or grape juice, our homegrown solution was a concoction of peach nectar grown right from Nana's grove on the Isle and some herbs and secret family ingredients. And it did more than act as a spiritual metaphor. This was Nana Ama's blessing for the island. It fortified the islanders, like how the mainlanders took vitamin C to keep from getting a cold.

The music's tempo increased and I downed the tiny shot offered to me. The taste was sweet at first, like drinking the nectar of a peach, and then spicy, like swallowing a hot fireball jawbreaker. I could feel it burn a trail all the way down to the pit of my belly, where it flared up inside and took over from the inside out.

I watched the dancers, then chanced a look at my grandmother. She motioned for me to go, and I didn't wait.

Nana never joined the dancers, but it would be different when it was my time to lead. I wouldn't be afraid.

I jumped off my chair and joined them. The tempo had moved from serious and ceremonial to celebratory. The elixir was beginning to take effect on everyone, livening them up as if they'd just taken a shot of caffeine, and I danced with them as the drumming increased. Those in the outer circle held large, body-length, thick staffs, stomping their feet and striking the bottom of their staffs to the ground in time with their stomps, which were in time with the pounding of the drums.

Nana Ama watched all of us, as she usually did, but it was like she wasn't there, like her heart wasn't totally into it. I kept dancing, singing with the rest of the Kin. I let myself get lost in all of it. But something was off and I couldn't place it. The feeling of unease and of being watched.

My body kept moving with the music, but my eyes scanned the trees surrounding us, picking through the flickering ring of torches at the outer perimeter of the ceremonial circle, their flames lapping at the humid air like hungry dogs, swirling lines of smoke stretching to the sky from them. I peered into the trees, trying to siphon from it the thing that didn't belong.

Nothing was there. I forced myself to refocus on paying proper respect to my ancestors. I certainly didn't want them coming after me for not honoring them in the way they were used to. The ancestors could be petty and vindictive like that if they wanted.

The music, the dancing, and the chanting increased. Songs asking the gods for goodwill and fortune, for good health and love, for security and an abundance of crops. The circles began turning in opposite directions, one going this way and the other going that way. Coming together in unison and then spreading apart. The blessing rejuvenated everyone, and they danced faster and harder. A once cool night ratcheted up in degrees and the whole place felt like a glorious sauna. Then they began slipping from the circles of dances to lay tributes at the base of Nyame's stool. Nana Ama accepted them with a graceful nod and a small smile, giving everyone the little piece of her they wanted.

When she stood, I knew it was time for us to go. I began to snake my way through the crowd of people, some laying their honoring, most dancing and singing with their hands lifted in the air. I drew closer to the tree and to my grandmother as a hush rippled over the Kinfolk and the drums softened to barely a bump, yet still maintained their slow, steady rhythm.

"On this night, the Thursday of our Harvest Festival, the night

I share my blessings with all of you, we pay tribute to all the ancestors who came before us and make way for all descendants who will come after. We ask for safety and sanctuary against any who wish us harm and ask our ancestors, Nyame, and the gods of the upper realm to continue bestowing their blessings on us, Kinfolk and all who reside here and step foot on this land. Most of all, we thank our ancestors for the nourishment they have given us."

She considered the crowd in front of her, taking them in. Beautiful Blackness in all different hues and cultures of the African and American diaspora. She raised her arms to them. "Honor our nsamanfo, my family, and welcome the good from the Asamando while the veil is thin and they can walk alongside of us."

The Kin cheered up to the sky and bared their teeth, stained red from the elixir in the firelight.

CHAPTER TWENTY-SEVEN

It was time. Silently my grandmother and I extracted ourselves from the celebration and walked into the woods.

The night air crackled with energy from the increasing music and singing coming from the square where the Kin still danced, deep in their celebration. My skin tingled and my breathing quickened, as I tried to tell myself I was finally ready and worthy of Lighting. This time I would be able to accept the gifts of my legacy that hadn't manifested themselves in their entirety.

We walked deeper until we couldn't be seen or heard, the transference that was about to happen sacred. Where I could accept my full gifts within the sanctity and protections from the island, and from my grandmother. It was dark, the light from the festival blotted out by the trees and dense foliage, leaving only the sky to offer dappled bits of light filtering through them.

I took my cue from her, every one of my senses amplified and ready for what came next. My grandmother studied me from within the shadows. Asking a whole lot of questions and looking as if she was leaving even more unsaid.

Nana Ama asked, "Are you ready?"

I took in a breath. "I am." I had to be.

She watched me more intently, as if she were trying to read me.

But I wasn't ready. I was terrified. What if I couldn't do it, like all those other failed times, last year and the year before? A gift that was as unknown to my grandmother as it was to me because I wasn't like her, one hundred percent. I was a first generation, only half of what I was supposed to be.

"To Light, you must truly consent and yield to it. You must truly want it."

I nodded. I did want it. I had wanted it all my life, watching my grandmother and mother.

"Then Nyame be with you," Nana said, smiling at me. "I will wait to celebrate you with our ancestors and our Kin."

She was gone before I could blink, leaving me alone. I listened for sounds of her retreating footsteps, light as they were, knowing there would be none. *Drive everything out. Leave only room to Light. Say yes. Accept it.* I told myself all these things. Over and over.

I refocused on what was around me, the noise around me, or rather the quieting of noise. The rustling of the wind through the dense forest. The echoes of singing back at the Gathering Tree.

The animals were equally as quiet. Waiting, as I was waiting. The snap of a twig sounded in the distance to my left. My ears homed in on it and my head snapped to. On the heady breeze, the aroma of cooking food from the ceremony marked the last parts of it drifting to my nose. I stayed perfectly still, regulating my breathing, letting out the air trapped in my body in one long blow. I ran my tongue over my teeth, baring them a little, crouching, zeroing in on where the sound was coming from, an unusual scent filling my nose.

I leapt in the air, soaring through the leaves and branches. My breathing deepened, each sense heightening, electrifying the air and my skin as I went through it. This was it, this was me finally receiving the Light, even though I had doubted, was doubting it this moment. I released myself one section at a time, doing as Nana Ama said and not forcing it. I was letting go, becoming this other me, my body changing, contracting and expanding.

I spotted movement ahead, and came to a stop in the treetops, tracking it. Its smell drifted over me, and my body reacted on its own, sailing down and tackling my prey.

The buzzing in my ear drowned out any other noise, any other cry I might have heard, because all I could hear was the thumping pulse of its life force, even as the animal staggered from my grip. It grunted in pain and surprise as we crashed hard to the compacted earth, roots and branches snapping beneath our combined weight, but as I now was, I barely felt the sting. My fingers grabbed it, digging into the rough skin so my catch wouldn't get away in a last-ditch burst of adrenaline. Its muscles pumped beneath me to buck me off of it, letting out a high, muffled whine of surprise. It kicked its feet as we rolled through the underbrush, connecting with something else, softer and more delicate, breaking my grip. There was nothing but my primal urge to hunt, and I pounced again, unseeing, grabbing what was there, not hearing the sound of retreating hooves.

My head tilted to the sky, my throat loosening a guttural sound as my mouth opened, my top canines disengaging in a satisfying slide. I snapped my teeth and I dove down, the points breaking through skin that seemed as thin as paper. This blood tasted as it never had before, rushing fresh from the animal's veins, making my vision hazy and unfocused. So delicious that I could barely contain myself, fighting to sink in farther, to drink from it. To drain it. Until it spoke.

"Ada, no!"

My eyes snapped open and I tore myself away, confusion and dread colliding in me along with the sweetest taste of blood I shouldn't have had. An ice cube moved coldly up my spine as my vision cleared, refocusing on Hailey's face, frozen as she stared up from beneath me, still half hidden in the brush, her face a portrait of horror and terror and revulsion as she finally saw me for who—what—I really was.

An adze.

A *vampire.*

CHAPTER TWENTY-EIGHT

My hands lifted off of her, afraid to move or hurt her.

I was horrified, staring at the girl I was beginning to like, the girl who shouldn't have been there with her delicious hot blood on my lips and tongue, dribbling from the light puncture wounds on her neck.

She came back to life before I did, shoving me off her, hands hard on my chest. I didn't fight back, falling on the ground as she leapt to her feet, cast one last terrified look at me, and held her fingers to the wounds I made on her neck; they came away with blood. Her breath hitched like she didn't know whether to scream or hyperventilate. She looked around—

How had she even found her way here?

—and chose a path and ran.

I remained there, unable to wrap my mind around the fact that she was there, had been in my hands, had stopped my journey to Light. The heat that had been bubbling up in me as I prepared to feed, the Light that would have burst from me, transforming me to the form of a firefly, one of my truest forms of self, as was my lineage, shriveled up back inside of me and died. Like I wanted to do. And I didn't think it would ever come back.

I would forever remain half human, half adze, never a whole of anything.

I stood up, failed, devastated, humiliated. How was I going to face my grandmother, who would inevitably know that I had not Lighted? That there was a disturbance on the Isle? She knew. And she would tell Elder James, and the rest of the Kin would know soon after.

Find her.

I didn't chase her. She was no match for me. I had had her blood and was able to follow her wherever she was. I put my finger to my lips, relishing the taste of her blood and hating that I loved it at the same time. But it was so unbelievably good. It was only a taste, just like Nana always said we should have if we chose to drink from humans—if we ever *had* to do it. But we mustn't.

Because if we drank from humans, if we killed them and from it became the monsters of lore, then there would be a boatful of consequences.

And yet. Maybe the consequences were worth it, if this was how they tasted. My tongue worked around my mouth, trying to get every bit of Hailey's blood. It was exhilarating. Mind-numbing.

And overstimulating. Sounds thundered in without my earbuds to keep them back, but Hailey's blood had opened up my senses, had opened her up to me, and I could hear everything—god it was torture—as if she were in my brain and crowding me out.

Oh my god. Oh my god. Oh my god. I'm gonna die. I'm gonna die. She's going to eat me. What the fuck!

Now, wait. That wasn't right. Her rambling words confused me, and I was kind of offended that she'd think I'd ever *eat* a person. I took a step in the direction where I was tracking her. I didn't eat people.

If all of that came from just a taste—No, not a taste. It was really more of a lick if we thought deep about it. All that knowledge of Hailey's thoughts and feelings from such a small amount. I couldn't help feeling like I had been cheated from something owed me, something that would make me more like who I was supposed to be. The flood of emotions was about to drive me up the wall, coupled with the crescendo of noise from Hailey crashing through terrain she didn't know, charging deeper and deeper in until she got lost and ended up at the cliff or lost in a marsh, where I wouldn't be the only thing she'd have to be worried about. I was nearly about to chase Hailey down and—

Shit. Shit. Shit!

Hailey was louder than the tiniest ant. And I needed to get to her first before they did.

The reality slammed me into the present, into the urgency of the moment. Not that Hailey had witnessed something private, something no human was supposed to see unless given permission, but that Hailey was about to be caught by the Kin, who had held this secret of ours for centuries. Even the islanders outside the gates didn't know about Nana Ama and me. If the Kin got ahold of Hailey, who shouldn't have been here, who I brought, they wouldn't let her leave.

The forest could be deadly. Hailey was not a person of the Isle. She was Mainland. She knew nothing about checking wind flow or the sky for where she was, nothing about checking which side the moss grew on to figure out which way was north, to lead her back to civilization, to the Gathering Tree, where the rest of the Kin would be. Hailey was now a threat. She'd seen too much, hundreds of years' worth of too much. And if our rules held fast, and I knew they would if I didn't stop them, Hailey would never leave the island alive.

My body was returning back to my usual human form, retracting—my senses normalizing from my heightened state of awareness, but I could sense another adze, my grandmother, transforming back to her human form, her own hunt interrupted from the chaos I had caused.

I heard joy and exaltation coming from the festival square as the Kin continued to drum and dance and celebrate at the Gathering Tree. Hailey was somewhere not too far, but I couldn't place where. I ran frantically through the undergrowth, trying to pinpoint where she was. Deepening dread built up in my chest thinking about how scared and repulsed she now was by me.

Then the drumming stopped abruptly. I sensed confusion and anger radiating from the square, and I could sense Sekou's energy especially, fury mixed with righteousness.

A scream I was now familiar with pierced the night, loud and clear like a beacon. It was Hailey. She sounded almost primal, her fear like that of an animal, caught.

They had found Hailey. And she was being taken back to where Nana Ama awaited her.

CHAPTER TWENTY-NINE

I burst from the forest, weaving through the homes in the Landing, heading straight for the Gathering Tree. My desperation intensified knowing Nana Ama had beaten me back, and they had gotten to Hailey before I could and were taking Hailey to her.

The ring of the lighted torches creating a square of illumination to cast off the darkness. The crowd huddled around the front with the tree looming above everyone. I searched for signs of Hailey or Sekou, but I couldn't see either, assuming that they were at the front of the standing bodies, craning for a good view of the spectacle happening up front. With each passing moment, my anxiety grew.

I started toward the front, but stopped when I looked down and saw the blood on my skin and clothes. They may know what Nana Ama and I were and swore to hide our secret, but they'd never seen those versions of us, the firefly traveling the night or the full-form being we could become—neither of which I could become because I had yet to Light. Even though the Kinfolk knew, I still didn't want them to see me bloody.

Taking a pitcher of water from off a table of trays of emptied serving dishes of food, I washed my hands and face and brushed off my skirt as best as I could, hoping nothing would be too noticeable.

There were still specks of blood and smudges of dirt and grass on my clothing, but I was presentable enough. I hurried through the crowd, people straining on their feet to see what caused the disruption. They parted for me as I walked through, trying to exude purpose instead of defeat and shame for exposing myself, for my poor decisions, and for my inability to control myself.

My steps slowed as I approached the front and saw what was there.

Normally, there were two chairs and Nyame's stool at the front beneath the Gathering Tree. Nana always sat in her wicker chair next to Elder James, or stood when addressing the rest of the Kin. Though Nana Ama was the leader of the Kin, essentially the "woman king" in Nyame's absence, she had never sat in the stool of the Sky God, the king of all gods. It was reserved for him alone and nothing serious enough had warranted her to sit in Nyame's place.

Until tonight.

When I saw her sitting upright on the stool, her expression stone cold gazing at the expanse of jittery Kin, my blood froze. Their chorus of thoughts crowded my mind, and I fought to push them out, wishing for my earbuds, which rested at home. Across the square, Nana Ama's eyes found me, her anger kept in check with preternatural ability, and followed me as I wound my way forward to accept my fate.

Nana Ama didn't have to say aloud what she was thinking.

Though her face was wiped clear of anything discernible, her entire vibe was clear.

I was in the deepest of shit.

Hailey stood in front of Nana Ama and Elder James. Sekou was positioned near Hailey as her protector or guard, I wasn't sure, but by the way his jaw tensed, maybe it was the latter.

"What's going on?" I asked. "Nana?"

James was looking at me like I wasn't much of anything. Hostility and disapproval sloughed off him and onto me. I didn't know what I'd ever done to him except exist.

I channeled my inner Nana and Sekou too, wiping my expression clean. I wouldn't give James or anyone who doubted me the satisfaction of seeing me squirm.

Nana Ama inclined her head, indicating that Elder James could begin.

"Your guest was found within the Landing perimeters unaccompanied and in a restricted area of the forest during the festival," James said, his voice reedy and accusatory. He fixed his bushy-eyebrow-covered eyes on me.

"I told her to stay in her bungalow at Freeman's."

"And yet here she stands," he said.

I didn't dignify that with a response. We could all see Hailey was there. James just wanted to flex his authority.

Nana Ama regarded me coolly. No special treatment just because I was next in line. I was not above anyone else when it came to reprimands and consequences. And I shouldn't be.

Hailey was a mess of dirt with the stains from her battle with the island's foliage, and I guess with me too, standing as evidence of her crime. Her body was riddled with scratches. I could smell the drying blood, saw the two contact points on her neck, and fought both guilt and thirst as I forced myself to focus elsewhere.

"What were you doing out of your quarters?" James demanded.

Hailey flinched at that question being directed at her, the once cool, dismissive rich girl who lived in the big city of Charleston a thing of the past. She trembled so hard I thought she wouldn't be able to stay upright for much longer.

"Ada and I . . . we . . ." She swallowed again. "We had an argument. I wanted to apologize."

"By coming to something she told you not to attend?"

She searched for an answer and spoke after a moment. "To apologize."

I swallowed a groan. Hailey's argument was weak, even she had to know it.

"And this all-so-important apology couldn't wait until morning. It was"—he paused for effect, pulling himself to the edge of his chair—"that urgent."

Hailey thought about it. There was no correct answer.

She whispered, "I thought it was."

The old man shot from his seat, throwing his hands in the air in exasperation. He implored the crowd. "Do you hear her? She says she thought some trivial argument was so important she had to come out in a place she didn't know, sneaking around people she only just met, to clear her troubled conscience."

Hailey's face crumpled.

"Your privilege knows no bounds." He pointed his short staff at her. It was topped with feather and horsehair, one of the ceremonial artifacts we used during ceremonies. "*She* wanted to apologize. *She* couldn't wait. So, *she* decided to reject the wishes of her host and seek her out to force an apology on Ada, forget this silly little traditional thing we had going on. Isn't that so, girl?"

"No." Hailey shook her head fiercely. "It wasn't like that at all. I just . . . I just . . ." Her words failed and she let out a sob. "Please." Hailey stepped backward into one of the men who stood guard behind her. They surrounded her like she was some kind of real threat. Like she'd run or something.

"Then explain," James said. "Silence is evidence of your guilt."

"Or of her fear, Elder James," I spoke up. "She's in a place where she doesn't know anyone." Hailey was dead wrong, but I'd had enough of his bullying. The crowd around me talked among themselves, surprised I had addressed him in that manner.

Elder James was about to address me when Hailey spoke again.

"I heard the drumming. It was beautiful and I only wanted to see what it was. I only wanted to apologize to Ada for being a—a jerk earlier. I am sorry I didn't listen to her. I am sorry for disrespecting you and not following your rules. I'll go home. I won't say anything about Ada bit—"

She stopped, her hand flying to her neck as she realized she'd said too much.

Dread rose in me. Hailey had cut herself off too late, confirming she'd seen something she shouldn't when no one really knew she had. She could have been lost and running aimlessly in the dense forest, trying to find me, for all they knew. But now Elder James—and Nana Ama—knew for sure that Hailey knew too much. Even Elder James, usually so smug, was speechless.

The mood was shifting from questioning to decisive action—permanent action. The last time there'd been an outsider who'd seen too much was decades ago. That person never left, their bones claimed by the island and lore among the young of what happened when an enemy came in.

Finally, my grandmother spoke, ending Elder James's inquisition and display of the little bit of power he wielded as head ceremonial priest and her second-in-command.

"What did you expect to see here, Hailey?" Nana Ama asked, her voice rich, smooth, and velvety with all of her knowledge and experience from a hundred and sixty years' worth of living.

Nana Ama wasn't sitting in her wicker chair as usual. Tonight, she sat on Nyame's golden stool, preparing to pass judgment on his behalf. Unlike my golden flecks of failure, her eyes were a deeper iridescent golden hue which I knew was from when she stepped out—feeding somewhere along the coast of the mainland—before I was discovered and thoughtlessly interrupted her and made her rush back early. I looked away to hide my guilt because she took so little, and so rarely, and I had messed all of that up. I hadn't Lighted, because of interruption or fear once again, and I stood before her a failure. I took a spot near the front of the crowd. I didn't go to her because tonight my place was in front of my grandmother, not beside her.

If Sekou knew I was there, he didn't show it, his face tight with anger, his hands fisted at his side. His jaw tightened and released, then repeated. There was judgment against me and Hailey coming from all angles, even my best friend.

I had fucked up royally.

Sekou wouldn't look at me. He was like a closed book. All I wanted to do was go to him and tell him sorry. If I had only listened to him back in Charleston, if I had heeded his warnings, we wouldn't be here. I didn't need him to say, "I told you so." The words radiated from his pores and from the way he held his fist so tight I thought it would break. How would he ever be my confidant like Elder James was to Nana, if I never took what he said into account? Had Naira said as much the night before she left?

Curiosity and fear rippled through the group as we all waited to see what she would do with this trespasser, and with me.

Nana Ama considered the crowd behind us, as if weighing her options on whether to handle this privately. But that had never been our way. Decisions were made in a group with nothing to hide.

"Ma'am?" Hailey could barely look at Nana Ama.

"Those things happening on Mainland," Nana Ama said. "Your family owns the Endowment, yes? The people who have been trying to get access to Golden Isle? Is that why you're here, snooping around?"

Hailey stuck to her script. "I'm not. I don't know anything about that, ma'am."

I prayed my grandmother would buy it. If pushed, I didn't know how far my grandmother would go to protect our secret. "I invited her, remember?" It was the same conversation I had with Sekou at Hailey's bungalow. I shot him a dirty look, knowing he'd told Nana his concerns. "Nana Ama, she didn't see anything."

Nana Ama turned toward me, the light catching her eyes like those of cat. "Don't lie to me, Addae. I can smell her terror."

Hailey shrank back like she was trying to get away again, crashing into the guards behind her.

"You are here on the island. What information are you seeking to take back to your family?"

"I don't know anything about that."

"Nana Ama, can we talk about this?"

"Quiet," Nana commanded, holding up her hand. "You know what it means that she has seen you. That she knows of our kind when she is directly and deeply related to the Endowment."

"She won't tell," I said. I couldn't allow us to kill to keep a secret. Whatever intentions Hailey had come here with, I didn't think she deserved to die.

"I took the liberties of having the bungalow searched while we were looking for the trespasser," James said. He produced a small leather bag from within the folds of the colorful robes wrapped around his torso and across one shoulder. He flipped open the flap, revealing several clear tubes and packaged syringes. Hailey's body sagged. "We found them in her bags when we searched her cabin, after she was spotted spying."

Hailey's voice rang out. "I wasn't spying! That's a lie."

Her eyes slid to me, begging me to believe her. The earlier fear she had at my nearly making a meal of her was gone, replaced by her need for me to believe that she didn't bring those vials here to get something.

But the vials . . . weren't they proof? Why were they with her if she wasn't going to use them?

Suddenly, I didn't know what was going on. All I thought I knew, I didn't. I hadn't just shown Hailey my precious island. I had shown her who I really was, beneath the stoic, dutiful front I was forced to put up.

Was it all a lie?

Was this all just a part of Hailey and her uncle's plan? Lure me in, make me trust her, make me *want* her, then use it to get whatever it was they were after on the island? From me and Nana Ama?

Nana Ama remained unmoved. She remained transfixed on Hailey, then me. She was unreadable, a stone statue with only her eyes moving from me to Hailey to me again. She didn't have to say what she was thinking, her eyes saying it all.

Addae, what have you done?

Hailey cleared her throat.

"My uncle runs the Endowment, yes, but it's research. We find ancient artifacts. We restore them and send them back to their place of origin. We try to help communities."

The laugh that came from Nana Ama was like thunder. "Oh ho! You think the Golden Isle needs your help? How magnanimous of you to offer something unasked."

Hailey shook her head emphatically. "No. I came here for Naira's Homegoing. I swear." She held her hand over her heart like she was making a pledge.

Nana Ama pointed to the vials in Elder James's hands. "And these?"

Hailey twisted around to look at me, silently asking for me to plead her case, but I turned away, my own thoughts conflicted. Hailey had violated something sacred, something intimate.

She'd seen me at my most vulnerable, when I was trying to finally Light and do something about those things we saw back in Charleston. My Light had been right there for grasping, and she'd ruined it.

Hailey turned back around, dropping her head. "We use those, but I forgot they were still in my bag from our last trip. I swear to god that's the truth."

"What do you use them for?" Nana Ama prompted. She would make me hear it. Make me realize how quick I was to trust. How I should have listened to her and stayed on the island instead of running off to find more trouble.

"For samples. Samples of the soil. Samples of . . . ," Hailey stammered.

"Of our blood?" Nana Ama's voice was low. "Of my elixir?"

Hailey was silent.

"You know what this means," Elder James said. "She has violated us in more ways than one. This is indefensible. This deserves death."

The word was poison to my ears. Death! Like we were those kinds of people. Nana didn't even kill to feed. But would she kill to protect?

I looked at her and her cold regard of a terrified Hailey.

Yes, she absolutely would.

"I would have never done it. If I was going to do that." Hailey found me again in the crowd. "If I was going to do something, I would have done it when you were in my home."

Elder James looked at Nana Ama, his body practically vibrating, his eyes wild and shining, his voice elevated and excited, like he was drunk on power, on bloodlust, on the chance to show his strength to Nana Ama.

He bellowed, "You see! She is nothing but an invader. They're trying to repeat history, Ama. They're trying to invade us again. To colonize what we've spent years building, cultivating."

Nana Ama was barely looking at him. She was looking at me. I held her gaze. What else could I do? All my bad decisions were on display for everyone to see.

"Where is this amulet you think belongs to my ancestors?" Nana Ama asked Hailey, but her eyes remained on me.

"It was gone when we went there," I answered. "Taken."

Nana barely registered a flicker. "By whom?"

"A scientist from the lab—Dr. Franco. He's—he's missing now, but we launched a massive investigation to try to recover it," Hailey said.

"A familiar." She spit the word out like it was garbage.

That word made no sense because Nana never mentioned it before in all her teachings about how to live as an adze. In books, movies, and typical vampire lore, familiars were human servants who served their vampire master and brought them victims.

She continued, "Do you even know what you have done, child? Here and there on Mainland? Your Endowment plays in things beyond its comprehension. And now?" She rubbed at her cuffs. "Now you have undone centuries of protection, of living quietly among humans undetected. You have brought her back."

She is gathering.

The square was silent. The only person who knew what she was saying was Nana Ama, and she didn't care to explain.

Nana Ama said nothing for a long time. Just stared with eyes that betrayed nothing. Her singular focus was boring into Hailey's center, as if determining if Hailey was lying or not. Hailey, trembling from exhaustion and terror, managed to stay upright beneath my grandmother's withering glare, one even I cowered at and didn't want to be the object of.

No one here, except maybe Nana Ama, James, and some of the really old elders, had ever dealt with something like this, an intruder and what to do with them. Not even me. I could sense their unease. They weren't sure if they wanted to know, or if they wanted to see what might happen.

The onlookers buzzed with nervous energy, unsure of what to make of this situation that I had caused. They whispered questions that worked their way through the crowd like a virus, their apprehension amplifying.

James wanted heads to roll, but I couldn't read Nana Ama. She wasn't throwing her weight like James. But she wasn't forgiving either. Not when it came to this island.

Nana Ama paused, regarding Hailey for another length of time.

"This is a most unfortunate matter," Nana Ama said gravely.

In that way of Nana's that let me know this was the end of everything I'd ever known, she said, "Take the girl."

This had to be some kind of sick joke. My grandmother wasn't about to agree to the execution of a mainlander, a young one at that. Never in my life had I disagreed with anything she said, but this . . . this went against everything we believed.

"Nana, please. Wait." I glared at James, and if I could will it, he'd combust where he stood. He pushed this harder than it had to be. There could have been a way to solve this with Hailey that kept us all safe.

He lifted his chin, daring me to speak against him in front of everyone, something that was never done to the unofficial consort to Nana Ama's queendom and her supreme power. I was not the matriarch, the Queen Mother, and should still be in deference to him. He was itching, had always been itching, to knock me down a couple pegs. His grandnephew was my best friend, and the two of them couldn't be further apart.

Elder James returned my glare with his own air of superiority, and with something else just below the surface I hadn't seen before. A malice that in the heat of the night among all the torches and bottles burned like hypothermia. He motioned for the guards to take hold of Hailey.

Nana Ama stood, facing Nyame's stool in silent contemplation as if Nyame would materialize on his seat to give her guidance. The decision she made tonight, to kill Hailey or not, would change the tide of the Kin, would vault us back a century or guide us to compassion and understanding that sometimes rigidity wasn't always the route to follow. I learned that the hard way, and now one of my best friends in the world was gone.

The buzzing in my head intensified, the pinprick enlarging. Nana Ama hadn't moved. She wasn't Lighting, wouldn't do it in front of the Kin anyway, so where . . .

James instructed, "Take the girl and hold her until Nana Ama has given her final word. We cannot let the others on the Isle see her again. The story will be that she left during the night, eager to return home."

Through Elder James's own words, he was giving me the start of an idea. I leaned over, trying to catch Sekou's eye. He wasn't looking, continuing to stand stock-still and glare out in front of me. A thousand I-told-you-sos probably still ran a marathon through his thoughts. I couldn't call his name. I didn't want anyone to see me trying to get his attention.

Hailey turned in a circle. "Wait. Please. Not in there. Please, please. I promise I won't tell. I won't say a word. I won't!"

Her words fell on ears that refused to listen. Just from the tiny droplets of her blood I could sense her panic. I could taste her fear of the unknown and the known. The guards around her hesitated only a few seconds to see if Nana would counter Elder James's instructions. When her back remained turned and she said nothing, they took it as a sign that she agreed and reached out to take Hailey.

"You don't have to do that," I said, taking a step toward them. "I said leave her alone."

Hailey fought against the hands grabbing at her. She begged to be let go, telling us it was a mistake and she didn't know the vials were still in her bag. That she didn't see anything. That she wouldn't tell.

There was movement to my right. Sekou finally pushed himself from his anger, activated by the commotion beside him. He seemed to see the struggle for the first time, realizing that this was not okay. As much as Hailey had done, she'd been caught up in it too.

She jerked away from my fellow Kin as they fought to get a better grip and began to drag her away.

"Nothing will happen," I called out, but she didn't, couldn't hear me. "I'll talk to my grandmother." I would. I could reason with Nana Ama, make her understand why it would be best to let Hailey go, why death was not the answer here . . . I'd convince my grandmother to listen to me because to not listen would make Nana Ama a monster, and *we* were not that.

Hailey saw me coming and her eyes grew double. She began to hyperventilate. My fangs were gone. My body, human. My mouth was not on her neck, and yet all she saw was me as an adze, or a version of one.

She threw herself backward, her mouth forming a *no*, wanting no part of me.

On the other side of her, Sekou looked at me, his face mirroring what mine must have looked like. Horror. Confusion. What the actual fuck? A fissure of anger sizzled in me. Her fault. If only she'd stayed in her quarters like I asked. If she'd just listened . . . then she wouldn't know a secret big enough to destroy me and all the Kin.

He made a beeline for the interior group that surrounded her. I came in from the other side, hoping to meet in the middle and grab Hailey, go to Nana Ama, implore her to listen to me and not to Elder James, whose eyes were wild with hungry power. The circle around Hailey closed in on her. She moved, her hand diving into the pocket of her jeans and lashing back out with a flash of pink in the palm of her hand.

I heard the alarm before I could register what she was doing.

The device I'd seen dangling from her key fob in her car. The contraption she never left home without. Good girl. She hadn't left home without it still. But no—the sound. It pierced at decibels incomprehensible to me.

Nothing had been this high or painful. It ricocheted in my brain, knocking through my mental defenses, opening me up to a world of voices and everything else crashing in. It startled the people around her, and she knocked into them, the surprise of her sudden movement making them fall like dominoes and her with them.

Sekou had reached her first, taking hold of her elbow despite her struggling. She slapped him hard and his face contorted in anger. He gritted his teeth, swallowing down his disdain for her, and pulled her up while Elder James shoved people out of his way, trying to get within the commotion.

Nana Ama moved from Nyame's stool, her face a mask of pain, anger, and confusion, echoing my own. Hailey pressed down on the nozzle of the alarm again. She inched away from those guarding her, away from the crowd she rendered senseless, their heightened senses from Nana's elixir becoming their Achilles' heel. The older Kin who had been taking the elixir the longest were more sensitive to the shriek of noise and dropped to the ground, clutching the sides of their heads. My hands clamped on either side of my head too, but the noise came through, as if she'd released the alarm inside my head.

Her alarm wasn't just around us; it reverberated through the trees, forcing its shrillness to echo and ping back in stabs of pain.

As if we were one, we shrank away from her and that thing as it sliced through our brains, immobilizing our every molecule.

My knees weakened from the way the shriek sliced through my brain, thundering in my head, setting my teeth on edge. Around me, Sekou, his granduncle, and the other Kinfolk contorted in varying degrees of suffering, all gripping the sides of their heads, grimacing in pain from our heightened hearing, once a perk of my being half adze and them consuming the elixir for years, now our kryptonite.

Nana Ama placed her fingers to her forehead as if she had a slight headache. She propped herself on the back of her wicker chair to keep herself upright. Her lips pursed in consideration of the chaos going on around us, watching as the people around Hailey receded from the front like a low tide.

Hailey used the chaos she created to make her move. She didn't hesitate to take it. I considered chasing after her, caught between preservation for our secrets and doubt that the solution for Hailey was right. That's what I got for thinking I knew more than I really did, like I had everything figured out. Watching this scene unfold in front of me, I knew one thing. Even if Hailey knew the truth about me and Nana Ama, it wasn't worth her life. To take it just to shut her up would go against everything my grandmother taught me. But I needed to protect Nana, the Kin, and the Isle too. I had to find another way to fix my mistake. Quick.

Hailey exploded out of there, whipping around the Gathering Tree with a speed I didn't think she had in her. She barreled through anyone in her path, overturning a table that had held a tray of empty cups of Nana's elixir. The cups and Kin scattered like matchsticks after barely recovering from the brain assault she'd just delivered.

Hailey mowed over them, arms windmilling, back into the hell she'd just emerged from, one hand gripping her canister of screams like a life preserver. She ran like the devil was at her heels.

And I guess we were.

CHAPTER THIRTY

HAILEY NEEDED TO GET OFF THE ISLAND AND BACK TO THE mainland. I needed to regroup and get space from my grandmother, who apparently was not above intentionally harming someone to protect the Golden Isle and the Kin. I stepped in the direction where Hailey ran, Sekou having gone after her. But a sharp, debilitating *pop* went off in my head, the buzzing pinprick that had annoyed me like a gnat destabilizing me. I staggered, and Nana Ama glanced up, her eyes homing in on me, blazing gold orbs.

Again my hand went to my head. Then I heard it. Or her. A voice as clear as if it were next to me, as old as time, as wise as my grandmother, spoke to me from within my head, my defenses obliterated if only for a moment.

Your friend, she lives, the woman said, her voice recognizable from two nights ago when Hailey and I were surrounded by bloodthirsty zombies.

I looked around, wondering if anyone could hear what I heard. If anyone could see that I heard. If Nana Ama could. She had turned from me, rendering aid to Elder James, who tapped at his ear.

The voice—otherworldly, terrifying, mesmerizing—continued. *Bring me her golden cuffs and you can have your Naira back.*

I wasn't that easy. *Prove she is with you.*

There was a pause. It stretched forever, each second pushing my heartbeat faster.

Then a voice I had yearned to hear for so long. *Ada! Don't, Ada. Don't give her the cu—*

Naira! I called out, reaching for a person who wasn't there. My hand curled into an empty fist.

The cuffs.

I understood what needed to be done, and that understanding firmed my resolve, made me angry that I'd been weak enough to allow something horrid to invade my mind. My mind's defenses, previously weakened by Hailey's stunt, resolidified and slammed shut, and that angry and demanding voice rooting around in it was gone, without a trace that she'd been there.

Hope made my heart soar, and I clung to it. I didn't doubt the voice. She had Naira, and she knew how far I'd go to save her. To the ends of the Earth. I would go that far, would bring her Nana Ama's cuffs to save my friend who I would never leave behind. And once Naira was safe, then I could figure out a way to save the cuffs too. Later, there would be many things I would have to ask Nana Ama's forgiveness for.

"Don't let her get away," James barked. Sweat streamed down his face from the complete chaos around us. He quickly began directing search parties to find her, which meant I didn't have a lot of time. And then I had to consider the message I'd received from Naira. The clock was ticking for Hailey and me, but most of all for Naira.

There were so many things to consider. So many people who questioned my choices, and maybe rightfully so. There was no time to wallow in my mistakes anymore. The breakthrough in my mind, the woman who'd spoken to me, was the first concrete evidence I had of Naira being alive. And when I linked up with Sekou and we found Hailey, convinced her it was safe to go back to the mainland with us, and I could tell her about the intrusion, she'd help too because where Naira was, Luke had to be, right? The thought, the plan, as shaky as it was, and believe me, it was shaky as hell, fueled me as if it was lifeblood.

I picked my way through the cluster as they separated themselves into those on the search and those going home. Sekou met me halfway, his eyes darting everywhere.

I stared up at him, got in close so we couldn't be heard. "I just heard . . ." I lowered my voice until it was nearly gone. Sekou had to lean in until we were practically touching. "Naira's alive."

He lurched back. "Not this again. This is the worst ti—"

I grabbed his arm. "I mean it. The woman I told you about. She just spoke to me." I tapped my temple. "In here."

Sekou's face twisted, his eyes narrowing in skepticism. "The alarm messed with your equilibrium. No one can punch through unless you let them."

"That's the thing," I said. "My everything was off. She was able to find me. As if we're linked. She was able to find a thread and follow it through. She has Naira. She wants a trade."

He eyed me. We were moving now, away from the cluster of people toward the edge. "What kind of trade?"

If I told him, he wouldn't come. I thought fast. "Hailey for Naira."

He did a double take. "What? The hell kind of deal is that?"

"We didn't sit to spill tea, Se, okay? Maybe because Hailey's family owns the Endowment with all those artifacts and the lady wants access. Anyway, will you help me?"

"What if it's a trap?"

I shook my head. "I sensed the honesty in her words." I searched his eyes, wanting him to see how I really believed we had to do this even if I was lying to his face. Just this time. For Naira. For the Isle. My stomach twisted in knots. Oh, Nyame, what the hell was I doing? I should tell Sekou everything. And Nana Ama too. She'd help. Right?

Who was I fooling? Nana Ama had already showed tonight what she was willing to do and not do. She would leave Naira out there as she already had, and she'd toss Hailey into the sea to protect and preserve our home and us. I understood it. But I couldn't abide by it.

The time was ticking. When Nana Ama settled everyone down, we'd be in her crosshairs. "Sekou?"

His lips twisted in thought, and he tapped a fist against his leg.

Tap, tap, tap.

His jaw flexed beneath his skin as he considered, watching James barking orders and waving his staff of power around as the other Kin moved about in organized frenzy.

When I looked for Nana Ama, she had disappeared.

Finally, Sekou made his decision. "Okay. I'm in," he said, splitting off in another direction.

At the same time, Nana Ama called to me, "Home, Addae."

CHAPTER THIRTY-ONE

The forest was illuminated with flashlights bouncing against sturdy tree trunks as the search party tried to flush out Hailey. Meanwhile, Sekou was on his own, tracking her himself.

I rushed back to Nana Ama's and my home, which was at the farthest end of the Landing, feeling like time was of the essence. When Sekou found Hailey and had the boat off the island ready, I had to be ready as well.

Nana Ama moved around the kitchen, plucking her favorite mug from the cabinet then going to the pantry where she got a bottle of palm oil she regularly had delivered from an international market in Bluffton. From the fridge, she pulled two of many cans of coconut water.

I winced.

She broke out both.

She eyed me first, then silently slid a can over to me. She poured a generous amount of palm oil in her cup then pushed the bottle to me too. She might have been angry with me, but she wouldn't let me starve.

We ate and drank like humans, even liked their food—maybe I liked food more than Nana because I was only half, my father being human. But their food could not nourish us enough to keep the thirst down. If it couldn't be blood, then adze could consume these. She didn't know why. I figured they were just the rules of being an adze. Nana said otherwise.

"It is by the grace of Nyame that I discovered these items could provide sustenance," she had said. "At least, he gave us that."

That was the only time I'd seen a flash of contempt when she spoke of the Sky God, and never again.

She drank the coconut water first, then the palm oil before her eyes began to lighten to their normal shade. The sting of guilt reared its ugly head again. She was supposed to have had a little taste tonight when she stepped out. I had ruined all of that.

Growing up, there had always been black holes of information about Nana Ama, areas that she would gloss over or flat-out refuse to discuss. I became used to those areas. If there was one thing I respected, it was giving someone the opportunity to have their private thoughts.

I sensed it was something beyond once being enslaved or the hardships the founding families faced growing and rebuilding their lives on the Isle. It was even deeper than the death of my mother, though my mother was one of the voids Nana Ama and I didn't really talk about.

I figured when the time was right, my grandmother would tell me whatever had been haunting her. Until then, I would be patient.

But now, when I reached the house and saw her there, moving

around the kitchen as if it were a regular night and not one where she was about to okay someone's death, I couldn't let it go. Not after all that happened back at the Gathering Tree. I needed to know who Nana Ama was forced to leave behind.

"Nana Ama, I know you don't trust mainlanders. I know you've been traumatized by what you've been through when you were—back at the plantation." She had her back to me, and it stiffened when I mentioned the plantation. I plowed on, thinking this would be my only chance to get her to open up. "I get all that. I even understand and have supported keeping us secluded on the island. Being strict about who gets to live here, who gets to become one of our Kinfolk. But no one's coming here to drag you, or any of us, back. That's not how the world is anymore." I thought about the precious minutes I was wasting, but feeling I couldn't just go off without at least trying.

"You have jeopardized everyone who lives here, all our Kin, for someone you barely know," she said. "And to top it off, she has seen you. No one is supposed to see you like that. Your true adze state is when you are most vulnerable. Any information about you makes you vulnerable. You know how this world is."

"Yes, Nana." Better not to anger her more. I needed to play it cool and show her nothing that would raise her suspicions.

I dropped my head. "I'm sorry." I meant it. I was sorry. Sorry for everything I did and everything I was about to do. I hoped she would understand me even when she realized her cuffs were gone. "I made a huge mistake in bringing Hailey here."

"Speak what you need, child," she said, reading my hesitation correctly.

I debated if this was the right moment. But my question had been burning all night.

"Speak."

"Would you really have gone through with it?"

She waited for the rest.

"Would you have killed Hailey? Will you kill her?" I corrected so she wouldn't get suspicious. I hoped Sekou was finding more success than everyone else. It was easier to track solo than in large groups where noise and distraction made it more difficult. "When you find her?"

Nana considered me for a long while. Finally, she said, "I will always do what I must. It's what has kept us alive for all these years."

I chanced another. "And the woman? Who is she? She's an adze? But not like you."

"She is what you should never hope to be."

I'D LEFT HER IN THE KITCHEN KNOWING WHAT I HAD TO DO. I'D known it the moment the woman broke through my defenses and spoke to me. When I heard the lanai door close behind Nana Ama as she took her seat in her chair, with her hot tea, and waited for James to tell her Hailey was found, I went to her bedroom. I felt a cyclone of emotion at what I was about to do, but I couldn't back down from it. I needed those cuffs. I was going to have to fight fire with fire, especially if the woman's amulet held any of the same kind of power as Nana Ama's cuffs.

I made my way to Nana Ama's dresser and to the top drawer where she kept them. The box was there and closed. I opened it, revealing the shining jewelry that lit up the room. I took them from the box, wrapping them in the towel I'd brought, and shoved them in the open backpack at my feet. Nana would know the moment the cuffs left the island. Probably the moment they left the house. I had to move fast and hope it was good enough to get us off the island, where we'd have a better chance to get Naira back.

As I was picking up the bag to zip it, my phone buzzed. Sekou.

At the cove. Ready to go.

I let out a relieved breath. At least something went right tonight in a sea of so much wrong. I'd run away. Lied. Brought home a stranger. Let said stranger see me as an adze. Defied my grandmother and the ways of the Isle. Why not add stealing to the mix?

When I left my home, heading for the cove with Nana Ama's bracelets securely in my backpack, I left a note explaining that I was borrowing the cuffs. I asked Nana to trust me and understand why I couldn't leave Hailey here or Naira out there and that if I was going to ever be the right kind of leader of the Golden Isle, then I'd have to learn how to take care of its people. No reason I gave for taking the bracelets was excuse enough, but I hoped she'd understand. And if she didn't, I'd understand that too.

As I ran from my grandmother like the thief that I was, moving through the dark forest paths so I wouldn't be spotted by the search parties, I pulled up Sheriff Lyle's number, a number I thought I'd never use. He picked up before the first ring completed, immediately asking what was wrong.

"I'll explain when we get there. I know it's weird to hear from me, but you're the only person I can think of now who can help and who's not on the Isle. Could you hear me out first, please?"

He took a long moment before he finally answered. "Alright then, Ada, I'll be waiting."

CHAPTER THIRTY-TWO

"Sekou."

My whisper sounded more like a bullhorn to me in the unnatural quiet of the night. I listened for signs from either of them. All I could feel was the subtle rocking of the dock and hear the gently lapping water against the wooden posts and the shore. Boats were moored up and down the dock, and it was hard to determine if there was anyone out there in the ink-black night.

Something rustled, and Sekou's head popped out from beneath the tarp he and Hailey were hiding beneath. I nearly ran to hug them. I was so relieved that they hadn't been caught. That the island wasn't trying everything in its power to keep them here. We'd better leave now before it changed its mind or we came across one of the Kinfolk.

"I can't believe we're actually doing this," Sekou muttered as I climbed into the boat. The moment I settled, he pushed off, using an oar to row us farther out into open sea where we could kick the motor on. I took up an oar too, following his lead.

Sekou glared at Hailey when she remained seated, scrunched down into the bottom of the boat. He raised his eyebrow.

"Oh," she said, finally getting the hint. She began feeling for the extra oar tucked at the bottom.

"Right," he confirmed. "This isn't *Driving Miss Daisy*." Sekou was channeling one of our elder aunties, but I wasn't about to tell him that.

We didn't speak as we rowed out into open water, afraid we'd be heard. What Sekou and I were doing went against every rule set by Nana Ama and the Isle. Even if I explained that Naira's voice had been in my head, they'd have thought I was delusional.

"You don't have to do this," I said quietly to Sekou. His arms pumped, guiding the boat effortlessly through the water. That was a lie. It took a lot of effort to row a boat. Sekou just didn't make it look so. On the other hand, Hailey struggled like she was rowing through molasses.

"Naira's my best friend too," he said. "It's the three of us, remember? You're not leaving me behind again."

I tried not to feel guilty about leaving him behind before. Instead, I concentrated on the water because it was easier than thinking about who had been left behind. I also didn't want Sekou getting hurt, or worse, because of me. We weren't heading to Disney World. But still, knowing he had my back was a relief. It allowed me to believe just a little that maybe we could figure out a way to get Naira back—together.

"Still . . ." I trailed off when no more words would come. We were heading into a world against something we'd never encountered.

"I shouldn't have told Uncle James about her connection to the Endowment," Sekou admitted. Then he picked up his rowing. We had to make up time. "It was—"

"A petty-ass move?" I offered helpfully, hoping to lighten the mood. Everything that happened tonight had already been too heavy. We deserved a little levity.

A range of emotions scrolled over his face as he determined my level of shady. "Have you been waiting all night to call me that?"

I nodded. It was easier to go back and forth with him than to deal with everything that had happened.

"Fair enough." He cut his eyes to Hailey. "But in all fairness, I just couldn't keep it quiet when I found out."

"When you snooped, you mean," Hailey reminded him.

Sekou snorted. "You should probably say very little, Mainlander. We risked our asses getting you out. We saved your life."

Hailey snorted back. "Yeah, right after you threatened my life."

"You put your own damn life in danger, had you not been so damn nosy and disrespectful," he snapped. White-hot indignation fissured up so violently that I could feel his energy taking me by surprise. My hand gripped the side of the boat to steady myself as I absorbed it, controlled it, didn't allow his rage to consume me. "You see how she's still thinking only of herself? How she's twisting it so *she's* the victim? Not even a thanks for going against your grandmother and our traditions. Not for getting her off the island that she weaseled her way onto. She's just like the rest of the mainlanders and people like her. They are always out for number one."

He wasn't wrong, but this time Hailey wasn't totally to blame either. Maybe my mind was all twisted from the past few days

I'd spent with Hailey and what we'd experienced. Or maybe it was the absolute terror in her eyes when she saw the other me. I should have never brought her here.

I couldn't let Hailey take all the heat. "That's enough, Se."

As the fishing boat glided along, Hailey and I stared at each other in the dark. I cut the oar in the water on the opposite side, trying to get us to a good place fast enough so we could start up the motor and go. Hailey did the best she could while eyeing me cautiously, as if I were going to make her my next meal.

"Can I ask you something?"

Most of me wanted to laugh in her face, thinking I owed her no explanation. But when you found out vampires were real and a whole town of people had been hunting you, I guess some clarification was deserved. She took my silence as the sign to go ahead.

"You're not what I expected vampires to be like."

"Because all vampires look alike, right?" I managed a wry smile and even Sekou had to chuckle.

"No," she said defensively, catching my meaning. "I mean from the books. You can be out in the day. You can change into a—"

How much to say without saying too much? "Every culture has a variation of the same ghouls and monsters." I began. "Same explanation for things they don't understand. Ours is the West African kind. Yes, I can go out in the day, but it can wear on me. The night is better."

I ran down the list of lore. "My kind doesn't turn into bats, but fireflies—lightning bugs. We're fine on holy ground. We're at one with the land and the spirits. Each can have a specific gift. My grandmother can heal. I'm learning as I go. A newbie."

"You don't have to tell her all this," Sekou told me. "You don't owe her anything."

I didn't, but tonight she had almost lost her life twice. It was the most I would do.

"I can sense emotions, the energy people put out."

Hailey asked, "Your grandmother is how old?"

"Over a hundred. Under two."

Hailey calculated the dates, her eyes widening. "So that puts her back when . . ." She couldn't make herself say the words that made so many white people uncomfortable.

"Back when Black people were enslaved on plantations for white massas?" I finished for her. "You'd have to ask my grandmother about that. If you dare." I smirked at her terror when Nana Ama was mentioned.

She was about to ask more, but I'd satisfied my guilt at her near death. It was Hailey's turn at truth. She wasn't the only one owed explanations.

"How about telling us the truth," I said. "No more bullshit."

Hailey said, "I didn't come to the island with some nefarious plan to expose you and your grandma. I had no idea you all were . . ." She paused. "The Endowment was created to be a help."

Sekou snorted. "Carrying around vials to take specimens from people. Really helpful."

"We take samples from artifacts for either carbon or archaeological dating to then get them to their rightful owners." She sighed, clearly exasperated. "But whatever. It's not like you're going to believe me anyway."

"First thing you've been right about since you got here," Sekou shot back. "I hope you don't try that guilt-trip shit here; you were only here because she was worried about your safety, and then you turn around and try to spy for your colonizing uncle and company."

"You!" Hailey pointed at him, but she caught my expression and snapped her mouth shut, sitting back against the side in a huff. "I'm not a spy."

I said, "Maybe research is all *you* want to do. Doesn't mean the same for the Endowment. It's usually not the same for big corporations. Maybe you don't know what your uncle's true goal of finding all of these artifacts really is; ever think about that?" I told her. Nana Ama's words earlier in our kitchen came back to me. "Maybe you don't know what your uncle Simon's real intentions for the Isle are, or for the artifacts the organization finds."

"Uncle Simon's not like that. He and Dr. Franco have only ever wanted to help give back by restoring and returning stolen items."

"And yet," Sekou threw in, "you came to our island with sample vials . . . to steal, not restore." He huffed out a laugh at her audacity.

She turned away. "A misunderstanding. When we get back, he'll explain. We're not all bad, you know? White people."

"Of course not," I snapped. "But enough have been. You're always 'well meaning' until someone threatens what you think you have a right to. You can't knock us for always being on guard."

"Right," Sekou said haughtily, pointing a long finger at her. "So don't play victim here, okay? 'Cause you're not one. You're the villain. Save the tears."

"Fuck you, Sekou."

Before things got any worse, I cut in. "What do you think

would happen if the world found out people like me and Nana Ama existed? What would they do with the power of Nana Ama's elixir? They'd take advantage of it. Don't you think that's what the Endowment is really trying to do?"

Hailey was defiant. "Then that would mean everyone has been lying to me my whole life—my uncle, Luke, our parents. I haven't seen any evidence of this."

"Guess lying runs in the family." I couldn't help saying. Whatever effect my words had on her, I didn't see it.

"Let's just get through the rest of the ride, okay?" Sekou interrupted when it looked like Hailey was about to reply. "Because I just can't deal with either one of you right now."

She snapped her mouth shut and settled down in the bottom of the boat, turning away from me, and I did the same, our backs to each other signifying the end of what could have been before it had really had a chance to begin. Sekou leaned over the motor and turned the switch. It roared to life, and we were off, cutting through the water, hitting the tiny swells, water spray and wind hitting our faces.

The mainland loomed in the distance, reeling us in over the dark water.

CHAPTER THIRTY-THREE

Sheriff Lyle's private dock was a bright beacon, guiding us in like a lighthouse. Sekou jumped out of the boat, the shallow water going just below his knees in the marshy brine. He grabbed the rope I tossed to him, pulling us in so he could secure the line to one of the thick round posts built into the dock.

I made sure my backpack was firmly on me and that it was still zipped, after I'd poked my hand in to make sure the cuffs were still there. Luckily, they were.

Lyle was supposed to pick us up from the dock, but I saw no evidence of him or his truck.

It was really quiet. A sort of dead stillness that was saying something was a tiny bit off. Sensing a disruption in the balance of nature here. And I was hearing something. Something moving through the woods on unsteady feet.

Maybe it was a hurt animal. I sniffed the air, trying to catch some sort of scent, but I couldn't tell exactly what was there. It was a faint smell of something diseased and malignant.

"Be careful," I said softly. "Watch out for animals. I think something's hurt out here and it could—"

I didn't get the rest of my sentence out because something slammed hard into my chest and I was sailing through the air. The once-faint scent of disease and rot was now heavy and oppressive, covering me like a dirty blanket. It was in my nostrils and my mouth as whatever it was wrapped itself around me.

I crashed to the ground, my backpack squished between me and the grassy earth beneath me. I kept my arms out straight to keep the thing as far from my face and neck as possible.

Sekou and Hailey were shouting as the thing over me came into focus. A pale snarling, snapping, clawing thing that kept gnashing its fungus-filled uneven teeth at me. No canines. It was like the things that had chased me and Hailey at the campus. How was it able to find us? What was it doing here out in the middle of nowhere?

Its nails were long and jagged like talons, and its face was a gruesome mask of bites and tears. It was a Black man from what I could tell. Or used to be. But its skin was pale and ashen, as if it'd been sitting in water and its melanin had lost its luster. Snaking up its neck were thick black lines. Its eyes bulged, the black pupils so dilated none of the whites showed. In the light of Sekou's bouncing flashlight, its eyes had barely a speck of gold that had lost its luster. They blazed bloodred.

It lunged for my throat. It was powerful, a shark, all muscle and power . . . an eating machine with thoughts of nothing else.

I struggled to fight it off, the blood I was able to take that night reinforcing my strength and letting me keep it from tearing a hole in my throat, but barely. It was either it or us if I released it, and it nearly overpowered me. I hadn't come this far to let one of these things beat me. I hadn't put everything I had on the line just to die here. It clearly had a one-track mind. Long ropes of saliva, thick like molasses and smelling like rot, dripped from its gaping mouth onto my face. It was all I could do not to gag.

Sekou was over it, smashing a large branch over its back. It lashed its arm backward at Sekou to get off, jerky like a marionette, and I scratched at it, digging my nails deep into the side of its throat. Blood, or something like it, seeped out, and I dug in deeper.

The thing let out an unholy howl that echoed in the treetops, and I was afraid more would come. It moved way too fast, but jerkily, like it couldn't control its limbs. With one gnarled hand, it tried pawing for my shoulder and the strap of my backpack, trying to hook its nail through.

I balled my fist and beat at its face while Sekou came back with the stick again. Hailey stepped forward, making small noises, unsure what to do.

The. Alarm. I wanted to yell. There was no way I was opening my mouth. No way that foul spit was getting in there. Bad enough I had to keep my eyes open and look into the empty, vacant, hungry ones of the thing above me.

"Alarm!" Sekou commanded Hailey.

"What?"

"Your alarm! Be useful for a change and sound the damn thing."

She dug in the pocket of her jeans, pulling out the small cylinder and pointing it toward the thing. The sound pierced the air, echoing among the treetops and sending bats fluttering into the sky. The thing above me reared back, howling. It clutched at its ears with its hands, covering them. It was enough that I could buck it off me, and it heaved to its side. I rolled up, wiping at my face to get the sticky, tacky substance off as I got to my feet.

Hailey's alarm died down and the thing immediately began to reorient itself.

But I was ready for it.

It jumped up to its feet, hulking and breathing hard. The saliva dripped to the ground. It bared its teeth. It zeroed in on me, the prey in its crosshairs. Behind me, Sekou readied his stick, having my back as he always had since we were little. And Hailey, surprisingly, stood beside him, her hands balled to her sides as if she, too, were ready to fight.

I crouched, preparing to launch myself at the thing and rip its throat out with my bare claws. My fingers had grown into talons. My energy crackled and I opened my mouth, allowing my teeth to let down, long and curved. My muscles coiled, and just as I was about to fly at it, a pair of high beams appeared out of nowhere attached to a black Dodge Ram.

The Ram bumped a high patch of packed dirt, bounced up into the air, and sailed into the thing as it leapt at me. The Ram's grill smacked into the thing, and its body zipped in front of us, smashing into a nearby cluster of trees. It hit one, and the tree shook violently from the impact. Its leaves rained down on the thing as it fell to the ground in a stinking, monstrous heap. It did not move.

The lights of the Ram illuminated the mound as I swayed side to side, watching it, waiting for it to recover and resume its attack. Still, it did not move.

Particles floated in and out of the high beams as they remained trained on the unmoving figure. The driver's door opened and Lyle climbed out, rifle in hand. He trained it on the mound in case it jumped up. Like all monsters did before their final end.

He rounded the front of the truck, staying out of the beams of light. He told us to stay back. Keep the light on the thing.

"Looks like you caught yourself an abalsom," Lyle said simply, as if pointing out a flat tire. He kept his rifle on the mound.

Abalsom. I racked my brain trying to translate the word, coming up with nothing specific. The sheriff noted my confusion, shaking his head like my ignorance was pitiful. Well, there was only my grandmother to blame.

"Simply put, this is what you'd call a zombie. This is the result of a turn gone bad."

Sekou and I shared a look to say Lyle was losing it.

"A turn gone bad?" I repeated. This man had was tripping and trying to take us with him. "You've got to be kidding." Nana and I would never kill, much less turn someone into *that*.

"Don't believe me? I'll let your grandma explain. Get in the truck while I square this fella away."

Sekou and Hailey didn't have to be told twice. They moved faster than me, and I could move pretty damn fast.

Lyle moved toward it, gun at the ready. I moved in sync with him on the other side of the beams. He stopped and I stopped too. He looked over at me.

"I said get in the car, Ada."

I wiped at my face again, then pointed in the direction of the thing. "You're gonna need my help. You don't know what I can do."

Lyle looked me dead in the eye. "I know more than you think. I know that if you wanted, you could rip him apart. Or suck him dry. Though what he's got, you want no part of."

An understatement. There was no way I was drinking *that*, whatever it was. I didn't appreciate Lyle's tone. No one ever spoke to me like that. What my grandmother and I were had always been inferred instead of spoken aloud and as bluntly as Lyle just had. He had been on the mainland for so long, yet spoke to me with a familiarity that made me uncomfortable and resentful.

The monster growled in its sleep, bringing me back to the dangerous present. "What if it wakes up? Aren't you gonna shoot it?"

He considered it. "Thought about it. But we're gonna need it."

My eyes nearly popped out of my sockets. Need it? For what? That thing just tried to eat my face off.

"We need it to figure out what we're dealing with," Lyle said, his eyes returning to the thing. Its body wasn't heaving like it was taking breath, but a whole lot of steam was coming off it in wisps, like it was running on hot.

Lyle said, "Always gotta know your enemy. Gotta study them." He inched closer and I inched with him.

Without looking my way, Lyle reached in the pocket of his plaid jacket and pulled something out. He bunched it up with one hand and tossed it across the beams at me. I caught it. A rough burlap sack. I held it up to him questioningly.

"To cover its face. We don't know what it can see. Or if it's a conduit."

"For who?" What Lyle was saying was unbelievable because for someone to speak through a thing like this . . . that was practicing dark arts. That was blasphemous.

"I'll tie off its hands and feet. Bind it up real good. You get the sack over its head and we'll cinch it so it can't see where we're going and call its friends or its boss."

I nodded, beginning to grasp what he was saying.

I looked into the inky voids of the monster's eyes and wondered what might be staring back.

CHAPTER THIRTY-FOUR

At Lyle's house, we tied the monster up out back, leaving it in his work shed, and finally made it inside, just as the night began to give way to morning.

I started in. "Sheriff. We've seen one of those before. A few days ago, in Charleston. A whole bunch of them tried to attack Hailey and me."

"Why don't you tell me what's been going on and why I'm up at this ungodly hour playing the role of vampire hunter with a bunch of kids?" he said matter-of-factly.

I updated him about the mysterious woman who could break through my defenses and probe my thoughts and all of the connections that pointed to her as a possible link to Naira. "What is it?" I asked when Hailey looked like she wanted to say something then thought better of it.

Hailey hesitated, and I waited impatiently. There was no time for this. Naira's life was on the line.

She finally said, "There is something I was keeping from you.

Not the stuff about my uncle eyeing your island, but about my brother." She took a deep breath. Then another. "Luke is still alive."

We stared at her, our shock mixed with disbelief. Me most of all because the lies and surprises from Hailey kept on coming, making me look even more like a complete idiot for trusting her. Luke had been the only one with Naira when their boat crashed. Hailey had pretended he was dead. She'd gone to the marina with me, and all this time he was alive? And what did that mean for Naira? Where was she while I was letting myself get played by Hailey?

"But he's sick," she said quickly. "And getting sicker."

"You need to explain," Lyle said sharply. "What kind of sick are you talking about?"

She wouldn't look at any of us, especially not me. I was trying to hold it in, thinking of every single instance that I'd let my guard down with her only to have it thrown back in my face, made to feel like an idiot every time.

"How's your brother sick? We don't have time for this!" Sekou yelled.

"Sick!" she cried. She covered her face with shaking hands, burying all of it in her propped-up knees. "He's sick like that thing out back, only not as sick. But almost like that."

Silence followed her outburst. Hailey's shoulders heaved as she cried with no sound coming out.

If Luke was *that*, then what was Naira?

Lyle stepped closer to her, pulling out a chair so he wouldn't intimidate. He had to get her to trust him so she'd open up.

"Can you tell me what happened? How'd Luke get . . . sick?" he asked.

Hailey let out a sob. Then she hiccuped. She peeked up at Lyle, seeing him near her and at her level. She hesitated.

"I want to help you, but I can't if I don't know what I'm dealing with," Lyle said.

"When Luke returned from boating that night, he was very ill. He couldn't eat regular food. He'd just throw it up. He kept saying he was hungry, but nothing he ate stayed down. And then he started speaking less until it was nothing but sounds. And his movements became jumpy and jittery. Like he was losing control of his mobility. His eyes were reddening and he was becoming so animalistic. It was like there was only—"

"A shell of him," Lyle finished.

Hailey shot up in her chair, throwing her feet down. "Yes!" she said, relieved. "A shell of his former self. That's it. He was steadily losing himself."

Lyle nodded. "I've seen it before." He walked to one of his kitchen drawers and rustled about in it. He pulled out a yellow legal pad and a permanent marker. Then he sat back down across from Hailey and proceeded to draw something.

Trusting myself to speak, I said, "What did he say about the boat accident? What happened to Naira?"

"Not much." Hailey had her head ducked down again. "He said the boat crashed but that some woman took them off first. A woman with red eyes and long teeth. And that"—Hailey's voice began to rise—"that—that she bit him and there was only pain. It felt like acid in his veins."

"And Naira?"

"He said the woman had taken her and left him."

She'd known they were alive this whole time. The betrayal was crushing. "Why did you come to the Isle?" I demanded.

"Naira told Luke about you and your grandmother, and the restorative properties of your blood," she stammered. "We had tried every possible treatment on Luke and nothing worked. I was tasked with procuring the blood in order to find a cure. Each day, Luke was getting worse."

Hailey wiped at her eyes and looked at me. "I was only trying to help him. I was only trying to find whatever the doctor needed to make the cure to save my brother. Then I was going to tell the police about Naira and the woman. But I didn't want the police to think Luke killed her or that he was on drugs, or worse, because of the way he was acting. You have to believe me, Ada."

I didn't have to believe anything, especially not from her.

"I didn't want to keep this from you," she said quietly.

I didn't answer her.

"I was going to tell you everything tonight, afterward. I realized I couldn't steal your blood. Not without your permission. Not even for Luke."

"Was that the first time you tried to steal my blood? At the island?" I asked.

She shook her head. "No," she whispered. "When you showed up at my house, it was the perfect opportunity. I thought I could do it that night or the next. But then we were attacked by those things. I was so scared Luke would become them that I went in where you were sleeping and . . ." She couldn't finish.

"And the first night," I continued. "When I felt something in the alley." I thought of the swirling, shaping black mass. The eyes had been the cat's, but the growing mass and the skittering had been—

"It was him," she whispered.

"Where is he now?" Sekou asked.

"Don't know. He wasn't at the facility when Ada and I went there. The night he came to my house was the first I'd seen him in days."

Lyle finished his drawing and pushed it toward Hailey on the table. It showed an arm with dark black lines zipping up and down the inside of it, where the veins would be. "This," Lyle said, pointing to the lines. "Could you see this on his arm?"

Hailey started to touch the sheet of paper, tracing the black veins on the sketch halfway before snatching her finger back as if she'd been shocked. Or burned.

She looked wild-eyed at Lyle. "It was light at first. I thought it was just bruising. Then it kept getting darker and darker each day. Throughout the day. And he kept scratching at it, like he was allergic. I was afraid he'd gouge a hole out of his skin."

"I was afraid you'd say that," Lyle said, pulling the pad back toward him. "That's the hollowing."

Sekou, Hailey, and I shared a look. "What's the hollowing?" I asked.

Lyle settled in his chair. I could tell he was worried. Whatever he knew that we didn't was affecting him. He hesitated, like he was weighing whether he should or shouldn't speak.

"We should wait for Ama," he said. "She should be the one to tell you."

I spat out, "Only she won't and she never will. So please,

Sheriff Lyle, tell me what she won't. I've known about adze, but she never mentioned *them*. I have to know."

He stroked his mustache, still thinking. Probably wondering how he'd let himself get roped into this when he'd chosen to leave the Isle to escape all of this. "You gotta think of it like a disease, or umm . . . an infection rather," he said grimly. "Like the flesh-eating amoeba they found in that water park up in North Carolina a few summers back. Eats you from the inside out? 'Cept the hollowing burns away your humanity. Makes you one of those things like the one out back that came after you. Makes you that shell like you mentioned, hollowed out with nothing left."

"Can it be cured?" Hailey looked up at Lyle hopefully.

"Only one person will know how to fix it." He snuck an uneasy look at Hailey. "*If* there's a fix. It will be Ama's elixir. It can do more than just prolong life and encourage good health. It might be able to reverse the hollowing."

As if on cue, I felt the force of my grandmother's presence as she arrived. There was no car. She hadn't come by boat, meaning she'd transported herself as an adze, something she never did in the day. It was too easy to be spotted and much too dangerous. She'd chanced traveling by day for me.

And if we wanted answers, we'd have to open the door to get them.

CHAPTER THIRTY-FIVE

AIR *WHOOSHED* THROUGH THE ROOM AS LYLE OPENED THE door, revealing my grandmother on the other side. My head jerked back when I saw her, looking not like the lady I left behind wrapped in African clothes of gold and black and a duke wrapped tightly around her head.

Nana Ama stood at the doorway taking us all in while Sheriff Lyle held it open for her, waiting. She finally stepped through, and the three of us petrified tree branches remained unmoving at the table. We were all still rightfully scared as hell about what Nana would say, what she'd do, now that we were back in her presence after disobeying her word and fleeing the Isle.

She assessed the room, her gaze going from left to right, landing on the each of us and staying there for a minute on Sekou. She pursed her lips down and turned in a disapproving manner to let him know that this was not what he should've done, following up behind me. Then she stared at Hailey with an inscrutable look. Her right eye kind of narrowed, like she was really trying to figure out who Hailey was and what the heck she wanted to do with her, but then she seemed to just give up.

The last look was for me. It told a whole story of grievances, and the disappointment emanating from my grandmother, in waves that nearly buckled me, almost made me fall back in my chair. She wanted to lay into me, but it was something she had never done. Her quiet storm of anger would just simmer until she decided what she really wanted to say.

"Lyle was my Abotisa, whom I chose as part of my sacred three, much like you, Sekou, and Naira," Nana explained impatiently, breaking through silence and the mental conversations. Sekou and I shared an unconvinced look, waiting for her to claim it was all a joke, only Nana Ama rarely joked. "One of my sacred passed on to the Asamando, the spirit realm, many years before you were born. Elder James is my second, though much has changed about him." She sighed resignedly. "But good Sheriff Lyle here. He remains so, even though he chose to leave the Isle for all of this." She gestured to the unimpressive room around us, cutting her eyes at him. He flushed, his caramel-colored ears reddening. Still a sore spot, clearly, and I suspected something more.

Nana Ama spotted the drawing of the arm on the table and studied it closely.

Hailey asked softly, "Is there any way to reverse the effects?" She looked everywhere but at us.

"Perhaps. If the victim is not too far gone. But there isn't much time. I can sense her now. She has been gaining strength. Where is it?"

Her?

Lyle pointed toward his backyard. "Around back in the shed."

In the backyard, the abalsom lunged toward Nana Ama in a rush of blurred orange and disjointed arms and legs. Though its movements were uncoordinated, it was still quick. And no match for Nana. Her hands struck out rattlesnake quick and snatched it up between her palms like she was catching a giant mosquito. The abalsom snarled and snapped at her, its mouth foaming, its teeth a mangled mess. It tried clawing at her, but she held it at arm's length, studying it intently as if it were a specimen in a petri dish.

Sekou and Hailey retreated from the action, having had their fill of killer zombies the night before. They clutched at each other, eyes wide and terrified. If we got out of this alive, I would tease them about this forever.

Ama held the writhing abalsom, in raggedy slacks, still. She raised her arms, its bulging head still firmly in her vise grip, its toes trailing the ground.

She looked deeply in its eyes. Deep, unmoving, saying nothing, until eventually its snarling, and snapping, and writhing started to slow, then stop. Its mouth opened, slack-jawed, and a long drip of slimy drool stretched from its mouth, over its lips, down its chin, heading to the grass between them. My mouth curled in disgust.

"He has the hollowing," Nana Ama said, giving her diagnosis.

"And what would that be?" I asked.

"Every adze has a poison inside them that, when injected into a human without a blood transference to counter the effect and complete a successful turn of a human, siphons their essence and rots their mind until they become a servant entirely under that adze's control. They are possessed by their master. No longer themselves. No longer human. And the master consumes everything about them. Their blood, thoughts, emotions."

I had no idea that the adze held such destructive power. I imagined, my horror intensifying, that this poison was somewhere inside me, coursing through my veins. That I could do this to another person. That *any* adze would do such a thing.

I looked up at Nana Ama, hit with a realization too big to understand. She and I were the only adze that I knew. "Who did this?" I asked, gesturing at the snarling monster in her grasp.

She ignored me and instead whispered, "Welcome back, Effie," to the beast. His hand seized, fingers curling. "You have been missed." His body spasmed. She returned the bag to his head.

"Who is *Effie*?" I demanded, panic rising.

My grandmother sighed, ignoring my question once again. She motioned for us to follow her back to the house. "Do you still sense that Naira is alive?"

"I do," I replied, hoping she could see how much I knew this to be true. "She spoke to me." Behind me, Sekou gasped.

Nana Ama was unfazed, as if she'd expected my answer. "What did she say?"

I would never forget her words. I wouldn't forget the terror behind them and the pain. Or the scream when something cut Naira off and our connection went dead. Miles and miles of cut lines.

. . . Don't, Ada. Don't give her the cu—

I relayed it all to Nana, becoming uneasy when my grandmother's face darkened, growing so severe I thought I was in trouble.

"Are you sure?" Nana got in close.

Instinctively, I leaned back. The look on her face was intense and fierce. It was as if my grandmother had been swallowed up and in her place was this warrior woman about to take my head clean off if I didn't give the right answer.

"Nana?"

"What you think you heard, Addae," she asked impatiently, "are you sure it was that she needed my cuffs?"

I nodded, my mouth going dry. Nana's eyes flashed gold so dark they were nearly bronze.

"Who is she?" I asked more firmly now because I needed some kind of answer. It was getting real old the way Nana kept things quiet, only feeding me tiny bits of information until she felt good and ready to let me know what was up. Nana's silence had kept me unprepared for whatever was coming.

It was the first time I saw Nana falter, as if the question destabilized her. "My sister."

Her answer slammed into me, fast and hard. It took the wind right out of me. Nana wasn't the only one destabilized. My whole entire being was rocked, and if not for me already being in a chair, I think I would have fallen flat to the floor.

Nana Ama had a sister. It wasn't just her and me in the world? We had blood family, not just people we called Kin because we grew to be. We had a person who just was. And if there was one, maybe there were more, like me, like us, who just . . . were. Family.

But from Nana's look, there was more behind the knowledge of a long-lost sister out there in the world.

"If she's your sister, can you figure out where she is? Do you still have a telepathic connection with her?"

"I only feel her now because her power has grown. I severed the connection we had as sisters who shared a womb. I couldn't sense her when she first woke. The Isle served as a buffer for the both of us, I guess. And she was likely very weak. But she has been feeding, much more than me. She's stronger and has made her move."

Lyle spoke up. "We're running short on time."

Shared womb stuck in my mind like big billboard letters. Nana and this Effie were not only related—sisters—but twins. Bound together before they were even born. And she never said a word. I spent my whole life thinking I knew so much. My truth had been cut up like fruit and baby-fed to me. I thought I was the one making my own decisions, when they were being made for me—what I knew, didn't know about who I was. Like I was some kid who wasn't tough enough to know the truth of my bloodline. There was a whole aunt hidden from me, and Nana would never have told me if Effie hadn't returned. The realization that I knew nothing, not even who I was, left me as hollow as the hollowing that the abalsom had. Betrayed and resentful, that's all I could feel. They thought they knew what was best for me, but turned out they didn't. Knowing was what was best. Now how could I trust anyone else, even my grandmother, at their word, when they obviously didn't trust me?

Sekou, who'd come up beside me, bumped into my side, arm-checking me, the vibe coming off of him telling me to be cool. He whispered, "I got you." It was all I could do to not break down, because Sekou was the only one who'd been completely honest this whole time. And I had done nothing but lie to him. The guilt turned my stomach.

"There's no need for us to link in any way." Nana Ama moved around. She was heading out front to where Lyle's cars were parked. "Because I know exactly where she is."

For now, I had to suck up all of my feelings. I asked, following her, "Where's that?"

She tossed over her shoulder without breaking stride, "The place where our paths diverged. Millner Manor Plantation."

CHAPTER THIRTY-SIX

We followed one after another toward the Explorer that Lyle said we were taking instead of his beloved Ram.

"Ram's already had enough action for a while," Lyle grumbled, no doubt thinking about the abalsom we'd captured. "Something like this, we'd better take a ride I can stand to lose."

But before I followed after Hailey into the back seat, Ama gripped my elbow, stopping me in mid-slide.

"I'll take my cuffs back now, you little owifo."

My mouth went dry at her calling me a thief. I'd forgotten just that quick that I'd stolen Nana's cuffs to give up to some unknown lady in exchange for Naira. I'd betrayed years of trust and bonding between my grandmother only to see her show up here, ready to help me clean up my mess. Returning her cuffs was the first thing I should have done when she showed up on Lyle's doorstep.

Hailey slid the backpack gently toward me, as if it contained a bomb about to detonate.

Last night, they didn't feel like anything more than two heavy pieces of cold metal. This time they gave off an energy like they were humming with electricity, and when my finger touched the first one, it zapped me like static shock. I snatched my hand back to my chest quickly, letting out a tiny yelp. Nana's mouth quirked in response.

"Do not do that again," Nana said.

I waited for her to get the cuffs herself. I didn't want another zap and hesitated going for them again. Nana waited me out. I'd taken something that didn't belong to me. I needed to give it back.

I sighed, learning my lesson, resigning myself for another jolt of current to my still-stinging finger.

I shoved both hands into the mouth of my bag and grabbed the cuffs hard, bracing my body, baring my teeth. When nothing happened, I looked at my grandmother, who watched me, amused, her eyebrow still raised.

A little embarrassed, I pulled them out and offered them up to their rightful owner. She took them, uncovering them. She looked down at them and they seemed to flash in the spotty sunlight.

She put on the right cuff. It molded like a second skin to her lower arm, a few inches above her wrist. She twisted it, positioning it just right so the blue gem gleamed so brilliantly, beams seemed to come from it.

Nana Ama held her empty hand out, open palmed and waiting expectantly.

It took a second or two . . . maybe three, for me to catch her hint, and I quickly placed the left cuff on Nana's outstretched palm.

As we raced through the back roads toward the city, Nana finally started talking.

"Before you begin your questions, child, I will say my piece. And then if you still have questions, we will discuss them after this is over. I can only share enough to help us get Naira back."

It was more of the same. Nana still keeping things secret when it was her secrets that got us here.

"And Luke," Hailey reminded. "He must be there too."

Sekou and I shared a look knowing Luke was the last person on my grandmother's mind.

Nana said, "If Luke is truly afflicted with the kwandamu—the hollowing—then it is too late for him. I am sorry for it, for what my sister, Effie, has done."

Hailey put her fist to her mouth to stifle the sob or cry that was going to come out of it. It sucked the air out of the car. Before I knew what I was doing, my hand found hers and gave it a squeeze. I felt Hailey take in a surprised breath and look down at where our hands intertwined.

"What is the kwandamu used for?" I asked.

"To control humans. It is a poison my sister and I learned we could inflict on humans if we were not careful when we fed or hunted. It put them under our sway. It is a violation, Addae, do you understand?" She looked at me in the visor's mirror. "It is an affront and no different than enslaving a person."

"But what if the person chooses it?" Sekou asked. "Is it like being an Abotisa?"

It was a question Sekou had to ask, one I wondered myself. But it hurt that he felt he had to ask. It meant he doubted our own relationship. Thought that somehow he might be another version of enslaved to me. All of that from one simple question.

Lyle spoke up. "Becoming an Abotisa is a choice you make, Sekou. And you can see it is a choice you can make to leave it. Like I did. The hollowing and being an Abotisa are entirely different, because you lose yourself from the hollowing. Even if you choose it, it would be because you didn't understand what would happen."

Sekou shot me an uneasy glance. I couldn't meet his gaze. I was too much in my feelings and fighting the insult that he'd think I'd ever take advantage of him in that way. Use him or anyone in that way. I thought my best friend knew me better than that.

"Sorry," he mumbled sheepishly. "This is a lot, you know?"

It was a lot. And for once I wasn't trying to act based off my emotions.

"I would never make anyone my slave," I told him, hoping he'd understand.

"The kwandamu is an evil use of our power," Nana Ama said. "No good comes from it, from what they become, if we do not take care."

Beside me Hailey deflated, no doubt thinking about Luke. Hell, even I felt bad for him. The way Nana Ama and Sheriff Lyle were telling it, Luke was done for, and there was no fix like Hailey believed. Luke was gone. Naira . . . she wasn't like him. Or, hadn't been when she'd finally been able to break through and reach out to me.

Lyle continued. "I believe Effie is using abalsoms as her army."

"For what?" Sekou asked.

Well, for nothing good obviously. She wasn't turning people into mindless zombie hordes to solve world hunger, that was for sure.

There was a more important question that needed to be answered. "What happened to Effie and where has she been?" I asked.

Nana said, "I thought she was dead."

"Why would you think that?"

Nana Ama paused before she spoke. "Because after the bounty hunters killed Effie, I was the one to bury her."

CHAPTER THIRTY-SEVEN

"I said I would never recount this story again," Nana Ama said. She shot Lyle a painful look, like she needed to draw strength from him instead of blood this time. "After I told you everything. That was . . ."

Lyle offered a quick glance and reassuring smile before returning to the road to focus on the many winding curves. It made me nervous whenever he took his eyes off. Plus he was going a little fast for my taste, making me think of Hailey behind the wheel. Nothing was that fast, thank Nyame. But Lyle could stand to take it down a bit. I kept my mouth shut though because there was no way I was going to ruin what would be a story of epic proportions.

"Nearly two hundred years ago—" She paused, her brows furrowing like she was unsure how to explain. "This thing we are is complicated. Before we came to be on that plantation, we never had the desire for blood, especially not human blood." Nana seemed to pick around parts of the story, giving us only the information she thought we needed to know. I wasn't sure if Hailey and Sekou could tell, but I knew how carefully she danced around her wording.

"We were caught by enslavers from Africa. One of the last ships here before trading enslaved people across the ocean was abolished. Effie and I didn't know how to get back home. We didn't know what it meant for our powers, as back home, we didn't have to deal with people like we did here. We were very . . . secluded, Effie and I.

"With the length of time away from home, we experienced untold horrors, along with all the other enslaved. We tried hard to assimilate. We didn't know how this new world would take supernatural people. But as more time passed, our needs became more primal. Food wasn't sustaining us. We were becoming weak, unable to work well in the day, unable to communicate telepathically between the two of us.

"Then I became pregnant, and we realized the craving we were having was for blood. We tried to deny it, but the hunger was too much. If we didn't become strong, soon the plantation owners would do away with us and take the baby.

"We held out as long as we could until we couldn't anymore. And that's when one of the overseers turned up dead in the forest. They thought he was mauled by an animal. I told Effie we couldn't feed like that, that we had to find another way. But the way human blood rejuvenated, reenergized, revitalized us . . . it was too much to pass up.

"More deaths started happening. Illnesses that presented as a wasting blood disease, or what was called consumption. Today maybe anemia. The hunt. The power was intoxicating to the both of us. But I tried to maintain for the baby—your mother.

"Superstition spread like wildfire across the plantation that we were witch sisters sucking the souls of the innocent. People were dying or coming up weakened from blood loss—that was me, because I learned how to take some blood without infection or death. The word that the plantation was cursed spread to neighboring plantations and word was that mobs were amassing to root out who was behind these killings and illnesses. It was a loss of money and production, you see.

"The others on the plantation came to us, begging for an end to it, for the killings to stop. Effie wouldn't listen to them. She'd decided to kill all the owners. She'd revolt and free the enslaved.

"But the bounty hunters got ahold of Effie's lover, Fitzroy, and killed him right in front of Effie's eyes. What they did to Fitzroy . . ."

There was a reason why Nana's stories were well known. She had a way of telling them. Of making them so visual you could see the images move across you. She was a true griot, a storyteller, and as she told this horrible story of my aunt, I could see it all as if I were there myself.

Nana looked to Lyle, and he nodded for her to continue. "Fitzroy's death was the final thing that did it, the final thread that held Effie together and allowed her to have reason. The men were coming for her next because they'd seen her with Fitzroy many times. She attacked them when they came for her. And she killed them horribly. I tried to help her. I told her we had to run, take the baby, and just run. But Effie wanted revenge for Fitzroy's death. And she had always wanted it for being stolen and for her treatment here. I couldn't convince her to run. She stayed and fought. I tried to fight, killing some alongside her. The plantation was in chaos. And I realized that we had made things worse for the others. We hadn't thought of the effect our revolt would have on them. We hadn't asked what they wanted to do. And then there was the baby. Who would care for her? She couldn't grow up not being free. I told Effie we needed to leave.

"Effie was enraged . . . There was no reconciling with her, and she just killed and changed, and the bloodlust took her over. She was not herself anymore. She could get not only herself killed but the baby and me. She could get all of these human Black people killed because the blame would fall on them. We were in hiding by now. I was terrified and I kept begging her that we needed to go. She changed into an adze. You know what that means."

Nana Ama looked pointedly at me. She wouldn't say aloud, especially with Hailey in the truck, the thing that was not only our greatest strength but our greatest weakness.

"I ran with the baby. They caught Effie, she lost her amulet, and they killed this devil monster they couldn't explain. They left her body so they could get other people to come see it, this monster that had been making everyone sick or dead. I knew they would search for me because if there was one, there would be the other. I asked one of the people running with me if they'd watch the baby. I changed and took my sister's body, burying her near Savannah, deep in swampland where I thought no one would find her. And that was the end of it."

"You didn't know that she was still alive?" I said, shocked. "When you took her?"

Nana shook her head. "I didn't know. She was dead in every sense of the word. I had no idea she was in a sort of living death. Remember, this was a first for us too. Being away from home transformed what we were. You being half human is new. That's why your Light—" Her eyes slid suspiciously to Hailey. "That's why we can't definitively say how and when, or even why, for you. I did what I thought I needed to do to save the baby and save myself and help to protect the others as best I could. Effie and I had wrought all these problems on them. We'd jeopardized them long enough, and I had to make amends. Effie would have eventually destroyed everything. She would have turned on our fellow Kinfolk on the plantation if she hadn't been killed and I hadn't buried her.

"I couldn't leave the proof of us, of adze. I couldn't let the men desecrate her body. We were on foreign land, but I needed to send Effie home properly, as had been custom in Africa. I spoke to the gods to protect her and see her to Asamando. I prayed and hoped she would never be discovered."

"But she was alive, Nana. Didn't you feel her essence? Her thread of life?" I thought about Naira's thread and how it called to me for help. The connection was weak, but it was still there. Wasn't there a connection between sisters?

"I didn't feel anything. Until that earthquake a few months back. Then I felt a faint emittance of energy, in and out. She has learned how to conceal herself from me. It's also been centuries, and our connection was severed. There, Addae, is your who and why."

I looked into Nana Ama's eyes, stunned by these revelations. I couldn't believe she'd kept so much pain and loss buried for so many years.

Out of the corner of my eye, I saw lights swing into view, growing brighter.

Then everything turned upside down and the world stopped cold.

CHAPTER THIRTY-EIGHT

The Explorer spun twice before crashing to a stop against a tree, the engine clicking like a time bomb. The unexpectedness and force of the impact was disorienting, the actions that came after happening in a flurry of movements and in a blurry haze. Hailey, Sekou, and Lyle were out cold, their heads against the windows and the steering wheel.

A pair of hands, fingernails long and sharpened to points, whipped in so fast I couldn't tell what was real and what was imagination. One hand wrapped its long, brown, elegant fingers around the seat belt that secured Nana Ama and plucked the belt right out of its housing like dental floss. Then they slid, almost lovingly, down to Nana, as if relishing in the feel of my grandmother, who tried in vain to beat at these powerful hands. They moved quickly because Nana's incapacitation and surprise were wearing off. The hands grabbed Nana by her jacket lapels and yanked her out of the car. The owner of those hands said nothing, but the intensity of its presence was staggering. There was no sound, no movement from anything else. Even the ticking time bomb of the stalled engine seemed to stop. I held my breath.

The next sound I heard was a *whoosh* and the wind blew harder, pushing a sickening smell into the car. And then the noises began. The noises from the alleyway outside Hailey's home. The noises of despair from my nightmares. All around the car, there were skittering nails on metal and scuffling on the dirt ground. Things, multiple things, grunted and keened as if in pain, as if hungry.

My vision went in and out as I fought to stay awake. My head throbbed and I was getting weaker and weaker, the nourishment from the small amount of blood I took from Hailey dissipating under all the pressure and exertion I wasn't used to. It was getting hard to stay awake and alert. To see who was prying open the doors and pulling us out. To fight against the sickly-sweet and rotting smell of infection flooding the car as the outside air blew in.

The voice I'd heard back in Charleston accompanied the glistening face of a pale Dr. Franco, with intelligent, red-rimmed eyes—Franco, the former lead researcher for the Endowment, bending down so he was eye level when it was only me left in the car. He held a phone to his ear.

"Thank you, Mr. Hall, for use of the Endowment resources. The . . . extraction went well. The lady thanks you and will provide you the samples you wish to have, as well as the return of your nephew."

I felt like I should know what he was talking about, but thinking was too hard at the moment. My head pulsated with too much sensory input. Too many of those things around me with the kwandamu steadily eating its way not only through their blood, but their very souls—there would be no Asamando for them. Franco wasn't like them, didn't have the hollowing devouring him from the inside out so he'd end up nothing but a human exoskeleton. But he didn't have the blood either. I wasn't sure what he was. He continued, speaking to whomever—whatever was waiting for his instructions.

His voice sounded far away, like he was moving away from me at lightning speed.

"Lock the others away until the lady is ready for them. And the girl—"

But the rest got swallowed up when I faded to black.

CHAPTER THIRTY-NINE

"Is she dead?"

"I don't think so? But, like, I don't know. We've been in here for a minute. I don't know what the hell is going on."

I recognized that voice as Sekou's. The other was the voice of a ghost. I forced my eyes to open, finding three heads peering over me like an umbrella. I blinked again as my brain fired on all synapses and called out names as my eyes jumped from face to face. Hailey. Sekou. Naira.

My breath caught. Naira!

"I'm not dead, yet," I croaked, waving them away so I could get up. I shot upright, unsure what to do first. Grab my best friend who I hadn't seen for what felt like an eternity? Punch her for scaring me and dragging me into all this shit? Cry? I was so happy to see her annoying self. I was happy to see the extra-long box braids with the electric-blue tips she'd been sporting before she left, her once fresh do now old with a lot of new growth at the scalp. Her clothes were dirty and torn. Like she'd been in a fight. Or, I guess, held prisoner by demented people, a mad scientist, and a royally pissed-off adze on a power trip. All things considered, Naira could have been worse off. She was alive. That's all that mattered.

"Where's my grandmother?" I asked.

I searched around the dank, dark cellar, once used to keep food supplies for a family centuries ago, now grayish, with contemporary lighting fixtures screwed into the stone walls. The lights made the whole thing look creepy and gloomy.

The room smelled of stale air and old dust and dirt and rot, lots of rot. A few dirt-crusted jars of preserved food still lined the built-in wooden shelves, among others that were broken either from someone or from years of rot and disrepair. I had so many thoughts sitting here. The first being that enslaved servants had bustled in and out of this room, grabbing items the cook needed for meals for the family, bringing in fresh jars and food to keep for the next meal. I could nearly see them going in and out.

"My grandmother?" I asked again, rubbing the fog away. I tried to concentrate, send feelers out for any sign of my grandmother, but there was too much noise around me, so much noise right on the other side of the locked door.

"They're keeping us in here," Hailey said.

"Keeping them out." I rotated my shoulders, testing what hurt and what didn't, finding myself feeling just fine.

If Hailey knew what I sensed, she'd prefer to stay in this locked room rather than out there with so many abalsoms, I couldn't count. Their hunger and want and need and pain and anger and all the bad things screamed out to me. They sounded like they came from one of Dante's nine circles of hell. And over the din of their noise I could feel the looming presence of Effie and another equal but lessened force that I knew had to be Nana Ama. Lessened and in pain. I could feel that. She was hurting and I couldn't help her.

"You came," Naira broke through my thoughts.

I hesitated. Ashamed for how we'd ended, how I'd turned my back on her. I couldn't ignore that Naira had brought me here, had made me bring my grandmother here, right to this woman's feet to probably kill Nana Ama. Because that's the only thing people with centuries-old vendettas had in mind.

We all made mistakes. It wasn't Naira's fault for wanting to go out and explore the world. To check out some history only to be kidnapped by an organization whose sole purpose was to take what wasn't theirs and own it. Just like the true invaders and gentrifiers that they were.

"Hey." I tried to smile and felt a cut on my bottom lip reopen. My arms opened and Naira crashed into me. Her body trembled uncontrollably against me. Her heart beat rapidly, so fast I worried it might burst through her chest. I could feel her terror, nearly taste it. It filled the room. I pulled away when I felt warmth on my shoulder and saw her face was slick with tears. I leaned forward, and Naira met me halfway, forehead to forehead. We were in the midst of hell, but this moment reunited with her was heaven.

Slowly, Naira explained everything she'd been through. The brief moments of happiness with Luke. The romantic boat ride. The storm that had been Effie, and being taken. Snapshots of broken memory. Luke becoming sicker and sicker. Naira trying to help him but him lashing out at her, scratching her, infecting her. Effie offering to help, and giving her blood that cured but not quite, making Naira open and accessible to Effie. Effie had seen the value in Naira. She'd seen Naira was the gateway to me, and I was the direct line to Nana Ama. But I also saw that all the while Naira fought against Effie. She couldn't become like the others had.

"She said I tasted like her. Like Nana Ama," Naira said out loud. "She said her blood healed."

Startled, I pulled away and looked where Lyle positioned himself near the door, standing sentinel, finding nothing in the room to use as a weapon. I understood now.

"What does that mean?" Naira asked.

"You know Nana Ama's elixir that she provides at the Festival?" I asked.

Naira nodded.

"The main ingredient is Nana Ama's own blood, which has healing properties and boosts your immunity. It's why the poison didn't have the same effect on you as Luke. The blood protected you."

From the floor, Hailey's breath hitched, drawing our attention. Her hand went to one of her ankles. She tugged at her sock.

"Have you been bitten?" Sekou asked sharply, having been quiet up to this point, not far from where Hailey sat. "Did any of them scratch you?"

She shook her head. "It's sore from the accident. I'm fine." She drew her legs up against her chest, clamping her hands around her ankles.

"We have to get out of here because she is not going to let any of us go. If she can't turn us, or make us abalsoms, or infect us with the hollowing, then she will kill us. No matter what she promises." Naira swallowed hard, averting her eyes from Hailey's. "She promised Luke and he . . . he . . ." She dropped her head into her dirt-crusted hands, blaming herself for being okay and for what happened to Luke. Luke was not.

Hailey said, "Luke's just sick. He can be cured just like you were. That's why I . . ." Her voice caught. "I was only trying to save him."

From the snatches of Naira's memory that she allowed me to extract, Luke was like the others, fed upon and too far gone. Whatever blood transference Effie had shared with him was only more of Effie's poison and had only prolonged his torture. Luke had been barely kept human for the sake of drawing in Hailey and using her and Naira to get to me, and then, to Nana Ama for the Endowment to experiment on her. For Effie to do . . . what to her sister?

Naira continued. "There are barely bits of him left. If we're lucky, maybe . . . but I don't know. I don't know what's going to happen now."

Sekou quietly processed everything. He had folded his long body up as small as he could make himself, and his right foot tapped beats only he could hear. I sensed how his mind repeated its mantra of how screwed up this was, how we were all going to die—it only stopped when Lyle straightened abruptly. The noise outside the locked door receded.

Lyle said, "Ready yourselves. They're coming for us."

CHAPTER FORTY

Franco, the lead Endowment researcher, opened the door with a couple of big burly guards on either side of him. Beyond them was a profusion of snarling and scampering, the abalsoms walking on all fours when they weren't being commanded. The smell of death from them was overpowering, and I nearly choked. Franco entered the room, assessing each of us coolly in his suit. His pale pallor and lightly red-rimmed eyes were the only indication that he was not bite free. Like Naira, Effie must have given him some of her blood.

"Come on. The lady awaits," he said pleasantly, as if inviting us to a grand ball or something. When no one moved, he barked, "Now!"

We jumped. The quickness with which he shifted from lord of the manor to terrifying villain was enough to give a girl whiplash. We scampered to our feet. Naira needed to be helped because she couldn't stand upright. She was bent over, spasms of pain hitting her with her sudden movement. I watched her, worried, wondering if she was going down the same path as Luke.

Lyle tried to put up a fight. But the two guards that came in with Franco were too much for him. They punched him hard in the gut and he doubled over, trying to suck in air.

Sekou tried to go to his aid, but he was no match for the guards. One stiff-armed Sekou, holding him by the throat at arm's length as if Sekou were nothing but a rag doll.

Franco sighed at me as if to say, *Must we do this?*

"It's easier if you just come along. Trust me, I know from experience." He looked around, assessing the scene. "Or I'll let them have you."

As if on cue, the noise from the abalsoms around us grew louder. Hailey cried out, covering her ears. She cowered, not wanting to go farther. As gently as I could, I nudged her along. We had to keep moving. I had no doubt Franco would do as he threatened.

I circled an arm around Naira to help her limp along. "Where does it hurt?"

"All over," she replied, "like from the inside out."

We had to find Nana the first opportunity we got and get out of this literal hell.

I was worried for Naira. She looked ashen, her lush, vibrant mahogany glow growing paler by the minute, her strength draining as if it were blood. We filed up the rickety wood staircase leading to the open space of the kitchen. Lyle swiped a palm over his bloodied nose, flicking the blood away.

The droplets flew into the abyss below us, to the abalsoms sticking their fingers through the spaces in the stairs. The zombies frenzied at Lyle's blood, a cacophony of their snarls and screams reverberating against the enclosed walls of the stairwell to deafening proportions. In this moment, we worked as one, all of us rushing, Franco and his henchmen included, hurrying up the stairs and closing the door to the cellars behind them before those things reached us.

We walked into the open kitchen and saw it was night outside, where more of the Endowment's hired goons stood around. The ones who'd rammed us and brought us here, I guessed. They had their weapons at the ready, their unease so thick, we could cut it with a knife.

"Don't linger out there in the dark," he continued. "With her preoccupied, they will be restless."

No one had to imagine who *they* were. We could hear them, rustling the trees, inhuman grunts and moans coming from out of the darkness. Not even the wildlife made a sound.

Franco continued, "Go straight to the van and back to the city. I'll check in with you in the morning."

"Mr. Hall said we're not supposed to leave without the blood samples and his niece and nephew," the guard who'd hit Lyle said gruffly. He pointed at the plastic biocontainer sitting on a make-shift workbench with empty glass vials and packaged syringes beside it.

"Do you want to tell her that?" Franco asked, head inclined toward the stairs leading to the second floor.

The Endowment guards shared glances that said they'd seen enough of Effie to never want to tell her anything.

They started to file out the back door, and I wondered: If they went with their guns, what would keep the things downstairs away from us?

Franco turned to us and said, "Let's not keep the new lady of the house."

We were ushered into the grand entryway, and there I was able to see it. I could almost imagine it in its former glory, if you could call it that. It wasn't glorious now, gutted out from the restoration project taking place on it and funded by . . . three guesses, the Endowment, this smarmy, mysterious organization. I couldn't tell you what their end goal was. All I could tell you was it was no good. Scaffolding and plastic sheets lined the walls, exposing the inner pipes of the house.

"They started putting in gas pipes for the fireplaces. Not trying to mess too much with the original makeup of the house, of course, but what do I know about restoring old houses? I'm an artifacts guy, myself." He laughed since he found himself so funny, and he was the only one.

"Watch your step. The floor is starting to go," Franco said helpfully as he led the group.

"Something is wrong," I said under my breath to the group so Franco couldn't hear as he continued his grand show of this decrepit place. Even if this was where Effie and Ama had been, why would she ever want to come back? There was nothing left of this mausoleum of horror but nightmares and angry ghosts. The energy of it rippled through the foundations of the building.

Effie bellowed, "It was not your choice to make!"

And then a crash, so hard the massive building trembled as if an earthquake had hit. Her rage, her howl of unrestrained rage, could only be directed at one person. My grandmother.

I didn't wait for anyone. I barely registered how the creatures below surged with renewed energy from their link to their master. They moved with her emotions. When she angered, they riled. When she was in control, they froze, like they did when they had Hailey and me surrounded.

Nana Ama said all of this was new. Abalsoms. The hollowing, a devastating infection that turned innocent humans to raging monsters. That the one person who'd kept them at bay and remaining below was confronting the one person for whom she harbored centuries' worth of growing hatred, and maybe for reasons anyone could understand if we really thought about it.

I raced up one side of the pair of curving staircases, jumping across the steps with holes in them, hoping I was going fast enough to not fall through to what was waiting below, to not get pulled back by Franco. Or maybe he was telling something else to stop, or maybe Lyle and Sekou had taken the opportunity to make their move. I didn't know. I didn't care. All that I could think about was getting up there and to my grandmother.

I reached the top of the steps, searching for where they were, trying to use both my physical and mental senses. But it was like I was being blocked, as if Nana was trying to keep me away. But she couldn't. The block she was putting up was being battered by something else, something like rage and revenge. Something like hate, and that was what I felt most of all when I finally found them in what must have been the rooms of the master and mistress of the house.

That was where I saw Effie, tall like Nana. Regal like Nana. Enraged unlike Nana.

I found Nana Ama was in the air, an invisible force holding

her against the wall that she had crashed into. Nana struggled against it, and when she saw me, any fight she had seemed to drain out of her.

She looked like Nana did when she didn't age herself to assimilate with humans. Effie looked no older than me. Except her eyes told of someone much, much older.

Effie's eyes, red to Nana Ama's gold, made their way down to me and caught me up in their snare. They froze me completely. She stared at me and I at her. She was beautiful. She was so young, as if she were no more than twentysomething. She watched me watching her, taking in all of her in her human form, with inhuman talons stretching from her fingertips.

And way below in the bowels of the house, the noise of the creatures amplified, Effie's hold on them loosening a bit more. I tore myself away from Effie to Nana, who had slipped down a little from Effie's distraction of me. If I could keep her busy, Nana could get free.

Two pairs of eyes looked up at me, one stunned and the other as if I was expected. I swung my gaze from my grandmother to her sister.

"There she is." Effie's smile was devious. "Fitting, don't you think, that the child be here to watch me rip your thieving heart out and drink you dry? You took everything from me. You have been living my life."

What did she mean Nana was living her life? My head felt like it would explode. I grabbed it, grimacing through its invasion.

"Because of that damnable choice," Effie said, answering my unspoken question. "Nyame, the supreme god." She said it like it was a curse. "Our choice to leave the pantheon of gods. Our punishment for doing so. Our father giveth and he taketh away."

Effie read my confusion with glowing crimson eyes, a stark and horrifying contrast to Nana's golden. One stoked fear and chaos to feed her rage while the other gave her life to use her damning blood to heal, to give life. Two twins with journeys vastly diverted. Different enough to physically change the same healing gift they had, their whole being, their adze into something like Effie, evil, vengeful, resentful, and wanting everyone to pay for what she'd been through.

"Dear child, you are mine." The word stretched for syllables, like she relished in my misery and shock, finding pleasure in the truth of where I came from.

"You are of *my* blood. She stole your mother, my child, from me and thus you as well. Look at the thief and the liar. She betrayed not only me, but you as well."

I looked at Nana, the only person who'd been there for me when my own mother couldn't. The one who'd still had faith in me even though my father was human and we didn't know how I would turn out from the first moment I started to feel charged, like I was lighting up from the inside out, and Nana said, "We'll ride out the unknown together." Nana still believed in me. More than I'd ever believed in myself. Yet that didn't keep her from lying to me my whole life.

Hadn't I thought those same things earlier? That Nana had betrayed me and lied? I was so angry and hurt then. I still was.

"Addae, look at me."

I did, caught in her hypnotizing eyes. Thinking how beautifully red they were.

"You are of my blood," she repeated, her voice like a snake charmer. Her words coiled themselves around me, constricting my brain in a vise, squeezing out any good thoughts I had.

How could I ever be of her blood and not of Ama's, who had spent years trying to pay for not only her mistakes, but Effie's as well? I could see that now. Centuries cultivating the elixir she had created from her blood and godly energy, offering the Kin choice of community and life if they accepted her gift. Ama had found a way to live and thrive without using humans as a meal ticket or thrusting them into mindless servitude, a new race of unthinking, unfeeling, forever-hungry shells of former selves. She didn't take lives unceremoniously.

Effie, on the other hand, had no care for life outside her own. And she would eventually only see me as one other thing to own. How was she any better than those who had enslaved her, who had traumatized her, whose evil had driven her to become this way?

I was the grandchild of *that*?

No way in hell!

I screamed, pushing Effie and her corruptive thoughts out of my head with everything I had.

The ground shifted beneath me, and Nana dropped like a sack of weights to the floor, released from Effie's mental hold on her already weakened body. She landed, one knee to the ground, steadying herself. She struggled to come to me.

I reached out. "Nana!"

"Don't call her that," Effie snapped. "Don't call her that ever again."

I tried to get to Nana, but Effie merely flicked her hand, pushing me back like I weighed nothing. I stumbled back with my arms pinwheeling to keep me upright as I careened into the narrow hall and into a group of abalsoms who had suddenly appeared with Luke stumbling ahead of them.

He was a complete mess. Thick, black veins had crawled all the way up to his scalp. His eyes looked rheumy, leaking tears of blood. His mouth looked horrible, teeth fighting one another for space in it. His once-blond hair was slimy and dirt- and blood-crusted, and hanging around his face like wet Silly String.

I struck my hands out to stop my backward momentum, hitting against the splintered doorframe. The wood caught my palm, snagging it, and ripped a chunk clean off. Bright blood dripped. Both Effie and Nana froze, both looking at me, one intrigued and the other in terror because they knew what blood spilled in this house of horrors meant.

On the other side of the doorframe, I stopped myself, where I'd noticed Luke and the rest hulking there, all semblance of their humanity lost because these were the ones most far gone. They breathed collectively. Like sharks, they circled me, the scent of my blood churning in the air, filtering into the noses they were sniffing the air with. Until they caught the scent of my blood.

And my being an adze or not made no difference to them.

They snarled, hissing at me as one, the scent of blood thick in their nostrils while inside, the two sisters went at it again. Nana

Ama made a run for me, breaking Effie's control of them. She couldn't control someone as strong as Nana and keep her monsters at bay and see to me at the same time. Even Effie had her limitations.

I backed out past the monsters, my hands held out to hold them at bay. Dumb move, because my hand was still bleeding and it only churned them up even more. The abalsoms' humanoid claws were ready to scratch every piece of skin from my bones. I shuffled back, trying to keep space between them and me. Could I take them on? All of them?

I snuck a peek over my shoulder, noting the banister and the railing overlooking the front hall of the plantation home only a couple feet behind me, with the abalsoms closing in. I could hear yelling from down below and commotion as Lyle and Sekou tried to get past Franco to the stairs.

The abalsoms pushed me toward the edge, closer and closer—toward the railing, the rickety one where a piece of rotted, hollowed-out wood had come off in my hand when I'd grabbed it to run up the stairs, spraying dusty petrified wood, now like sawdust, in the air.

There was no time for any more thought before the mob of them turned their doomed, reddish eyes on me and lurched forward in a throng, throwing their bodies into me, slamming into me like a cement truck. My body reeled back, my hands windmilling to gain a hold on something, anything that would stop me from falling over. Nothing was there but air. And to the horrified screams of Hailey, and Sekou, and Sheriff Lyle below, I catapulted over the banister.

I sailed through the air, watching the falling zombie creatures coming in behind me. The world began to go out of focus. A ball danced in front of me, or dots of light from the stars in my vision, and there appeared a blurry image of a woman. She smiled down at me. Nana Ama? My mother? Come back from the sea?

Her whisper was a den of snakes coiling themselves in a tight ball around my brain. She pointed at me with her long-nailed finger. Touched it to my forehead.

"Go back, child, and learn." Her voice was low and menacing.

Everything around me brightened, became hot. Too hot. I thought Effie had sent me to hell. I burst through the rotting floor below like it was paper. I kept falling, crashing through layers and layers of colors and temperatures, and smells and climates and times of day and night.

So this is how I'll die were my last thoughts.

Then, suddenly, the stale, old, putrid smell of decay was replaced with one of honeyed fragrances and savory spices. The air warmed and became as bright as the sun. As bright as the Light that would emit from my grandmother in firefly form. I hit the ground.

My body smashed to the earthen floor below in a plume of brown copper dust, the impact so hard my bones felt like they shattered, crunching, splintering apart.

CHAPTER FORTY-ONE

Spurts of laughter forced my eyes open to blinding sunlight. Or what I thought was sunlight. It was too bright. I snapped my eyes back shut, afraid the brightness would burn my retinas. *This was what it feels like to be dead.* My body felt crumbly, like cookie dough with not enough butter mixed in. All signs pointed to dead. Yet there was sensation tingling in my body, my fingers and toes were wiggling. Wherever I landed must have been the afterlife because nothing else made sense.

The laughter came again, sounding like kids. I started taking a mental scan of my body, going down section by section from my head until I reached my toes. They wiggled back at me. I was fine.

I opened my eyes, adjusting them to the brightness of a sky. There was a slight breeze that was neither too hot nor too cold, soothing. The place, wherever I was, felt soothing. It's the best I could explain it. I sat up, my hands landing in soft carpet-like grass, and took a good look around. I was in a garden. No, maybe woods. There were trees of every kind all around, from southern oaks to baobabs.

The forest surrounding me was filled with tall trees. Taller than I'd ever seen. The path I was on curved, cutting though them. It was endless. The flora, plants and flowers I didn't recognize, were vibrant with colors, as if I was looking at them through the latest high-def TV screen.

From Nana Ama's stories, I was in the world of the Skies, the Oosoro, which stretched over Akanland. Her true homeland.

I recognized it all. Ahead, a mountain loomed into the sky, its peak hidden, with lights of gold and white moving slowly around it like a wispy haze. Behind me, the path I was on continued down, and I could choose to head up to the mountain where the Sky God must live or down the winding path to the human world of Asase.

I heard laughter again, so close to me, and suddenly running past were two young women—maybe my age, maybe in their twenties. Both wearing white gauzy fabric that shimmered when it caught the sun. One had a top that wrapped like a bandeau around her chest. The other's top came over one shoulder. They wore skirts that hung low in the back and swept up over both legs in folds in the front. With the skirts was a thin length of roped fabric, which knotted up beneath the belly button and cascaded down the front in several golden threaded ropes.

Sisters, wrapped in beaded jewelry of cowries and precious gems from head to toe.

The first sister, the one leading the way, wore what almost looked like a breastplate of golden chains and multicolored gems matching the cuff about her neck. Rows and rows of singular strands hung low between her breasts, and in the middle of these hundreds of thin, golden strands sat a large blue gem, where they all attached and spilled out from.

The other wore a set of wrist cuffs that nearly took up the entire length of each forearm. They were thick, forged golden metal with intricate designs and etchings that crisscrossed around them. And in the middle of each sat brilliantly blue stones. Stones within a pair of cuffs that I'd seen all my life.

They were heading straight for me, looking nearly identical, looking like child versions of my grandmother and her sister, looking at me.

No, looking through me. They could not see me even though I was right in their path.

The sister who led them said, "Come, sister, let us go see if what Uncle says is true. You know he is known for his stories and his little tricks. I want to see if he tricks us now. Before the gates close."

My breath hitched. *No way.* My real world colliding with the countless spoken tales of Anansi the Trickster God.

"We mustn't, little sister," the elder sister said. Her perfectly shaped eyebrows frowned with worry as she looked at the sky. "The time is getting late for the gates to close. And the baby . . ." She gestured to her sister's stomach where the tiniest round bump could be seen beneath the armor-like amulet.

That was when the younger one, who had stopped to face her sister, rolled her eyes, annoyance clearly written on her face.

"The baby, dear worried sister, will be just fine." She said it with the impatience and attitude of a younger sister done with her older sister's overprotection. "As will we."

The elder sister continued, "Father says we are not to go to the human world. We are not to interfere in their matters. No one is unless he allows it, and he never does. It is his command."

The younger twin in the lead stopped suddenly, spinning on her heels to give her troubled sibling her full attention. I inched closer to get a better look at them.

"Father should walk among the people more often, as he used to do. Then he'd remember that sometimes it is necessary for us to intervene. Those of us with power have the responsibility to help those of us who do not."

She left her words hanging in the air, heavy with meaning that would stand the test of time. She took a deep breath as she placed a hand on her sister's shoulder and patted it gently. Her voice became light. "But fear not, we will not 'interfere.' You, nervous one, don't even have to go."

Unease lined the elder sister's face, so much so that everything about her drooped. "You are much too headstrong."

"And you are much too safe. Like Father. Let your fears keep you here, sister," the younger sister quipped, two tiny canines barely peeking out as she smirked.

She was about to resume walking when her sister told her to wait. Impatiently, her weight switching from one foot to the other, she played with the strands covering her chest. Her whole vibe said, *Well?*

"We must obscure the safoas that permit us reentry through the gates. Should something happen and they get into the wrong hands . . ." The elder sister trailed off, blinking away sudden tears, unable to continue. She let out a breath. "At least let us listen to Father in that regard."

The younger twin wasn't buying it, but she humored her sister anyway. Anything to stop her worry.

The elder twin placed her hands over the blue gem at the middle of her sister's chains. The younger twin intertwined her sister's arms so each hand rested on the opposite cuff. Together they bowed their heads, closed their eyes, and waited.

Three tiny specks of light like fireflies appeared beneath their hands and began to grow until they were the size of orbs. I could barely understand what I was seeing. Their hands glowed as they eased down, like when the sun's rays moved throughout the day, shrouding the cuffs and the amulet in its yellowish-white glow. I could hear a tiny sizzle as wisps of smoke rose from the jewelry.

The twins absorbed the pain of their jewelry being branded into their skin. I felt the pain with them, my own face a mask of grimaces. I hissed through my teeth imagining how the burn must be feeling. Then, as quickly as it had started, the whole thing was done. The cuffs and the amulet had been absorbed into their skin, becoming a part of them, looking like masterful art. A network of designs etched into their skin, and the blue gems, no longer brilliant, were now dulled and branded on them.

The younger sister was the first to open her eyes. "There. Are you satisfied? Can we go or would you rather stay here? We don't have to do everything together. You certainly didn't marry like I did or make a child." She rubbed her barely there belly.

The elder sister slowly opened her eyes. "I didn't fall in love like you did, sister."

"Stay. I will not mind." The younger sister turned heel and made a break for it, running straight through me.

My body fragmented from the disturbance of her energy with mine. I reassembled as she shivered, muttered something about the chill, and charged forward, her arms pumping at her sides, into the woods on the trail to the Asase.

The concern was so evident in the elder twin's face that I reached out. Her fear was palpable. She grimaced, and when she spoke, there was a whole lot of resentment packed behind her words. "Where you go, Effie, I go."

Her words froze my incoming hand in midair, the confirmation of who she was making its way to me.

Ama, my grandmother, moved through me like a ghost, our energies merging, then separating when she went through. But unlike her younger sister, she slowed until she stopped. Ama turned back, her face full of wonder and question as she looked back at where I stood. She stared hard at where I was, putting myself back together again. But unlike before, when it was like they couldn't see me, this time it was as if she did. Not only was she staring where I was, it was like she was looking directly at me. Like we were looking at each other.

"Who is there?" she asked, squinting.

I tried to answer, to tell her to stop and to stop Effie from going down the trail, but no words came out. In this world Above—or in the memory of it—I was the voiceless.

CHAPTER FORTY-TWO

Like a flick of a light switch, I wasn't in the forest where I'd started out. I was deposited at the end of the path that wound in the steep curves of one continuous S up the mountain and deep into the realm of the Above. In front of me were two massive, ornate closed gates.

They were also made of gold with luscious, thick vines of ivy and moss winding through and on top of each of the closely placed golden pillars, which were as thick as small tree trunks. I realized each of the pillars were spears, the tops of them pointing dangerously in the sky. I couldn't help thinking about if something fell from the sky and was impaled on one of the many sharp-edged tips. Tiny, cupped flowers of every color imaginable dotted the vines.

There were no levers or latches to open or close the gates. Carefully, because I didn't want to damage any of the delicate petals or smudge the shiny gold, I placed my palm against the metal, finding it cold to the touch, cold to the point of burning. Reflexively, I pulled my hand back, not expecting the sensation.

But I could hear commotion on the other side, could see a mass of people who looked like me and the backs of the twin sisters as they approached them.

"Wait," I called after them. I'd seen scenes like this before me in history books, on countless movies. Scenes of masses of people being lined up. Having their hands bound. Being tethered together by rope, one after the other, by the waist, or in the cases of these people, by the neck.

But seeing it in person was a completely different experience.

I watched as the men on horses holding rifles and handguns corralled the people as if they weren't . . . people. Screaming curses at them, spit flying as they looked down at the dazed and shocked African people as if they were nothing. My heart and my body ached at the sight of it.

I knew where they were going. I knew what would become of this hundred, as it had so many before them and so many after. I'd seen plenty renditions of it, but it was nothing like seeing it with my own eyes. It was something that would stay with me forever.

I pushed and pushed against the gate, but it wouldn't give.

"Wait!" I yelled after the sisters. "Come back. Don't go down there."

But they couldn't hear me. I still had no words. And I wasn't really there. This had already happened and I hadn't been there.

They got farther away from me, but even as they got farther and farther, they grew closer and closer toward the people and what I now saw was a gray shoreline lined with tiny boats being filled with people to be carted off to the tall, dark, massive ships bobbing ominously in the whitecaps, their stained sails fluttering in the wind.

It was as if I were seeing Effie and Ama through a mirror, as if they were right there. But they were not. They had gone well beyond their realm. They were not as close as I thought, even though it felt like they were right there and I could touch them, feel them, as I did when they ran through me back in the clearing.

They inched along the bushes, trying not to be seen. They hid behind big ones and I could see them arguing between themselves, so deep into what they were saying—I could imagine it, Ama begging Effie for them to turn back. Effie shaking her head vehemently, refusing to come back without helping the captured people in some way. Intervening as their father had told them to never do among humans. They didn't know they'd been heard. They didn't see four of the invaders coming up behind them, their guns pointed. Didn't see them at all. But I did.

"Behind you!" My warning was absorbed into the ether. I wasn't really here. I was just a witness to something that already happened and couldn't be altered.

Screw the cold. I placed both hands to the gates, ignoring the sting, and pushed. The gate didn't give, not an inch. I pushed again with more force this time. Nothing. I backed up a couple steps, trying to see where the gates ended or if there were places where I could get through. Nothing.

But it was too late. The men were upon them. The twins turned, fear so plain in their eyes that it pierced me where I stood—where I had to watch, unable to help, unable to do anything at all.

"How'd we miss these two?" one of the men asked. He pointed at them. "And what are those markings on them?"

Ama shielded Effie and her little round belly. Ever the protector, ever the big sister even if only by minutes. Her arm was fully exposed, showing that instead of the gleaming, golden cuff, dark raised markings like a tattoo and a fraternity brand were embedded in her skin. And when another of the assholes yanked them apart, Effie's regal amulet was revealed, now embedded into her skin, the once brilliant blue gem having lost its luster in this setting.

The man gripped her face, though she fought hard to get from his grasp, and twisted her head left and right as he decided if she'd be too marked up to sell.

"Just markings of her people. That's what they do, paint and cut each other. They think it makes them beautiful."

"Nothing will ever make them that," another sneered.

But the man on the horse studied them keenly. "These two are the most beautiful I've seen yet. Black or not, they are striking. Plus, have you looked upon a mirror yourself lately, Thorson? No woman would have you. Not even one of these savages."

In a blur, Effie lashed her hand out as if she were throwing something at him, like a beam of godly light, a curse, something that would spew forth and strike him where he stood. Nothing happened.

She stared down at her hands, first the backs, then the palms, in horror and disbelief. She looked up at Ama, wide-eyed, who stared back. They could not fight. They'd lost not only their way back home, but whatever powers they possessed as well.

The men gathered the twins without any more fight, and neither of the goddesses reacted. They only stared past the gates and through me at their home in the Skies, their eyes giving away their anguish and disbelief that they were truly lost. Then they were carried down to the shores where the last of the rowboats would push them off to the looming, dark ships waiting just beyond.

As they set sail, the twins watched their home—with its majestic gates, the bounty of multicolored flowers, the outline of the highest mountain draped in mists, with a ringlet of golden Adinkra signs circling its peak just as they had in my dream—begin to fade away, as they were warned it would. Their world folded into the thickening mist, closing itself off to them forever, their keys no longer able to open it.

There was a sensation building in me, and I touched my lips. My fingers came away red with blood; the rich metallic tang filling my mouth tasted like life. My tongue ran across the ridge of my top teeth, stopping where my canines had descended.

I flipped around, pressing my back against the gates, nestling against fragrant foliage to see the last images of the Oosoro, wavering before me like rising heat. The deep sadness was overwhelming, was nothing I'd ever felt in my life. The grief cascaded over me because I knew what would come next for Ama and Effie, for all of those African souls on that ship with them, the ones who came before and after, and the people who'd be born enslaved on foreign soil for years to come. There was nothing I could do to stop it. There was nothing *they* could have ever done. Even when they were gods.

This was how the story of the adze had begun.

CHAPTER FORTY-THREE

For the second time, I woke up, but instead of to the tranquility of a magical forest, it was to chaos. My head was pillowed in a lap. She was calling my name, bringing me back from the past, from the time I'd spent in Ama and Effie's world. I woke up feeling the pain of their loss and their fear in my heart. And a sense of disbelief that I was a descendant of Nyame, the maker of gods, that not only was I an adze, but half goddess—or a quarter. Something like that.

Not only that. Ama wasn't my actual grandmother.

It was Effie.

I tried to sit up, woozy, and held my head in my hand until my vision cleared. I realized then a couple of things: I could move without any problem when I knew that every bone in my body broke when I hit the ground. And the person with me was Effie.

I startled, moving quickly away from her as she remained kneeling on the floor. She put her hands up in the air as if to say she meant no harm. Blood trickled from her chin and my own mouth tasted of iron.

"This batch was faulty," she said, moving to a more comfortable position on the floor. She propped her arm on her knee and studied me. We were in another room, maybe the parlor. I had been lying on an old dusty lounge chair that had become hard and brittle over time. The room was clotted with thick, swirling dust, and the rot from the abalsoms permeated the air, even in here, though it was not as strong. There was the faintest whiff of gas in the air, and I remembered what Franco had said about the renovation. I looked back at Effie with new eyes.

"Where—where is everyone?" I stammered.

"Awaiting our return. Because I am going to give you a choice." The way she looked at me was unnerving, so calculating and curious, like she was trying to learn me.

Effie's voice was like honey, but there was poison and the promise of death lacing every syllable. She spoke like she was from an ancient world and was trying to become accustomed to our way of speech. Hers was old and rustic whereas Nana Ama's had been softened and molded over the time she'd spent living among the Gullah Geechee people, the people who had reminded her most of home.

Franco, haggard and aging, looking nothing like the vibrant picture of him I saw at the Endowment offices, walked in.

"My abalsoms are still a work in progress, as I am still figuring out the—what is it I heard the human say the other day, Franco? The arrogant one who simpered like a baby before I drank him and his arrogance dry?" She grinned wickedly, her long, curved teeth showing.

"Kinks," he volunteered.

She snapped, her long blackened nails and fingertips catching in the light. "Kinks. I'm still working the kinks out. So, I regret they caused your fall. But you are well now, yes? I have mended you?"

The iron taste in my mouth was unfamiliar, and I realized it wasn't my blood.

It was hers.

I could feel its power surging through my veins like liquid fire, healing my body and filling it with vitality.

"We shall not be much longer." She waved away her servant, the Renfield to her Dracula, with a flick of her fingers. That's when I noticed the cuffs on her wrists. Nana Ama's cuffs. They looked so wrong there.

"Where is your amulet? The one I saw in the dream?"

She watched me for a long time before answering. And instead of speaking, she pulled apart the opening of her cloak, revealing the amulet against her chest. "For safekeeping until I return back to my homeland and to the front gates of the Oosoro. My memory has told you what they are now, yes? My amulet and Ama's cuffs are needed to unlock the door. Together. Our father always wanted us together. Not one twin without the other. Except Ama and I will never be together again."

She sounded a little wistful.

"When I return without her, the trick will be on him. I guess Anansi is not the only trickster in the family?" She laughed, but there was no humor in it, only bitterness.

"You did not know of your lineage? Of our history?" Effie asked, her head cocked to the side as she studied me. Her teeth glinted and her dark pupils held a crimson circle in the low light. Crimson, not gold like Nana Ama's.

"Because I do as is our nature now. I feed how we're supposed to feed. On humans. Often. Until they are dead. I do not care. Your auntie's"—she emphasized the word and made it sound as if it were a curse—"eyes glow gold because she is weak and would rather take bits and pieces than accept who we have become. We no longer have palm oil to sustain us in the Skies. We have what this damned world of humans has provided for our sustenance, their blood. Their essence. Their obedience as our abalsoms."

Our abalsoms. Monsters *was more like it,* I thought.

Effie balked. "What do you consider these humans who live with you and Ama, these—" My head pulsed, my mind being raked too hard. "Kinfolk?" she finished.

She had no problem invading minds without permission. The act was so invasive and a violation. I wanted so much to push her out so my thoughts could be my own.

"Are these humans who swear fealty to you nothing but better versions of my followers?" Effie asked.

"Yours are monsters. Yours are sick with the hollowing, and they'll never be human again. They're zombies," I replied.

She laughed. "Zombies. Is that what they are here? What makes your Kinfolk any different or better, girl? They follow your ways. They do your bidding. Even though Ama doesn't always feed to kill, she has killed to feed, and still might on occasion, which makes her no better than me."

It was way too much coming in at once. I needed space from her. From Effie's words that made too much sense. From Nana

Ama's love and care, the only parent I'd really known even when my mother was alive.

A small smile played on Effie's lips as she read my thoughts like I was an open book, stoking the confusion, the rage, the betrayal of a denied history and lineage.

I shook my head, still woozy, images of the dream that wasn't a dream crystal clear in my mind. I was having a hard time remaining in the present. I wanted to go back. I wanted to see the god who was my great-grandfather.

Effie said, "Good. That anger you are beginning to feel toward the liar. Keep that, Addae, hold it in you and thrive from it. Then you will really be like your true grandmother. Like me."

She was right. My anger was an oncoming train with its horn blaring.

I was enraged at Nana—at Ama—for the lies she told me. But they weren't lies. Not directly. She omitted the truth. Lies of omissions were just as bad as lies told directly. Weren't they? But what was the harm in telling me where I came from? Why did she hide the fact she had a twin sister, that the Above was her home, and what had happened to her and her sister? Nana Ama had even hidden her age. Not centuries old and a former enslaved. But thousands of years old, maybe millennia.

Why didn't she trust me enough to tell me any of that?

A red mist clouded my line of vision, and I closed my eyes to clear it. I couldn't think this way. I wasn't in control of my emotions. The blood Effie used to repair me was affecting me in ways I didn't like. It was like a bad acid trip, like the inability to trust anyone seeping in. Paranoia and rage.

Ama had lied by omission, yes. But there had to be a reason why she'd left Effie behind.

Effie's anger simmered and her eyes blazed, making me waver even with her blood and her story. I couldn't throw away the last eighteen years of my life. Nothing compared to how long Ama and Effie had lived and what they'd been through, but I'd been around long enough to know all the good Nana Ama has been doing. Despite all Nana kept from me, she loved and protected me. She'd tried to raise me to be a person who helped, not a person who hurt. Nana would always be my grandmother.

"And what's wrong with a little hurting after what they have done to people like you and me on this godforsaken rock?" Effie said.

"There is a difference between your abalsoms and the Kinfolk. *They* have choice. They are human. They live without fear from her," I said weakly. "But most of all, they are our family."

Effie drew back as if I'd struck her. The red of her eyes flashed and her hand raised like it would hit me. I flinched, waiting for the blow that would take my head off.

"*I* am your family, Addae. Ama has denied you that. Had denied your mother *me*. Your mother might still be alive today if I had been afforded the chance to raise her."

I swallowed the knot in my throat. I didn't want to think about my mother. She wouldn't have wanted this. I just knew it. I didn't answer, waiting for Effie to kill me.

She took a cleansing breath, channeling the last bit of patience she had for me. She rose to standing in one fluid motion, not needing anything to assist her.

"Get up," she commanded. "This ends now."

CHAPTER FORTY-FOUR

Effie pulled me up by my elbow. My knees buckled beneath me, and she held me up until I could get my footing. She was supposed to be my grandmother, but there was nothing at all grandmotherly about her.

She led me back into the grand foyer, to where I'd fallen through the main level and down into the cellar with the abalsom horde.

Simon Hall, with his perfectly tailored suit and Italian leather shoes and sharp facial features, was there in the middle of a heated argument with Franco: "I need the damn samples, Franco. I'm not leaving here without—" Simon stopped when we entered, bowing his head in fear or reverence. I thought he would have stayed back at the college commanding his guards from the safety of his research facility. Guess not.

"Why is he still here?" Effie asked, scowling as she prodded me ahead of her.

Franco shrugged. "He's demanding his samples."

"Just a little, Awuraa." He stumbled over the unfamiliar word.

"Something to begin our research right away." He looked at Luke. "For my nephew."

Effie sneered at him, baring her teeth so he shrank back, his arms drawing up. "You'll get what I give you when I give it to you. Or you can be the one that feeds them." She cast her eyes down at the jagged hole in the floor where abalsoms writhed.

He slammed his mouth shut, and Franco cackled with immense pleasure.

The foyer was littered with the dead ones who'd toppled over with me from the second floor, except one was still alive. Luke. His head was in Hailey's lap as she whimpered. She looked around, making sure no one was watching, and she leaned to the side, her ankle drawing up to meet her. I thought it was bothering her again, but instead of rubbing it, she slipped two fingers between sock and skin, and pulled out a tiny clear glass vial, the size of trial tube of perfume, with a black rubber stopper.

I checked to see if Effie had noticed. She wasn't looking Hailey's way. Hailey shielded her movements, plucking the stopper out. She held it in one hand, using her other to pry Luke's ruined, blackened lips apart. She tipped the vial upside down, pouring the shimmering reddish liquid into his mouth, murmuring in his ear.

He didn't move at first. And then he bucked once, his body arching. His bloodied fingers went to this throat and he struggled, grimacing. His arms flopped to his sides. Then he stopped moving. Hailey looked at me with huge, wide eyes begging me to understand why she'd hidden the vial from us. She held his ruined hand, watching to see if he'd come back to her.

Meanwhile, Simon continued to stand guard, glancing at his nephew and niece with a worried expression. He hadn't anticipated all of this. He probably thought he'd be able to control an angry ancient goddess. He had thought wrong. Between Simon and Franco, Simon could be reasoned with. Franco was too far gone, having taken Effie's blood and becoming her familiar. Franco was irrational and jittery, alternating from foot to foot as he kept arguing with Hailey's uncle Simon. Franco kept his gun on Sekou and Lyle to keep them in line. Lyle tracked Franco's every movement, waiting for the right moment to make his move.

Nana Ama was in bad shape. Signs of a fight painted her body in hues of deep crimson and purple. Blood ran from her nose and from a cut above her eye. I had never seen her look so breakable, and my body ached knowing she was in so much pain.

Below us, in the hole I'd opened up, was the horde of abalsoms, crabs in a barrel clambering over one another to get at the blood they smelled from Ama.

I was happy to see everyone was there, alive. I shared a look with Sekou, shaking my head so he wouldn't come knocking at my mind's door. Effie would hear us as easily as Nana had.

Effie inspected them one by one, her disgust growing until her eyes finally rested on Ama. She took stock of Nana from head to toe as her sister nursed a wounded arm, sitting against the wall, a couple of dead abalsoms at her feet. Gingerly, Nana Ama rose to her feet, wincing as she did.

"Can you not heal yourself?" Effie asked incredulously. "What have you done to yourself? You are the daughter of Nyame the Sky God. How is it I can bind you with ropes and make you bleed?

You should feed as is your true nature. You have your choice here. How about the girl you came to save? Your Kin?" She stretched the word. It was an insult coming from her.

Effie released me, setting Naira in her sights. Naira's eyes widened; like Simon, she shrank back, crab crawling backward until she was next to Luke and Hailey, against the scaffold leaning on the wall, long plastic sheets swaying in the wind. She stuck out her arms, making as if to ward Effie away.

Effie stalked over to her, ignoring my demands to leave Naira alone. I blocked her, trying to slow her down or stop her, but Effie flung me away as if I weighed nothing. Naira kept shaking her head, pleading *no, no, no*. She didn't want to be in Effie's clutches. Never again.

Franco cackled in the background, cheering Effie on like the sad little man he was. He swung his gun from Hailey to Luke, then Sekou to Lyle, enjoying the way they swayed to avoid the gun's barrel. I heard a long, low moan. I turned my head to see that Luke, who not too long ago had attacked me with nothing but emptiness in his eyes, was moving slowly as if waking.

His eyes shot open, and the previous vacantness, like no one was home, now showed signs that someone had returned. His pupils normalized as he studied us, his ravaged face showing the faintest semblance of humanity in his eyes, eyes I realized were much like his sister's. His mind was a muddled mess, his body warring with itself, the hollowing against the taste of elixir Hailey poured down his throat, each trying to regain control. I let out a burst of short breaths. Luke's mind was lucid, if only temporarily, and he was sorry. He was in pain. He was in a panic, knowing he could not hold on for much longer and that Hailey needed to get away from him before he lost his inner battle.

Effie was too lightning quick, lunging for Naira so fast it was like a movie on four-speed fast-forward. She grabbed Naira's braids, wrapping them around and around her fist to tighten the hold, and yanked her away from Hailey's and Luke's outstretched hands.

Effie's eyes narrowed to slits, noticing Luke for the first time, that he was there when he should have been gone, like the others down below or lying dead around the room.

"What is this?" she asked in complete surprise. Her head turned toward Franco, and a sheen of sweat popped up on his face. "How is this possible?"

The gun trembled in Franco's hand. He blubbered, stammering an unintelligible response as he searched frantically for an answer that wouldn't incur Effie's wrath. Hailey tried too late to slowly put the vial where she'd gotten it, and it slipped from her hand, dropping to the floor with a *ting*, and rolling.

He zeroed in on the vial. "His sister. She's given him something. I couldn't stop her *and* hold them." He pointed at Sekou and Lyle, who ducked away with every careless wave of his gun.

Simon studied the vial, his greed quickly replacing his fear. Slowly, he inched closer to his niece and nephew as if a lion were in front of him.

Effie stared at the vial, disbelief clouding over her face, then her head snapped around, zeroing in on Hailey, who shrank beneath her glower.

"What," she growled, "did you do to him?"

"She gave him a taste of my elixir," Nana Ama answered from the other side of the room. Naira yelped, her hands clamping over Effie's where it gripped her hair and pulled.

"You think you are still the healer and I the warrior as Father and the undergods would always say? You think the Adinkra etched on you means anything? Father would disapprove of you giving them your essence in this elixir of yours. We are not supposed to intervene, remember? You gifted the humans longer life, yet you let your sister die." Effie laughed, and I detected hurt and betrayal in it before her brief exposed emotion calloused over and her voice hardened. "Well then, dear sister, heal this one too."

There was nothing I could do to stop her even when I screamed for her to stop. But Effie held me fast in a vise grip with one hand while pulling Naira to her opening mouth, her saber teeth unsheathing, terrifying even me. She sank her teeth deep into Naira's neck. Naira howled, her body going rigid. Her hands seized and her body began to shake violently in reaction. Effie pulled from Naira's neck, blood spraying from the extraction, and flung Naira as if she were a balled-up paper towel.

Ama reached out, bracing herself. Naira crashed into her. The momentum of Effie's throw and Naira's weight were too fast and too much. In Ama's weakened state, the two of them smashed onto the floor in a jumbled heap, rolling head over heel. Ama took the brunt of the throw, but Naira's forehead still cracked hard against the edge of the wall in a sickening thud. She lay there unmoving as blood began to trickle from the open wound in her scalp and from Effie's bite on her neck.

The smell of fresh, hot, pungent human blood permeated the

air, filling my nose. To my horror, my fangs descended. My stomach rolled in enticement and my mind filled with nothing but thoughts of delicious blood and my increasing need to have it for myself.

Effie's breath warmed my ear. "That's it, my girl." She took a deep inhale, her mouth twisting to a lecherous, bloody grin. "What you smell is your life force. What you smell is our power over these humans."

I struggled to fight against Effie and against the adze needs battling inside me to dive down and lap up the wasting human blood.

Sekou jerked, attempting to make a break for Naira, but Franco hit him with the butt of the gun and Sekou stumbled into Lyle, who saved him from falling through the splintered wood beneath their feet.

"Be still," Franco yelled, his gun trembling. "Don't be a hero."

Another voice rose up above mine. It was weak and gravelly, as if it hadn't been used properly in a long while.

"Naira!"

Hailey cried Luke's name, grabbing at him as he attempted to lunge in Naira's direction.

Ama looked down at her and at the blood. Her nature to feed and restore herself gaining strength over her duty to heal and protect.

"Heal the girl," Effie said simply. "Or feed and heal yourself and regain your strength. Be who you are. My gift to you."

Ama looked at her sister, defiance blazing like lasers from her. "I will not."

Effie's face slipped, revealing her surprise and dismay at the rejection. A second later, she swallowed that moment of weakness, hardening again.

"You see?" Effie turned to me. "After all she's done, betraying me, leaving me to those hunters, burying me to make sure I was dead, and stealing my child, she still refuses me. She still refuses to embrace who we now are. She is ashamed of herself. Ashamed of me and of you."

Ama worked quickly, biting the inside of her wrist, and allowing droplets of her blood to land on Naira's lips while we all watched. This was what Effie must have done with me. Only the outcome would not be the same. Ama could heal. Effie could only destroy.

"This was not the way we were meant to be. Not killing humans or enslaving them ourselves. That was not our father's teachings," Ama said.

"Yet the humans taught us differently. This world, dear sister, has taught us that there are masters and there are those who are mastered. You would choose to be the latter?"

"I would choose life, yes." Ama inhaled the scent of Naira's blood. "I would choose it again and again."

"Human life over that of your twin?" Effie growled, the energy around her crackling. "Over your own?"

"If it means I do not become a monster like those who stole and enslaved us were—like you have become—then yes."

Effie gripped me tightly, practically lifting me to the tips of my toes. "Make your choice, Addae. Your rightful grandmother. Or the impostor."

CHAPTER FORTY-FIVE

Drop!

The word beamed from Nana Ama's mind as clear as if it had been said out loud. I went down.

Nana Ama launched into the air and attacked Effie, who struggled to fight her off. At the same time, Lyle lunged at Franco. Simon bent down, crawling on the floor among the blossoming chaos of the room, before getting to his feet, slipping in his expensive shoes, and running out of the door. Lyle grabbed the gun, forcing Franco to move the barrel in Effie's direction. They fought over the gun and it went off. The bullet hit her in the side and she fell to the ground next to me. I rolled over her, trying to keep her down. The bullet was no more than a mosquito bite to Effie. But my suddenly being on top of her disoriented her. I felt the power of the adze flushing my system, Effie's blood bolstering me enough to put up a fight.

But she was too strong for me, and she recovered, hitting me in the chest with hammer-like hands. I flew back into a wall. Plaster and rock rained over me. Nana Ama launched at Effie once again, pinning her to the floor.

Another shot went off wildly in the air. Franco cried out, no match for Lyle's brute strength. Lyle knocked him out.

Below us, the abalsoms began to churn. And Luke began to convulse, the monster beginning to take over.

"Gotta get out," he managed. "Get . . . her . . . out."

Naira. That's who he meant as he struggled against the monster trying to free itself. He looked at his unconscious girlfriend. The most innocent of us all.

"Get her out!" he howled.

The door from the cellar exploded, setting the horde of abalsoms free.

The first abalsom barreled toward me, and I grabbed its forearms, calling to my other nature. It came to me naturally. My nails grew into sharp points and I swiped at the thing, gouging out a chunk of its neck. Lyle and Sekou attempted to block the cellar to keep more abalsoms from entering and overpowering us. But we all knew there were too many, much too many to take out at once. I ripped the throat out of another and another while Lyle and Sekou did the best they could.

We were outnumbered.

Behind us, the fight between the sisters intensified and they flew at each other above our heads. The air crackled with electricity as the two of them transformed into their full form. Effie, fueled by more human blood and rage than Ama, was bigger, more monstrous, with razor fangs. The cuffs were still on her leathery skin, the amulet still embedded in it. And Ama with nothing at all but her smaller adze form.

Sekou and Lyle stopped and stared, the first time they'd seen an adze in full form.

They lunged at each other with such force that the whole foundation shook. The impact blasted them apart and into walls that crumbled, causing huge chunks to rain down on us and on the abalsoms that piled in. The large slabs of stone and wood fell off and onto some of the monsters trying to get at us as we retreated farther and farther back.

The ground below us was opening and some of the abalsoms fell through the jagged hole. Falling debris and bodies slammed into the exposed pipes. Something like a teakettle whistled, light and high-pitched. The exposed pipes had been punctured.

The abalsoms jumped on Franco like locusts. His screams were horrible and the mass over him writhed and undulated as they ripped him apart.

With epic strength, Ama sent Effie crashing down to the crumbling floor. Effie stopped cold, suddenly confused. Her head cocked to the side as if she were listening for something, receiving something. Then she looked where her abalsoms had gathered around her. All of them froze.

Together, they turned toward her with their horrible, ruined faces. They breathed in unison. Effie looked down at them, disbelief all over her face as her creations stood there, staring at her. Waiting for something.

She got to her feet, favoring her left side. "What are you doing?" she said to them. "Move! Attack them. Get her!" Effie pointed to Ama still hovering in the air, her powerful gaze locked on the abalsoms.

Collectively, their heads craned up and looked at Ama, but they made no moves to attack her.

"What are you doing?" Effie flicked a hand and sent a few of them flying. "What are you doing?" They slowly crawled toward Effie, disobeying her commands. She took a step back, unsure. "What? What? What?" she sputtered.

And then they attacked her, creating a pile of jerky bodies. They muffled her scream.

Luke wheezed, using the few seconds Ama had bought us. "Go!"

Hailey was fighting with him, begging him to come too. He pushed her away toward the closed door.

"Go!" he growled again, using his arms to pull himself toward the pulpy mess that had been Franco. "Go. Get Naira. Please, save yourselves."

Suddenly, the pile of abalsoms blew apart, revealing Effie in the middle, her arms outstretched. The bodies went flying every which way, and we had to take cover to avoid being hit by them. Effie shot up, bloodied and with murder in her eyes. Ama had turned her creations against her. She barreled into Ama and drove her into the chandelier hanging from the ceiling. The ancient pieces swayed precariously, then dropped like deadweight, and we scrambled to take cover from the flying shards and metal pieces.

The abalsoms regained their footing, coming now at anything that was living, no longer controlled by either sister. They were in a free-for-all and they wanted blood.

The sisters ripped and snarled at each other, battling, rolling around intertwined as each fought to gain the upper hand.

I yelled for the others to get out. I had to figure out another way to help my grandmother, but there was nothing I could see. I couldn't even see her.

And there was no opening for us to get through the abalsoms.

Sekou screamed over the roar of zombies and the sounds of the battle above us, "Hailey, you got any more juice in that thing? Just like last night!"

Yes! The whistle. That could buy us a little bit of time to get everyone out.

Hailey stood up, taking in a deep breath. We all put our hands over our ears. She pulled out the cylinder, shook it hard, and pressed the button.

In the crumbling house the sound was louder, reverberating against the weak and porous walls. The abalsoms dropped to the ground writhing, screaming. Some fell back through the huge hole in the floor, crashing into the exposed pipes below. Fumes of gas began wafting up from it and we started to cough.

My grandmother and Effie broke apart. Effie roared, her hands flying to her ears. Nana Ama bared her teeth and went after her sister. They flew up into the second floor.

Lyle picked up Naira from the floor, threw the front door open, and went through. But I wasn't going to leave my grandmother. No way. I wouldn't leave her, not when she'd come back for me.

Luke had found a lighter, golden cased and bloodied, in Franco's pocket. I knew what he meant to do. I tried to tell him to stop. To wait because my grandmother was still in here. Somewhere upstairs where I could hear her and Effie still going at it.

Luke flicked it open. "Tell Naira I love her," he said as Sekou pulled me toward the front door.

"No. Let me go. We can't leave her. Not here," I cried. I tried to pull myself away from him, but he was unbelievably strong, even for me.

Lyle had returned for Hailey, who refused to let go of her brother's hand. "No, Luke! Not when I've just found you again," she said. "You can beat this. You can."

But he couldn't. He knew it. I knew it. We all did. Even Hailey. This was Luke's last stand. A way to absolve himself of the things he'd done these past weeks under Effie's control.

"Too late for me," he panted out. "I feel her will running through me. I'll be like them soon. I . . . can't."

Lyle yanked hard on Hailey, just as Luke managed to slip his hand from hers. They ran out the door.

Nana Ama reappeared. She held Effie in her claws and was about to rip her throat out. Nana looked at me. Looked at Luke and what he held and at the abalsoms once again emerging through the broken floorboards. My grandmother understood.

"Let her go, Nana! Please," I begged, my hands reaching out to her. Sekou flung me over his shoulder and ran toward the door.

"Nana!" I screamed once more.

But she'd already turned, tossing an unmoving Effie and lowering herself to face the horde of abalsoms advancing on us. For a suspended second, our eyes locked—mine terrified and pleading with her not to stay, Ama's full of fire and fury—I saw the entire world of my people, Nyame, and his kingdom Above in her eyes.

I saw the strongest person I'd ever known and would ever know in my long, long life.

I tried to change into my form, to break free and snatch her before Luke lit the fire. But I couldn't concentrate. My adze self would not come.

We jumped over the threshold onto the brittle porch that nearly caved in from our weight.

The legion of abalsoms swarmed Ama.

We hit the last step, onto the path, then began running over the uneven dirt away from the house. Luke flicked the lighter, but it failed to produce a flame.

Effie bellowed, "No!" and I could feel the anger, the fear, the hate coiling like vipers all around us. She tried to escape through the door, but Ama tackled her and held her down as the abalsoms swarmed around them.

The lighter finally flicked. And then with a spark and a *whoosh,* the flames caught on the gas fumes. Then I heard the swell of abalsom screams as the fire spread like the hollowing, consuming them all.

CHAPTER FORTY-SIX

WE MUST HAVE BEEN KNOCKED OUT BECAUSE SUDDENLY SOMEone was calling my name, shaking me. My eyes opened and I hoped this had all been a bad dream, that my grandmother hadn't given her life for me. But the acrid and sweet smell of burning aged timber told me otherwise. Told me, *Ada, this is nothing like a dream.*

My eyes focused on the shapes hovering above me, and the image cleared. It was Sekou and Hailey. Their voices sounded as if they were a million miles away but were growing closer, rushing in like a semitruck.

I didn't know what was going on. Where I was.

But then it all came back like a punch to the gut. Nana Ama! I had to save her!

I shot to a sitting position, my head on a swivel as the massive heat from the raging fire came at us in waves. The plantation home burned like a box of matchsticks. I searched the flames as if I could see through them and pick out where my grandmother might be.

"Nana Ama!"

I stood, moving several steps toward the house, but the fire burned so intensely my face felt like it was melting. It illuminated the entire area, casting all the trees in a murky glow. They looked like they were dancing a ceremonial dance in the firelight.

Who could have survived that inferno?

My insides burned, matching the heat from the fire. I doubled over in pain. Sekou tried to console me, but I pushed him away. I didn't need his pity. What I needed was for my grandmother to be okay. And for all of this not to have happened. I needed Sekou to have let me help Nana Ama back there in the house before everything went to hell.

Behind me, Lyle was back in sheriff mode, telling us to get back to a safer distance, telling us we had to go because the local police and the people who maintained this land would be arriving soon to see about the fire.

But I didn't want to leave. Part of me still believed that she would emerge from the house, charred and triumphant. I still felt her life force, as I had felt Naira's. I would wait for her, look for Nana Ama, just as I had done for Naira.

"Come on, Ada, we need to go," Lyle said. He spoke with such tenderness my knees nearly buckled. But I couldn't go.

The fire roaring like a demon. How would I have Nana Ama's Homegoing and release her light properly? How would I be able to send a goddess home to her father without her body cared for the right way? How would I say that final goodbye when she was in there with the very things she worked years to prevent, her final resting place in her personal hell? I didn't know how I would be able to forgive myself for that. For the fact that Nana Ama would be a part of this place, the place that nearly made her forget who she was and where she came from forever. How could I ever live with that?

Then I heard it.

A low buzzing that sounded more like angels singing. I stared hard into the flames, until I finally saw it. A ball of light floating in a jagged line back down, heading straight for me.

She blinked in and out like the light of a true firefly, moving drunkenly, barely able to control its path. She lurched along, growing bigger on her approach, dimmer than I'd ever seen her before. Growing dimmer and dimmer as Lyle and I watched. I held my hand out to her, trying to catch her so she wouldn't fall, but she couldn't control herself. She crashed hard into my chest, the size of a grapefruit, but the force of her impact made me fall back into Lyle and we hit the ground.

She landed in my lap and began to re-form herself, growing, lengthening into an adze and then, finally, into my grandmother.

Nana Ama blinked her eyes open after much effort. Everything for her was an effort. That she was able to change into her Light and get here said much for her strength and power. But it was still not enough. She swallowed, trying to speak. Her wounds, where the fire had severely burned almost all of her body and where Effie had gouged out parts of her, were wet and oozing blood.

I couldn't bear the unimaginable pain she had to be in. Her wounds weren't self-healing. I was losing my grandmother.

"What can I do?" Sekou asked frantically.

"I don't know. I don't know!" I wheezed, trying to catch my breath. How did you heal the one who was the healer?

It was Nana Ama who always knew the perfect remedy to help, the perfect word to say during times like this. It was Nana Ama who'd led the first founders of our island to safety with bounty hunters and enslavers at their backs and an unknown world at their front. She made the pact with the island to provide sanctuary to those who needed it against those who'd do them harm. And now, my grandmother, the greatest woman I'd ever known, a goddess and daughter of Nyame, was dying in front of me.

I opened my mouth, letting my teeth disengage from their shafts. They slid down and I bit into my wrist. "Take this, Nana, please," I begged, pushing my bleeding arm to her mouth.

The droplets dropped on her lips and around her chin because she was shaking her head. I wanted to scream. Why was she shaking her head?

"Use me to heal yourself," I cried.

I tried to put my wrist to her mouth, but she pushed it away with more strength than I thought she had.

I hiccuped out a sob, unsure what I could do next. How could I force her to drink? "I can't do this without you. Please, it's not time."

I could barely see her clearly through the hot tears filling my eyes. I couldn't imagine a world with Nana Ama not in it. I wasn't ready. I'd already made so many mistakes, so many bad decisions in this short amount of time. I wasn't ready for any of it.

Nana Ama gritted her teeth as a shock of pain rippled through her. I slid my hand in hers. She gripped it tightly, not exhibiting nearly the strength I knew her to have, but strong enough. I took it, waiting for the pain to pass, wondering what we could use around here, in the woods, to ease her pain, or better yet heal her enough so I could get her back to the island. I tried to call upon all her lessons during the walks through the Isle, but nothing came to me. What kind of poultice? What about a mojo bag? I needed an asanka and tapoli to grind the herbs and berries with a bit of my blood. Enough to form a salve for her burns. Bones from a small animal to sew her torn body. Anything for right now until I could do more.

Nana Ama opened her mouth, trying to speak. At first the words struggled to come, but then she whispered, "Drink." It was low and croaky. Her throat was closing up, burned and filled with smoke, but I heard her. Too clearly.

I shook my head hard. I wouldn't.

"You must, child." Her voice was stronger, forceful like Effie when she had me in her clutches. Nana Ama's words weren't coming from her mouth. She was in my head, now. Only I could hear her.

Take what I gift you.

I sputtered through tears and snot. "But—but—but then you'll . . ."

Be gone? She gave me a blood-smeared smile. *Yes.*

"No, Nana. We can fix this. Tell me what I need to do." I made a move to slide out from beneath her and channel every prayer or incantation she'd taught me in her cabin back home. Anything to set her back right.

Be still.

I stilled.

Be strong, my girl, and lead and do whatever it is that you will.

Keep the island for those who need its sanctuary, but live as you must. Drink what I gift you and take all that is me and my history and legacy and live your life.

I choked on my sobs. I didn't want to take her last bits of life. I didn't want to do this thing.

She reached out to me. *Quickly, before it's too late. There isn't much time.*

She lifted a hand to my face, touching me on my cheek in a gesture she'd never really done. For all the love she bestowed on me, my grandmother had never touched me as tenderly as she did in this moment.

Then she spoke so the others could hear, "You are everything I was and more. I waited too long to tell you that. I shouldn't have shielded you from the world, and all that I've done was for you." A solitary tear slid down her cheek as she whispered, "You, my child, are . . . my everything."

She looked deep into me as if assuring herself that I was ready. I didn't feel I was, but something in my eyes must have shown her otherwise. Even during this moment, in which she was the one in need, she took care of me.

"Never forget, Addae, that you are my granddaughter. Mine. Always was. Always will be." She pulled me closer, the words clearly difficult to speak, but she pushed through. "What Effie never understood was that everything comes from choice and consent. You can create another, but only if there is true consent and acceptance between you. They must always accept the gift in its entirety. That is what Effie didn't know, or accept."

"Nana."

"Listen, because I don't want you to make the same mistake. She took her gift for granted. Let it destroy her. That's why the only thing she did right was to create your mother."

"Okay." I nodded.

"Now drink. Don't stop. It will be hard. You will see too much because you will take everything I have ever been and learned. Tell our stories. Keep our history and heritage alive and the island safe."

My grandmother, the original adze, slid her hand to the base of my head and pulled me toward her neck, to the artery that pulsed beneath her skin.

To drink. Her blood. Her Light.

I bit, and her blood was like drinking a soothing balm compared to the fire that raged from the few drops Effie gave me when I'd fallen. Nana's was an elixir of life and of gods. And I saw it all. I knew all as Nana Ama had known. Every single joy, sorrow, and hurt. My body felt like it might burst with the force of so much feeling.

When I took the last drop, my grandmother's body began to blacken and grow small, and smaller still, until all that remained of it was a dark bulb, its light extinguished like that of a firefly. The connection Nana Ama and I shared that I always believed was strong and unbreakable, finally broke. I thought my grandmother would be forever. I didn't want to believe that she wasn't.

And that I was left alone in this world.

CHAPTER FORTY-SEVEN

We had to leave the plantation's raging inferno quickly. Lyle wouldn't let me look for Nana's cuffs, even though I begged him. The cops would be coming. And firefighters. All the people who maintained the forest and property. And we'd have no explanation for our being there and for the bodies they'd find inside. I let Lyle guide me away, holding on tightly to the ball that was my grandmother. She needed to be sent home.

We made it to the Charleston marina, where Lyle was able to hire a late-night boat to take us back to Golden Isle. The captain didn't question why we smelled of smoke or looked like hell warmed over. While Sekou and Lyle got a still-unconscious Naira on board, Hailey and I stood off to say our goodbyes.

She looked as if she'd aged a hundred years. Her eyes were as red rimmed as her brother's from crying. Her heart was as broken as mine.

"I'm sorry about Luke. I was wrong about him."

She tried to smile, sighing. She looked out at the water and the lights glinting off of it. "I'm sorry about your grandmother."

Hailey hesitated. "She turned out to be less terrifying than I had thought."

My eyes filled, and I shook my head. I couldn't talk about her yet.

"What are you going to do now?" Hailey gestured at my hand where I still held my grandmother. "With her? With everything?"

I couldn't begin to think of how to be the Isle's matriarch. I couldn't even wrap my mind around the fact that my grandmother, *my* grandmother, was gone.

"Release her light," I said, trying keep it all in. If I broke down here, I would never get back up. I would literally die.

I wiped an errant tear. "And then I don't know."

Hailey grabbed my hand, squeezing it. She pulled me into a hug, holding me tight. Slowly, I wrapped my arms around her. I didn't want to leave her. So much had happened between us in so little time. We'd lived a lifetime in a matter of days.

"You'll be better," Hailey whispered in my ear. "You already are."

We left with that and a promise that we'd be in touch when things were settled for both of us. Hailey had to deal with her family and the Endowment. And I had Golden Isle and a Homegoing to plan, and . . . I couldn't even imagine it without Nana Ama.

All of the Kinfolk came out for Nana Ama's Homegoing. We all wore our traditional robes of white. We wore arm and leg bands, and headbands made of white beads and cowries. We drew designs with white powder to represent our cultures, traditions, and we adorned ourselves in our chosen Adinkra symbol that best represented our character and the blessings and protection that symbol would provide for us.

My Adinkra was the Dwennimmen, ram's horns that symbolized humility together with strength. The ram fights fiercely against its adversary but also knows when to be humble and submit. All my life Nana told me to not always be fierce, to know when to back off, and I hadn't listened. I thought being humble was weakness. I'd give anything for Nana to give me that lecture again.

The lighted lanterns symbolized Nana Ama's light as we released her on the water she loved so much, from the island she never stopped fighting for, and sent her on her final journey home. I wished I had been able to take her *home*, home, back to the Above and to Nyame like she'd wanted her whole life. I wished I could have done that for Effie too, for whom I sent out a lantern too. Because bad or not, Effie had been family. I sent a prayer as the water lapped at my feet that her final journey would be in peace and not in the suffering she endured, and inflicted.

That night I went to bed. It was the first night I was able to sleep fully, where I wasn't plagued by dreams of a world and place and people I never knew. Or of an uncle I'd only heard about in stories. Anansi. But it wasn't Anansi's voice I heard that night. Or Sekou, who sometimes came knocking, though I hadn't been letting him in. It was another voice. One who never asked to be invited.

Addae.

I shot up in my bed, the string lights off because ever since I'd come back home, I hadn't felt in the mood for them. I twisted every which way, looking for the source of the voice. I wasn't sure if it was a nightmare or if I'd really heard her voice. I licked my lips, and opened my mind, checking for any sign there was anything but a nightmare approaching.

I found a thrum. A connective line.

Addae, I am home.

It was Effie.

I threw off my covers, panic bubbling from my toes, making my scalp tingle. I was near panic. My heart beat in triple—no quadruple—time. Why was it her? Why not Nana Ama? And with Nana Ama gone and me the Isle's matriarch and protector, how could I win against an adze as old and angry as Effie when I hadn't even Lighted?

But how could I not win? The lives of the people on this island and on the mainland were in danger with Effie roaming. The weather had called for clear skies, no storms. But thunder cracked its whip, and lightning illuminated the sky. The boom rattled the house, and I ran out of my room, taking the steps two at time.

I ran outside in my pajama shorts, dread a huge stone block sitting on my chest and growing bigger by the second. A list of places where she could be ran through my head, but the list was short if she wanted to make an impact. She was at Naira's house, reclaiming the one that got away. Or she was at Sekou's, or where Lyle was at the guest cabins up front. But I didn't feel anything from Sekou, or Naira, nothing that indicated any of them were in trouble.

But the lightning cracked something fierce and the thunder boomed seconds later. Thunder that meant a storm was right upon us. But the sky was cloudless, except an eerie light emitting in the distance from near the Gathering Tree and the cliffs. And I knew then where to find her.

CHAPTER FORTY-EIGHT

Again the thunder rocked the earth. It was a sound that would shake islanders wary of sudden gales and storms that could wreak unexpected havoc. And the island itself pulsed with unease. It recognized someone was here that shouldn't be. Something had blown through the protections.

The wind whipped, and as I left the skinny walk leading to Nana Ama's house, there was Sekou pulling up in his cart.

"What the hell is going on?" he asked, yelling above the wind.

It howled something inhuman, and I was terrified that Effie hadn't come alone. That she'd brought some surviving abalsoms with her or made new ones when the others burned. I didn't know what she could want here since she had what she wanted—the cuffs and her way back home.

"What is it?" Sekou asked again.

"Effie."

Usually Sekou was cool under fire, never showing his fear, but her name shook him and his eyes responded in kind. "What? How? I thought she was dead!"

I didn't have time to answer. I screamed for him to call Lyle and make sure the people kept the area clear. And then I ran toward the Gathering Tree.

I found Effie standing in front of it, in her human form, wearing her amulet beneath her cloak, the cuffs visible on her arms. Nana Ama's cuffs. Mine, by right. My blood boiled. I flexed my fingers, approaching her. But I wasn't the only one. There were some Kin there, slowly approaching the circle that surrounded the Gathering Tree. She watched everyone, a knowing smile on her face. She watched me. Her cold, red eyes assessing me.

Who is she?

Where'd she come from?

Look at her eyes.

Thoughts, a multitude of thoughts, crashed in on me. The blood from Nana Ama had changed the mechanics of my body, heightening my senses to levels I'd never even imagined. She'd remade me by giving me her blood, her Light.

Get to Lyle.

What the hell is going on?

Tie down my boat.

Why does she have Nana Ama's cuffs? Did Ada invite her here?

She's not ready to lead.

I tried everything to push the thoughts out. They were coming at me fast and hard.

This girl can't run this island. I'll get Lyle off again. And then I'll take care of her.

My steps halted, that stream of thought different, more treacherous, than the others infiltrating my mind.

Meanwhile Effie grinned horribly. She was enjoying the fear snaking from her to all the people approaching, as sick and poisonous as the kwandamu that she inflicted on the people on the mainland.

"Surprised to see me?" Effie grinned, looking around like she was taking in the scenery.

My mind whirred with questions. How had Effie gotten here? Had I really failed the island so much as to not consider the protections at all? I had, whether the protections held or not. I had failed the island.

Maybe Awuraa Effie will do what Ama could not. Keep Golden Isle pure with only Kinfolk. Build our power. Keep outsiders out. Keep that damned child from inheriting the throne. A new Abotisa, with me as the lady's counsel.

I gritted my teeth as I heard James's snake voice.

Effie bared her teeth in an ugly smile, the length of them making the growing crowd gasp and fall back. These were things they hadn't seen. It was one thing to believe Nana Ama and me were medicinal women with direct lines to the gods, the founders of the island; it was another thing altogether to see the teeth and glowing red eyes in the light.

"This place," she drawled, advancing toward me slowly, methodically, like she was stalking me. "This little island is quaint. I shall be comfortable here when I do some . . . renovating." She knelt down, placing her slender fingers on the ground. She dipped her head, turning it to the side, listening.

"This island lives," she said, practically purring. "How is this so?"

"You have what you want, Effie," I finally said. "You have the cuffs. Just go. Leave the island alone. This is not your home."

Effie's eyes flashed at me. "Any place I am is my home. No one will ever tell me what I can or cannot have again."

She rose from her kneeling position.

"You let your little pets have too many liberties here. They do not see you as their leader, Addae. Let your rightful grandmother take the burden from you. I will get everyone back on track. Restore the order of what a queen's kingdom should be."

"Stay back!" I commanded the Kin.

She held her hand out, and one of the Kin, a man, was lifted off his feet. His legs pumped in the air, finding no ground to stabilize himself on. His arms flailed as he was brought close to her.

"Stop it!" I yelled. I launched myself at her in an attempt to break her focus and release the man. I crashed into her, propelling her into the trunk of the tree behind her. The tree shook violently, the leaves rustling and falling, a storm of foliage. Effie grunted at my impact, pinned between me and the tree.

Effie looked at me incredulously, her eyes blinking as she sought to understand where my strength and speed had come from, realization hitting her that I had done it.

Behind us, Sekou finally arrived with Lyle and approached, yelling at the rest of the Kin to fall back. They obeyed, bumping into one another in an attempt to get out of Effie's line of fire.

With a push of strength, Effie overpowered me. She flicked her hand and threw the Kin man, smashing him into one of the peach trees.

I launched at her again, and we tumbled backward, heading fast toward the cliff at speeds I couldn't clock, fast enough for the wind to cut as we fought each other for control. I had to keep her off track, unbalanced, and not knowing what was coming next. That was the only way I could win this, I thought. Throw her off before she had a chance to react and recover.

With one final, massive shove, I sent Effie careening off the edge of the cliff, her arms outstretched to me, her red eyes glowing and scared. She keeled backward and screamed as she went over. The wind reduced and everything was still.

I dropped to my knees, my chest heaving in and out, pulling in mouthfuls of air. My hands hung at my sides.

The first thing to come from the void was a streak of lightning. It shot up from the darkness into the air. Everyone dropped except me. Another bolt zipped its way past us, striking the ground. Beneath me the ground bucked, the island groaned, reacting to the attack on it.

I approached the cliff's edge, Effie hovered, suspended over the cliff of the inlet, above the raging waters below.

Above her the moon was crystal clear and sparkling, looking luminous within the black void that surrounded it. There wasn't a star in the sky. It looked so large I felt I could reach out and touch it.

The sky began to fill with storm clouds, like it did in my nightmare when me, Naira, and Sekou were on the boat. Like Naira and Luke when they were on their date. Thunder rumbled like an oncoming train and then boomed.

"I wish Nana Ama had finished what she started that night," I said.

Effie looked down at us and for the briefest moment I could have sworn there was sadness there. Hurt. Disappointment. Betrayal.

"I wish your grandmother had," she said, "because a true end would have been better than the hell she imprisoned me in all this time, only to be awakened and betrayed once again."

There was another crack of thunder, a ragged line of brilliant lightning that looked like it would rip the inky sky in half. The light was so bright I could see clouds gathering in the darkness, undulating and growing, looking as if they'd trickle down and swallow us up. It was like this was the end of the world. Or maybe, the end of my world.

The ground beneath our feet began to shift and then shake. Screams came from the islanders as they fell to the ground that rippled like a blanket being shaken out. A deep groan seemed to emit from deep within the island, as if it were wakening, as if it were wanting to roll over and die. The islanders were running now, running away, understanding what I was beginning to understand.

This would be our end, I couldn't help thinking. Effie was going to destroy every last one of us. But not before I did everything I could to stop it.

I launched myself into the air and grabbed on to Effie. "You'll sink the island. You'll kill them."

I tried to yank her arms down, to break the connection she'd made with the oncoming storm she was gathering. But I was no match. She was like a statue, her strength immovable and mine incomparable. She was a goddess and me . . . not even half of that, not even with the blood Nana Ama had given me.

She caught me easily by the neck, holding me before her. All the weight of her loss, her grief, the life she should have had flooded behind it. Her hands held me up in midair, and through them I could feel her, the real Effie, goddess and child of Nyame, the Sky God.

How she used to be before the invaders took her and Nana Ama, before her hell on Millner Manor Plantation, before her rage, before her thirst for human blood overtook her, and then her revenge. Before she was buried—asleep but alive—by the only family she had left, her sister. "I thought I wanted what Ama had," Effie said. "I thought I'd come take this island and rule as Ama did. Have my own little oasis here, untouched, and perfect with nice little humans to adore me and drink my elixirs. Just as Ama had done. I'd put her to sleep for two hundred years as she'd done me."

Beneath us, through the swirling typhoon of a storm that had gathered, lightning struck again, and this time, it struck the Gathering Tree where Nana Ama had held council and led this island and its people for hundreds of years. It split, shearing in two halves, while everyone ran.

"But now she is gone, I will not hide behind mists and superstitions. I will rule out in the world where I will be their superstition, their greatest fear, made real. They will fear me."

Her last words came out like ice. I could see the world exactly as she said. More abalsoms, stronger, hungrier. A world of death and carnage all at her whim. She was the last god left.

"Will you join, my child?" she asked. The silence around us was louder than the storm Effie had summoned. "I won't ask again."

I gripped her iron-like claws, struggling to break free. "Never."

Effie tightened her hand around my neck. She glowered at me, her glowing red eyes lasering into me, igniting a tiny spark that began to spin and spin and grow.

"Then have it your way." She began to squeeze the breath out of me. It was like she was pinching a straw. I felt my vocal cords and my windpipe crushing and all air being cut off. I pried at her rock-hard fingers, but she only squeezed harder and harder, preparing to twist my head off.

Effie began to transform. Her shoulders curved into a haunch and her arms drew in. Her eyes enlarged, becoming luminous disks, more bright red than amber. Her mouth elongated, as if she were yawning, extending lower to unbelievable proportions. Her joints popped and crackled, disengaging and rearranging. She was terrifying and beautiful all at once, both Effie and adze.

In her natural self, with the cuffs and the amulet, her strength intensified. Her long hands pulled, attempting to separate my head from my neck. I closed my eyes, focusing on the spinning ball of heat within me as it rippled, and grew, and heated.

Please, Nana Ama. I didn't know if my grandmother could hear me. I wasn't sure if she was with me, or if she was just dead and buried at the base of the tree under which we gathered. But I begged just the same. *Show me what to do.*

But a strange voice, thick with the heavy accent of my nsamanfo, my ancestors, whispered, the voice from my last dream. Anansi.

To kill adze, you must be adze.

I hadn't understood it then. But I did now. My body took on a mind of its own. I gave myself to it. To the spinning orb glowing and growing in me, stretching itself to every limb, filling me with heat that grew and grew. I thought we'd made it to sunrise, but the Light, the heat, wasn't coming from around me, but within. It was like looking into the sun, something Effie's insect eyes couldn't take. She let out a shriek of shocked pain, her claws releasing me. I began to fall back down to earth.

My body collapsed in on itself, the world spinning around me. I was not in control but only knew what I needed to do, what I needed to be.

For the first time, I was drinking the Light. Truly. I was becoming the obogya, the firefly with its golden orb, the part of me I had yearned for but was always too scared to accept. I stopped my downward spiral. I reversed, shooting up faster and faster, a rocket, launching myself into the very heart of Effie.

Effie audibly sucked in air. Her body bent inward from my impact as I took up residence within her, absorbing her essence from the inside out. She was too powerful with so much rage she'd siphoned from the countless lives she'd taken by force, so alone, so utterly broken—the storm of emotions and unbridled power she could barely control nearly expelled me from her. But I held on, refusing to give up because only an adze could kill an adze in this form.

When I had absorbed all I could, taking her core within me, I shot out, going through her back, and leaving a small hole. Exhausted and nearly passed out, my body started to fall. I almost passed the cliff's edge, heading down to the sea, but with the last of my energy, I managed to launch myself at the cliff, hoping I wouldn't miss.

I hit the ground in a hard roll along the grass and over the protruding rocks, until I came to a stop. As my body began to reshape, returning back to my human form, my friends gathered around me—Sekou, Lyle, and Naira.

"Are you okay?" Naira asked frantically.

I barely got out, "I think so—"

Someone below shouted to look into the sky, and we all did.

Effie was still suspended in the air where I'd left her. She still wore the cuffs and amulet that glowed turquoise blue, but she no longer commanded the storm. The island shuddered itself to a complete stop, like the earthquake that started this whole thing. She remained completely still. She gazed down at her chest and studied the palm-sized hole that I had left in the middle of her chest. The hole I'd made expanded, eating away at her. She looked like the golden edges of a piece of paper as it smoldered with fire, the edges blackening, curling, flaking off, then floating away.

Her mouth opened as if to speak, but no sound came out. She studied the growing hole, now up to the base of her neck and down to her abdomen.

Then she looked at me, the red within her irises changing to gold. She looked relieved. She looked like she didn't hurt anymore. She'd lost everything. Her daughter. Her granddaughter. All for fleeting rage and a desire for revenge on people and a world that would never truly understand her or her kind. She looked up to the sky, her right arm stretching up to it as the burn crawled up her skin. It was a different kind of hollowing.

Effie reached up toward the sky above her.

"What is she doing?" Naira asked.

"She's trying to use the keys to open the gate to the Oosoro," I answered.

I knew it because in taking her heart, I learned what had always been in it. Her father. Going home. That had been the root of everything, as convoluted as it had become for her. She had wanted to be seen by him. She had wanted to go home.

Her body blackened in that final pose, reaching for the sky, looking to her father, who wasn't there, or maybe he was. Nyame was supposed to be everywhere. Even on this foreign land, though it was beyond his African realm. The father who would not interfere in the ways of the human world nor aid those who did.

The burned-out, charred husk of Effie's remains floated back down. Slowly, it dropped, settling softly onto the grass, petrified in its ash state in the same position Effie had died. Still reaching up to the sky.

The ground once again began to shake.

"Now what?" Sekou groaned, looking around frantically.

Lyle held out a steadying hand. "Wait."

Where Effie's lightning had ripped the tree in two, it had struck where I'd privately buried my grandmother. Beneath the Gathering Tree, at the foot of Nyame's stool.

The cuffs and the amulet began gleaming on the ground as black ash from Ama's grave drifted into the air, between where the tree was split, joining the bowing two halves back into one, as it had been. The ashes lifted into the air. Swirling like a tornado. On the other side of us, Effie's charred remains began to do the same, swirling up from the ground, into the sky. Their two ashes intertwined, revolving upward into a deep funnel that suddenly appeared in the heavy clouds above.

There was something on the other side of those heavy clouds. A looming presence, big and meaningful. Something familiar and yet not, which had never been there before but was now.

The jewelry shone so bright, their light shot skyward, piercing through the black mass of the clouds like a spotlight, as if all the fireflies coalesced together to create a lit guide for the ashes' path into those impenetrable clouds. They went straight up in that funnel, the brilliant light guiding them the entire way to whatever—whomever—waited for them on the other side. It stayed like that until every last piece of them had made its way up.

And then the light followed them, growing shorter and shorter as if it, too, were joining them wherever they had gone. A long, jagged stretch of lightning cut through the sky, and a sonic boom of thunder exploded—the sound was so deafening it forced us all to cover our ears.

Then the billowing clouds began to collapse in on themselves until they dissipated and there was nothing left but a cloudless night and a million stars shining bright and a big-ass moon to accompany them. The cuffs and the amulet lay there in the dirt as if they hadn't just opened the gates to the Skies and lit the way home for Ama and Effie, returning them to Nyame the Sky God's imperial kingdom, the beginning of our story.

I picked up the cuffs and clasped them on my wrists. Naira helped drape the gleaming amulet around my neck. I expected them to feel heavy, as weighted as the responsibility of being their keeper, but the jewelry was surprisingly light, like air. I held Nana Ama's cuffs up, watching the gold catch the moonlight from different angles, their brilliant blue centers radiating like the stars above and the blinking fireflies floating around me.

The cuffs and amulet vibrated, warming against my skin, and I recognized it as power.

But what would I do with all of this power?

First, I had an island full of people to tend to. I was sure the locals were confused and beside themselves. I had to make sure

I still had a home and parts of the island hadn't crumbled into pieces into the Atlantic during all this family drama.

And I'd call Hailey, because after all that'd happened, I thought about her all the time and of how free I felt when I was with her and how chill she could be with me. I thought we could work it out. I thought . . . together we could do some things, explore the world, and see what other beings were out there, because it couldn't just be me.

And, one day, I'd go to Africa, visit the lands of the Akans. I'd go to the Kakum Rainforest, in Ghana, from my vision—the one that was the gateway between the Oosoro and this world. I'd check out the ancestral grounds where the twin adze goddesses once roamed free, to see if maybe there were more of my kind.

Maybe Sekou and Naira would go with, or maybe they would go wherever they wanted. Didn't matter, because in the end, we'd all end up back home where we belonged.

I'd have a word or two with my great-grandfather about some of his choices. I now held the keys into Nyame's kingdom, the power of my ancestors. One day I'd tell him that he was a day late and a dollar short for a lot of things, the first being his daughters. But that was an entirely different story and could wait until another time.

Wherever my travels took me, I would always return home to the Golden Isle to be with my people.

I didn't know what tomorrow would bring, or what challenges I would face as the Kin's leader, but I had Sekou and Naira, and most of all, I would always have the Light of my grandmother, Nana Ama, and my ancestors to guide me, because I was Addae Ewiem, the morning sun of the sky.

ACKNOWLEDGMENTS

First, thank you to the readers. I hope you enjoyed Addae and that you get to see more of her and her world in the future.

Thank you Alli Dyer and the Temple Hill Publishing team for providing the opportunity to write this story and open the literary world to more African stories with these Akan folktales and mythologies. Thank you to my editor Kat Brzozowski and the entire team at Feiwel and Friends for their excitement and support. That means a lot. Additional thanks to Rich Deas for the gorgeous cover design that blows my mind.

Kat and Alli, you worked really hard with me on many iterations to get this story right and help it to become what it is. I truly appreciate you both.

A special thanks to my amazing agent, Melissa Edwards and everyone at Stonesong Press.

My mom, Evelyn, and Uncle George for their help with pronunciations and meanings of the Akan languages used. And to my kids who humored me with deep, deep discussions about the history and methodology of the adze and how to fit it all in today's society, or not.

Margeaux Weston and Terry Benton-Walker gave advice,

suggestions, and comfort when doubt and fear were eating me up. I owe you two bigtime.

I had a lot of help while researching the land and location where the book "takes place." To the ferries who took us over and regaled us with barrier island facts and nautical information to maneuver the surrounding waterways, Hilton Head, and Charleston, South Carolina. And a special thanks to Daufuskie Island, my muse, which I totally fell in love with the moment I stepped foot on the marina and drove a golf cart throughout the island for the first time, thinking what a great place this would be to live and the stories it could tell. The island has a long, deep, painful but hopeful history. The families who are native to the island going back centuries and have thrived and remained rooted there served as inspiration to me and for the reimagined world of the Golden Isle. I am grateful to them, along with the Gullah Geechee people whose strength, welcoming ways, and pride in their rich culture always makes me feel like home.

Lastly, the books that rounded out my research to help make *SDTL* an immersive experience language-wise: *Learn Akan English-Twi Dictionary* by Stephen Awiba; *Let's Speak Twi: A Proficiency Course in Akan Language and Culture* by Adams Bodomo, Charles Marfo, and Lauren Hall-Lew; and *A Comprehensive English-Twi Dictionary* by Kofi Oteng-Gyang.

Thank you for reading this Feiwel & Friends book.
The friends who made

SHE DRINKS THE LIGHT

possible are:

Jean Feiwel, Publisher
Liz Szabla, VP, Associate Publisher
Rich Deas, Senior Creative Director
Anna Roberto, Executive Editor
Holly West, Executive Editor
Kat Brzozowski, Senior Editor
Dawn Ryan, Executive Managing Editor
Kim Waymer, Senior Production Manager
Foyinsi Adegbonmire, Editor
Rachel Diebel, Editor
Emily Settle, Senior Editor
Brittany Groves, Assistant Editor
Maria W. Jenson, Designer
Helen Seachrist, Senior Manager, Production Editorial

Follow us on Facebook or visit us online at mackids.com.
Our books are friends for life.